P9-DWC-919

11/15

A Specter of
Justice

Books by Mark de Castrique

The Buryin' Barry Series
Dangerous Undertaking
Grave Undertaking
Foolish Undertaking
Final Undertaking
Fatal Undertaking
Risky Undertaking

The Sam Blackman Series
Blackman's Coffin
The Fitzgerald Ruse
The Sandburg Connection
A Murder in Passing
A Specter of Justice

Other Novels
The 13th Target
Double Cross of Time

Young Adult Novels
A Conspiracy of Genes
Death on a Southern Breeze

A Specter of Justice

A Sam Blackman Mystery

Mark de Castrique

Poisoned Pen Press

Library of Congress Catalog Card Number: 2015932053

ISBN: 9781464204722   Hardcover
       9781464204746   Trade Paperback

Poisoned Pen Press
6962 E. First Ave., Ste. 103
Scottsdale, AZ 85251
www.poisonedpenpress.com
info@poisonedpenpress.com

Printed in the United States of America

For Linda

"Better that ten guilty persons escape than that one innocent suffer."
—Sir William Blackstone, 1765

Chapter One

Eating a jelly-filled doughnut takes concentration. I hadn't been concentrating and my first bite sent a glob of red jelly squirting down the front of my white shirt. Thank you, Hewitt Donaldson, Attorney-at-Law. He was the reason for the doughnut. He was the reason for the white shirt.

Hewitt's office was down the hall from the Blackman and Robertson Detective Agency. My partner, Nakayla Robertson, and I had a three-room suite in the Adler Court building on Asheville's historic Pack Square. Near both the police station and Buncombe County Courthouse, the location was overrun with attorneys. And where there are attorneys, there's potential business for private investigators.

I sat in my office, trying to scoop up the glob of jelly with the edge of a manila folder containing the notes for the sworn testimony I would be delivering later that morning. Bad idea. I managed only to smear the red filling across my shirt and the folder. Maybe the jury would think the defendant shot me on my way to the witness stand.

"Nice look. Definitely you."

I swiveled my chair around to face Nakayla standing in the doorway. She shook her head like she was reprimanding a five-year-old.

"It's Hewitt's fault." My whiny excuse sounded like it came from a five-year-old.

2 *Mark de Castrique*

Nakayla held her arms away from her side and pivoted in a complete circle. Her neatly pressed navy blue dress was unscarred by stains or crumbs. "Hewitt gave me a doughnut and I ate it. I didn't try to wear it."

I looked at my watch. "It's eight thirty. Think I can make it home to change?"

"Maybe if I drive you and then drop you at the courthouse so you don't have to park. Let me get my purse." She crossed the middle room that served as the client conversation area and entered her office.

I stood, clutching the file in one hand and reaching for my suit coat with the other. The door to the hall opened and a ghastly pale face peered through the crack.

"Oh, good. It worked. I brought you a matching tie." Hewitt Donaldson's office manager stepped inside. Shirley the Strange.

At some point, I must have been told Shirley's last name, but I'd forgotten it. She didn't look like she had a last name, unless it was Underworld. Her white makeup was caked on like frosting, and her black eyeliner and lipstick would send little children scurrying under their mothers' skirts. She'd recently permed her hair into a tangle of inky black coils that bounced as she walked as if demonic Slinkys had sprouted from her head.

She was also one of the smartest and funniest people I knew.

"What worked?" Nakayla joined Shirley in my doorway.

The women stood in stark contrast. Nakayla, a tall, slender African-American whom I dearly loved, projected both warmth and regality. Shirley, white, short, and wispy, projected a life force from some other astral plane.

"Hewitt's idea," Shirley said. "Although it pains me to give him credit. He didn't want Sam going into court looking too slick."

Nakayla laughed. "Too slick? Sam?"

"I have my days," I said. "I was the hit at my senior prom."

"Then you must have been home-schooled," Shirley said. "Here, Mr. GQ. Wear this."

She handed me a god-awful powder blue tie with misshapen polka dots.

"These dots are stains," I said.

"Wow, Nakayla, he is Sherlock Holmes. Here's another hint. You'll find a nice assortment of ketchup, mustard, and barbecue sauce gracing that fine polyester fabric. What does that tell you?"

"Hewitt wore it to lunch only one time."

"Impressive. Those detective correspondence courses are paying off."

"And his reason?" I asked.

"Ah, Sam. I thought you were going three for three. I bet your smarter partner knows."

"To have the jury identify with him," Nakayla said.

"Right. Hewitt doesn't want them thinking Heather hired some big-time P.I. who framed poor Clyde."

Clyde Atwood was on trial for shooting and wounding a police officer in the course of a domestic violence incident. Hewitt was representing his wife Heather in the separate, contested divorce case, and in this rare instance, Hewitt was allied with the criminal prosecutors seeking to put Clyde away for a long stretch in the penitentiary. A guilty verdict would make Heather's divorce and settlement a slam dunk.

"What's Hewitt wearing?" I asked. "A seersucker suit from an all-you-can-eat buffet?"

"I'm wearing nothing."

Nakayla and Shirley stepped aside to reveal the attorney behind them.

Shirley threw her hands over her eyes. "If you're wearing nothing, then the jury will require post-traumatic-stress counseling."

"I mean I won't be in the courtroom. I've just learned one of the jurors wound up on the losing side of a case I litigated and won. He'd be prejudiced against Heather if he thought I was connected to her. I alerted D.A. Carter, so when he asks you, emphasize that you were hired by Heather and keep my name out of it."

Instead of a suit, Hewitt wore a Hawaiian shirt so bright I thought Shirley might have shielded her eyes to prevent burns. His long gray hair hung to his shoulders, and the faded jeans and sandals made him look more like a sidewalk vendor of beaded jewelry and leatherwork than Asheville's most successful defense attorney.

Hewitt came of age and stayed of age in the 1960s. A hippie who never did cozy up to the establishment, he loved nothing better than to run through the halls of power shouting, "The emperor has no clothes!" I wouldn't put it past him to do it bare-assed naked too, if it furthered his cause.

"So, I'm on my own?" I asked. "Nakayla planned to work in the office."

Shirley pointed out my window. "See that building across the square? That's the courthouse. I can walk you across the street if you like."

Nakayla took pity on me. "It's good to have someone hear his testimony for debriefing afterwards. We're not called as witnesses that often."

"I agree," Hewitt said. "Cory's already there. She'll take notes. We might need to polish you up if the divorce goes to court."

"Polish me up? You're the ones coating my clothes with spilled food."

"Forget the loaves and fishes," Shirley said. "Jesus could have fed the five thousand with the food particles on the jury alone. You'll blend beautifully."

Neither Nakayla nor I were big on domestic investigations. Sneaking around motels snapping photos of cheating spouses seemed as sleazy as the actions we were documenting. Hewitt Donaldson refused divorce cases unless a criminal element was involved, and spousal abuse brought out the crusader in him.

Nakayla and I had intended to verify Heather's claims to the extent that we could turn evidence over to the police without her having to confront her husband. But my surveillance put me outside their house one night when Clyde's mercurial temper spiked. I heard Heather's screams and phoned 911. Then I pounded on the front door. Clyde yanked it open, cursing and ranting at me to get off his property. When I refused, he retreated into his house, only to emerge brandishing a pistol. Two officers arrived, and as they approached from the side, Clyde swung around, yelling at them to leave. The gun discharged. One of the officers was struck in the shoulder and seriously wounded. I punched Clyde hard in the throat and disarmed him. He was arrested and the subsequent legal process brought us to the moment where I entered the courthouse wearing a blotched shirt and a necktie that looked like it had been dragged through a condiment tray.

When I was summoned to testify, I found the courtroom nearly full. Heather and her friends and kinfolk sat behind the prosecutor's table. Clyde's supporters, five men who looked like they were drinking buddies, occupied the row behind Clyde and his public defender, Tom Peterson, a newcomer to the Asheville legal scene. Clyde's mother and father sat alone on the second row, each looking uncomfortable as if they had wandered into the wrong trial. The rest of the observers were family and friends of the wounded police officer.

I understood young Peterson had urged Clyde to plead guilty and ask for mercy. His client refused, claiming he wasn't abusing his wife, he was disciplining her in accordance with God's will. "Wives be submissive to your husbands." Therefore, he had a right to protect himself against me, an intruder. He was sorry about the wounded officer, but the pistol had discharged accidentally.

The photos I took of Heather immediately after Clyde's arrest showed his alleged discipline was nothing short of an abusive assault. Her swollen jaw and bleeding nose spoke far louder than anything I could say. I hoped the jury would clearly understand why Heather feared for her life and that their guilty verdict would not only provide justice for the wounded police officer, but put Clyde away where he couldn't touch her.

I took the stand and swore to tell the truth. As I sat, I glanced around the room. Clyde Atwood glared at me. He was sober, clean-shaven, and dressed in a coat and tie. The last time I saw him, he was drunk, scraggy, and wearing an undershirt that lived up to its name, wife-beater. Clyde was a few years older than me, probably thirty-five. He worked in a lumberyard and was well muscled. His wife was no match for his brute force.

Behind Clyde, his buddies put on their meanest tough-guy faces. They must have rehearsed because they all leaned forward and sneered at me. I winked at them. All of them broke eye contact.

On the other side, Heather Atwood sat pale-faced, her lips drawn tight. She wore a loose-fitting dress that made her look small and vulnerable. She cut her eyes to her husband and then back to me. I gave a reassuring nod and she returned a weak smile. An older woman sat beside her. I recognized Heather's mother from when I accompanied Hewitt to her deposition. She studied the jurors, probably willing them to put away the monster who married her daughter. I wondered who was watching the Atwoods' three-year-old twin boys, the heart of the conflict in the divorce case.

Directly behind Heather sat Cory DeMille, Hewitt's paralegal and the third member of his practice. Unlike Shirley, who appeared as if she stepped out of *The X-Files*, Cory could have starred in *The Brady Bunch*. In her preppy attire, she played the role of designated grownup for the firm, looking more like a lawyer than Hewitt. Cory raised a legal pad just high enough to show me she was ready to take notes.

"Mr. Blackman. Please state your name and occupation." The prosecutor, none other than D.A. Derrick Carter himself, flashed me a confident smile.

"My name is Sam Blackman. I'm a private investigator and a partner in the Blackman and Robertson Detective Agency here in Asheville."

"Very good. Would you share with the jury your qualifications as an investigator?"

Carter omitted the word private because he wanted me to lead with my military experience. I quickly summarized my years in the Army, beginning after high school graduation, my training as an MP, and then finally my role as a chief warrant officer in the U.S. Army Criminal Investigation Command.

Carter frowned when I skipped over the reason for my military discharge and simply stated that I settled in Asheville to use my skills as a private investigator. I listed several high-profile regional and national cases that Nakayla and I had solved.

Carter nodded enthusiastically. "And am I correct in that convictions were forthcoming in each and every one?"

"Objection!" Tom Peterson rose from his chair. "Mr. Blackman's prior cases have no bearing on the charges against my client."

Judge Ronald Clemmons, a seasoned jurist, sustained the objection.

"Very well," Carter conceded. "Then tell us how you came to work for Mrs. Atwood."

I went through the chronicle of events from Heather's initial visit to our office, twins in tow, to my stakeout of her house. I explained how she was afraid to contact the police for fear of repercussions unless she had definitive proof. Heather told me Clyde was particularly volatile when he'd been drinking and that was usually on payday Fridays.

Carter walked me through the Friday in question, culminating with the color photographs of Heather's injuries. I had immediately given the camera's memory card to the police at the scene to establish the proper chain of custody with no opportunity for Photoshop or any other enhancement. The judge allowed the photographs to be entered into evidence as exhibits and passed to the jury.

Carter and I studied each juror's face and saw the reactions range from revulsion to anger, the emotions we wanted the pictures to generate. When the last juror had viewed Clyde's "discipline," Carter turned me over to the defense.

Tom Peterson stood at the table, but didn't approach me. "Mr. Blackman, did Mrs. Atwood know that you were positioned near her husband's home?"

I noticed how he was subtly reinforcing Clyde's lordship of his castle.

"Yes. She had called me to say he was becoming intoxicated."

"Called you at your office?"

"No. On my cell. I was already outside Mrs. Atwood's house."

"So, she knew where you were."

"Yes."

The public defender nodded like I'd admitted to some major revelation. "Mr. Blackman, you testified that Mr. Atwood was screaming so loudly that you could hear him in your car."

"Correct."

"But that you couldn't hear what Mrs. Atwood said."

"No. Not directly from her house."

Peterson pivoted slightly to angle toward the jury. "Then if Mrs. Atwood knew you were outside, you have no way of knowing what words she might have said to incite Mr. Atwood to lose his self-control, do you?"

Poor Peterson had fallen into the trap, the trap Hewitt Donaldson had devised and that I had shared with D.A. Carter.

"I heard what she said."

Peterson blinked. His turn toward the jury let all twelve see his confusion. "But you just testified that only Mr. Atwood's voice could be heard."

"That's true. Directly from the house to my car which demonstrated to me how enraged he was. But when Mrs. Atwood placed the call to me, she left her cell phone on. That's how I heard her. Would you like me to repeat what she said?"

The defense attorney's face glowed like a stoplight. He'd made the rookie mistake of asking a question for which he assumed he knew the answer. In our depositions, Peterson had only asked about making the call, not when the call ended. When Hewitt learned that, he urged me to hold back the fact, and, for once, D.A. Carter was happy to take the advice of his old nemesis.

For a second, it appeared Peterson might choke on his tongue. To his credit, he took a deep breath, and then said, "That won't be necessary at this time. I'd rather hear the testimony from Mrs. Atwood herself."

His sidestep was the best play he could make until he could regroup. He picked up a legal pad and studied it thoughtfully. I knew he was buying time to compose himself.

He dropped the pad. "Mr. Blackman, would you say Mr. Atwood saw your arrival at his home as a provocation?"

"I can't attest as to how he saw me. He became more enraged when I refused to leave."

"You were clearly on his property, weren't you?"

"Yes, but I made no attempt to enter the house."

"And it was only after you refused his order to get off his property that he retrieved the pistol, isn't that true?"

"That's correct."

"And if you had obeyed his order, a police officer wouldn't have been accidentally wounded."

"I'm under oath, sir," I said. "I can't testify as to what might or might not have happened."

"Come now, Mr. Blackman, don't you think if you had run back to your car and waited for the police, the situation wouldn't have escalated like it did?"

I hesitated. It would be a cheap shot, but Hewitt had instructed me to set it up if I could. Carter started to rise to object that the question asked for speculation, but I shook my head, signaling that I wanted to answer.

"I couldn't run, Mr. Peterson. I have only one leg. I lost the other one in Iraq. I have a good prosthesis, but it's not the same thing. I'm sure you understand."

Tom Peterson froze. He was attacking the testimony of a wounded vet trying to protect a woman who was being beaten by her drunken husband. The damning photos were already etched in the minds of the jurors.

Tom Peterson might have been new to his profession, but he wasn't stupid. "I have no further questions."

Carter stood and addressed the judge. "Redirect, your Honor?"

Judge Clemmons nodded. "Proceed."

Carter smiled and I knew he appreciated why I'd gone off script and not mentioned my war injury earlier.

"Mr. Blackman, is it your opinion that if you had gone back to your car, Mr. Atwood would have continued assaulting his wife?"

"Objection," Tom Peterson shouted. "Calls for speculation on the part of the witness."

Carter stood as tall as he could, indignation on his face. "Your Honor, Mr. Peterson has certainly asked his share of questions requiring the speculation of this witness. Mr. Blackman is an experienced and highly decorated former U.S. Army investigator who has been in numerous situations similar to what he experienced at Mrs. Atwood's home. I'm asking the opinion of a trained law enforcement officer."

"Objection overruled," Clemmons said. He looked at me. "You may answer the question."

Now it was my opportunity to turn toward the jury. "Without a doubt, I was afraid that if I left, Heather Atwood would face the wrath of an intoxicated man waving a pistol. And speculation or not, that pistol nearly killed someone."

"No further questions," Carter said. "Thank you, Mr. Blackman. And thank you for your service and for your sacrifice."

Two days later, I was back in the courtroom. This time I sat directly behind Heather Atwood between Cory DeMille and Hewitt Donaldson. We'd been alerted that the jury had reached a verdict after only an hour's deliberation. Although I took it as a good sign, juries can be fickle. Nothing is a sure thing until the verdict is read.

Heather turned around. "What do you think?" she asked Hewitt.

"I think we trust our fellow citizens to provide justice."

She looked at me.

"Clyde will never hurt you again," I said.

Heather bit her lower lip and blinked back tears. "Thank you for what you said and did."

I was saved from making protests of modesty by the arrival of the jury. As they filed in, I looked across the aisle. The row behind Clyde was empty as if no one wanted to be near him. The buddies present on the day of my testimony had disappeared. His parents were in the same spot on the second row and seemed to be sitting closer together. Mrs. Atwood clutched a lace handkerchief in her right fist and stared at her son. Clyde sat turned in his chair. He wasn't looking at the incoming jurors; he wasn't looking at his attorney. He was staring at Heather.

"Mr. Foreman, have you reached a verdict?" Judge Clemmons peered over his reading glasses at the lanky, retired business executive who had been elected by the other eleven.

The man stood. "We have, your Honor."

The clerk took the verdict form from the foreman's outstretched hand and brought it to Clemmons. The judge studied it for a few moments.

"The verdict is in order." He handed it to the clerk, who returned the form to the foreman.

"Will the defendant please rise," Judge Clemmons ordered.

Clyde Atwood stood by his attorney. D.A. Carter also rose. Clemmons nodded to his clerk.

The man stepped back and cleared his throat. "On the count of felonious assault on a police officer with a deadly weapon with intent to kill and inflicting serious injury, how do you find?"

The foreman kept his eyes straight ahead, ignoring everyone but the clerk. "We find the defendant guilty."

Out of the corner of my eye, I saw Clyde Atwood stiffen.

The clerk continued. "On the count of assault and inflicting bodily harm, how do you find?"

This time the foreman cut his gaze to Atwood for the final pronouncement. "We find the defendant guilty."

The verdicts on Carter's two indictments, one for the shooting of the police officer and the other for the beating of Heather Atwood, meant mandatory sentencing guidelines would send Clyde Atwood away for years. The shooting was the big verdict. Hewitt had been afraid the jury might break down over whether the pistol discharged by accident or was fired intentionally.

On the stand, Clyde had been a less than credible witness, and upon cross-examination, Carter managed to make him angry. The decision to have Clyde testify had backfired, although I doubted Tom Peterson had little choice in the matter. Clyde wanted to vent at what he saw was his unjust arrest, and with just a few character witnesses, the defense was doomed.

Judge Clemmons thanked the jurors for their service and ordered the court deputies to take Clyde away.

As he crossed in front of the bench, Clyde yelled at the judge, "I'll see you in hell for this."

The deputies looked up at Clemmons, expecting a response. In that brief moment, Clyde wrestled free and grabbed the pistol from the duty belt of the deputy on his left. Then, instead of springing for the judge, he lunged toward the stunned spectators, pulling back the semi-automatic's slide to chamber a round. He fired point-blank at Heather. The shot sounded like a cannon. Then he aimed the pistol at me. A second shot erupted and the top of Clyde's forehead exploded, spewing blood and brains in the air.

Screams filled the room.

Hewitt shouted in my ear. "Are you all right?"

"Yes." I looked down at Heather lying on the floor in front of me. Her mother cried over the still body. I turned to Cory. She had sat down, her face turned up to me. Her lips moved and I read the single word, "Sam."

A bright red stain was spreading across the front of her starched white blouse.

Chapter Two

On the first Monday afternoon in August, I was taking a nap on the leather sofa in our conference room when the office door opened. I sat up quickly, hoping I wasn't drooling.

Shirley stepped inside. "Sorry to interrupt. I can see you were deep in thought about one of your many cases."

"Deductive reasoning," I said.

"Hewitt does the same thing. He claims what sounds like snoring is his dynamo of a brain working."

I waved for her to sit in one of the two matching leather chairs. "And you buy that?"

"I asked why I never hear that dynamo when his eyes are open." Shirley glanced in Nakayla's office. "Where's your smarter partner?"

"She ran to the bank. I expect her back in a few minutes."

Nakayla had actually gone to make a wire transfer from our offshore Cayman account to put a little more capital in our checking account in Asheville. Nakayla and I first met when her sister was murdered, and our pursuit of her killer had uncovered a fortune that was best left off our books. So, although we ran our detective agency as a professional operation, we had the luxury of taking only those cases we wanted to investigate.

"Were you looking for her?"

Shirley sat across from me. Her pale face softened, and I sensed she was turning off her rapier wit. "I have a favor to ask of her. Well, both of you actually."

I leaned forward. I'd never seen Shirley so serious. "Sure, what is it?"

Her hands fidgeted in her lap. "You'll probably think it's stupid, but I believe it can make a lot of money."

I didn't know where this was going. Was Shirley looking for investors in some side business? "Tell me what it is and I'll tell you if it's stupid."

"We want to do a fundraiser for the Atwood twins."

Two months had passed since the shooting in the courtroom left Heather and Clyde dead and turned the twin boys into orphans. The outpouring of sympathy had come from all corners of the city, but sympathy and cash donations are two different responses. Then, the custody battle Hewitt sought to avoid through Clyde's conviction returned with amplified animosity between the grandparents. Heather's mother, Helen Wilson, saw Clyde's parents as a dysfunctional couple whose childrearing practices created the man who slaughtered her daughter. Mrs. Wilson wasn't about to allow her grandchildren anywhere near them. The Atwoods considered Heather an ungrateful shrew who drove their son to the breaking point that absolved any responsibility he bore for his actions. They felt entitled to the boys as a replacement for their loss.

Helen Wilson had temporary custody. She was a widow with limited income, but Hewitt Donaldson had agreed to represent her. Tom Peterson had resigned his position as a public defender and taken the Atwoods as his first private client. Neither family had great financial resources and I wondered if this fundraiser was for Helen's legal expenses.

"The custody fight?" I asked.

Shirley drew back. "Oh, no. Hewitt's not charging Mrs. Wilson a dime. He feels an obligation to pursue the case for Heather's sake."

"Who is we?"

"Cory and me. The doctors won't let her return to work for another two weeks and she can use the time for planning."

Cory had undergone not one but two operations. The first had been an emergency procedure to stop the bleeding caused by the bullet ripping through her chest at an oblique angle. Forensic evidence determined that the shot that killed Heather also wounded Cory. As the second victim, she was struck by a mangled slug that nicked the aorta as well as damaged lung and muscle tissue before shattering her shoulder socket.

I survived unharmed because the second deputy had dropped to his knees and fired upwards into the back of Clyde's head, a quick-thinking maneuver that saved others from the bullet's exit trajectory.

"Is she coming back full time?" I asked.

Shirley shook her head. "A couple of weeks working from home and then half days at the office. She's anxious to return to work, but Hewitt insists she pace herself. Her arm's still in a sling from her last shoulder operation."

Nakayla and I had visited Cory several times in the hospital. When Cory was discharged, Nakayla teamed with other friends of Cory to provide meals. And every morning, a delivery man brought fresh Starbuck's coffee and pastries, courtesy of Hewitt. He was particularly distraught because he thought the trial tricks we used on the defense attorney had contributed to Clyde's rage, especially since he targeted me as the victim of his second shot.

"So, what's the money for?" I asked.

"An educational trust fund. Cory thinks if we can get enough seed money, in fifteen years when the twins graduate from high school, there will be a nest egg large enough to send them to college."

"Count us in. That doesn't sound stupid at all."

Shirley bounced up and down on the chair cushion like a kid. "Thank you! Thank you! Cory will be so pleased. She didn't think you'd do it."

"Of course, we'll do it. Why would she think otherwise?"

"Well, not everyone believes in the supernatural. Cory was afraid you wouldn't play your role with conviction like she said you did on the witness stand."

The conversation had suddenly spun in a direction that left me adrift.

I made a stab at regaining my bearings. "This is the stupid part, right?"

The joy vanished from Shirley's chalk-white face. "You're backing out?"

"How can I back out when I don't even know what I'm in?"

"The ghost tour. You'll be a host on the ghost tour."

I made a time-out signal. "You neglected to mention any ghost tour and it sounds pretty important. Why don't you fill in that little detail."

She took a deep breath. "You know several companies conduct ghost tours through Asheville. Something for the tourists."

"Nakayla and I went on one last year. A walking tour after dark. Yeah, it was fun."

"Some are walking, others go in open-air buses and vans, and the guides spiel the history of who was killed where and what spirits have been reported. Well, Cory and I would like to do something more elaborate. Have some re-enactments and hosts at the various sites so there's not just one guy talking on a PA over traffic noise."

"I'm not dressing up as a ghost, Shirley."

"No one's asking you to. There's a difference between being a ghost and being a host."

"It had better be more than the letter g."

Shirley looked confused for a moment, and then laughed. "The letter g. That's a good one. Use it in your speech."

"You need to finish your speech first."

She stood and started pacing between the sofa and the chairs. "I've lined up people to play the ghost parts. I belong to a spiritualist group."

"Really? You?"

She either missed or more likely ignored my sarcasm.

"Yes. The Asheville Apparitions. For about five years now. We meet every couple of months. Share articles and books of interest. Describe any paranormal activities we've experienced."

"Working for Hewitt's got to be a paranormal activity."

"I'm talking about out-of-your-body, not out-of-your mind." She stopped pacing. "But Hewitt's all for this."

"You had Cory ask him, didn't you?"

"Of course. Right now she can ask him anything. Hewitt suggests we do it in early fall when it starts getting dark earlier."

"Aren't you going to be stepping on the toes of the other ghost tours?"

"Not really. We're only doing it one night, and we'll be selling sponsorships. That's where the real money comes from, not the ticket sales."

"And you and Cory are organizing the event and lining up sponsors?"

"We'll have a steering committee. Mostly Asheville Apparitions, but we're looking for other volunteers. We'll need drivers and food preparers for snacks we can sell along the route."

"Walking or riding?"

"Both. The tour will go for a couple of hours. We'll walk through central Asheville but then take buses to some sites too far to walk. That's where you come in."

"I'm a bus driver?"

"No. You'll be the on-site storyteller. You've heard of Helen's Bridge, haven't you?"

"No. Does it have something to do with Helen Wilson?"

Shirley's eyes widened and she seemed to be peering into a different time zone, one measured in decades, not hours. "Maybe," she said to the corner of the ceiling behind me. "They both lost their daughters."

"Hello? Shirley? It's me. Sam. I'm down here."

She blinked and stared at me as if I'd materialized out of thin air. "Very weird. I wouldn't have made that connection, Sam."

"Exactly what I was thinking. Weird."

"Helen's Bridge is up on Beaucatcher Mountain near where College Street ends. It's a stone arch bridge that once was a carriage road for the old Zealandia Mansion. College Street passes under it."

"Is that the big house that's now the office of some online timeshare rental company?"

"Yes. But the bridge was reinforced and preserved by a special fund raised to protect it. The shock waves from the blasting for the I-240 loop around Asheville threatened to bring it crashing down if repairs weren't made."

"I take it the bridge is old."

"1909. Thomas Wolfe mentioned it in *Look Homeward, Angel.* How he would shout beneath it to hear the echo."

"Did he call it Helen's Bridge?" I asked.

"Not that I remember." Shirley returned to the leather chair across from me and sat. "The legend is a woman and her young daughter lived in a small house near the Zealandia Mansion. This was in the early nineteen hundreds. The mansion was unoccupied at the time, and the daughter would sneak inside to play. There was a fire in the house. Maybe the child was playing with matches, or it started from some other cause. Anyway, the girl died in the blaze. The mother was so distraught, she hanged herself from the bridge. Only her first name remains to tie her to the story. Helen."

"And she haunts the bridge?"

Shirley nodded solemnly. "Yes. Not as a hanged woman, but as a mother desperately trying to find her child. The story is if you go up there at night under the bridge and call out three times, 'Helen, come forth,' she will appear."

"Have you seen her?" I asked.

"No. But I've felt the chill of her presence. I drove up alone and gave the summoning cry. The air temperature must have dropped ten degrees, and my car, which was idling, stalled. I managed to jumpstart it coasting down the mountain, and when I got home, do you know what I found on the hood?"

"A hangman's noose?"

"Don't be ridiculous. How could a hangman's noose stay on the hood of a car all the way down Beaucatcher Mountain?"

I felt defensive, even though the whole discussion was nonsense. "I don't know. It seems to fit your story."

Shirley held up her hand. "A palm print. Not just surface grime but a discoloration of the paint itself."

"Is it still there?"

"No. I totaled the car five years ago." Her voice dropped to a whisper. "And every bit of the hood was dented except for that print."

"Too bad she didn't run her hand over the entire car."

Shirley stiffened. "Go ahead and laugh. Cory and I are just trying to help two little boys who've lost their parents."

The rebuke stung. "I'm sorry. I didn't mean to make light of what you're doing. But really, is that the best use of time and resources? A ghost tour? It's not very dignified, given that Heather Atwood was murdered."

"This isn't about dignity and it's not about murder. It's about raising the most money so that these kids have a decent shot at life. What do you think Heather would want? Dignity or her children taken care of?"

Heather Atwood's tearful face floated before my eyes. I heard my own voice—*Clyde will never hurt you again.* She took that as a promise, a promise I hadn't kept.

"Okay. I'm in. What do you need me to do?"

"Speak for Helen. Tell her story at the bridge. I'll give you the facts."

Facts and a ghost story were an odd combination for a detective who makes his living collecting hard evidence. But, how difficult could it be to spin a yarn to a bunch of gullible ghost stalkers?

"And Nakayla?" I asked.

"I'm going to ask her to be the guide on one of the buses. If we have any problem, that's probably where it will occur. Nakayla thinks well on her feet." Shirley swept her eyes along the length of the sofa. "Whereas you, by your own admission, think better lying down." She stood. "I'd better let you get back to work."

"So, what's the next step?"

"An organizational meeting. I was thinking we'd hold it at your place."

"My place?"

"Sam, you live in an ancient, haunted hotel that was once a hospital and a mental institution. Where else would we meet to plan a ghost tour?"

◇◇◇

The Kenilworth Inn stands on a hilltop overlooking Biltmore Village. The village had been constructed over a hundred years ago on the site of a little crossroads community called Best. I guess Best wasn't good enough because the man who purchased the property, George Vanderbilt, changed the name to match that of the spectacular estate he was creating.

The Kenilworth Inn, completed in 1891, predated Vanderbilt's summer home, Biltmore, by several years. In fact, the story goes that Vanderbilt was an investor and was particularly impressed that the Kenilworth had a bowling alley in the basement. So he had one installed in the basement of the Biltmore House.

The original inn burned in 1909, but it was rebuilt in the Tudor style in 1913. Its life alternated between stints as a grand hotel and as a military hospital during the two world wars. Later it was converted into a mental institution known as Appalachian Hall. In the late 1990s, a developer saved it from being razed and he converted the former hotel/hospital rooms into apartments. Each had a unique layout because of the challenge of working around the existing infrastructure.

I rented a one-bedroom apartment on the fourth floor. The fourth was the top story, although some apartments on this level had lofts that took advantage of the building's five-story height.

I don't believe in ghosts, but I understood how Shirley would claim that the Kenilworth Inn was haunted. The old structure had more than its share of creaks and groans. Several of my neighbors swore they heard whispers in the night, particularly right after they moved in. I heard no such eerie conversations, but I had taken over the apartment rented by Nakayla's murdered sister Tikima. No question Tikima's ghost could keep any other spirits including Beelzebub at bay.

Two weeks after Shirley sprang her surprise request upon me, the organizational meeting for Cory and Shirley's fundraiser took place. At seven in the evening, Nakayla and I watched from the Kenilworth Inn's wide terrace as members of the planning team parked in the lot at the far end of the expansive lawn and began the trek up the circular drive to the main entrance. Nakayla had convinced me to host the gathering, but when I learned ten to fifteen people were expected, she agreed to move the site to a large room off the side of the lobby. I'd set up folding chairs in a circle and slid a table against the wall where we could lay out cheese and crackers, nuts, and oatmeal raisin cookies. Bottled water and assorted soft drinks nestled in the crushed ice in my cooler. The only problem was the room also held the mailboxes for all the tenants. I hoped by now most of them had collected their mail and not walking in on our discussion.

"Do you know if the contingent from the Asheville Apparitions will come in some special garb?" I asked Nakayla.

"Yes, black robes and turbans. Don't worry. I checked your lease. Nothing prohibits a tenant from conducting Satanic rites."

"If I'm evicted, I'm moving in with you."

Nakayla shuddered. "Now that's a scary thought."

Nakayla and I were not only business partners but also lovers. I'd suggested combining households several times, but she insisted on maintaining her own place. Her space, as she called it. She wasn't ready for working together and living together. I'd give up my apartment, ghosts and all, if she ever changed her mind.

"Looks like Shirley drove some of her friends," Nakayla said. "Four people are getting out of her car. Look at those cult outfits. Jeans and shirts."

Shirley started walking across the lawn with a man and two women.

"Obviously disguises," I said. "Do you know them?"

"No. She just gave me a head count. There's you, me, Cory, Shirley, and Hewitt. I've never met any of the others."

"I hope they're workers and not just talkers," I said. "The problem with volunteers is you can't fire them."

More cars pulled into the parking lot and Nakayla waved to the approaching group. Through a smile of gritted teeth, she whispered, "Remember, this is Cory and Shirley's event. Don't turn into a chief warrant officer and try to run things."

"That only happens when the moon's full. Believe me, I have no interest in doing anything other than telling my little story about Helen."

Nakayla and I led the volunteers through the lobby to the corner of our meeting room farthest from the mailboxes.

"Please help yourself to drinks and snacks," Nakayla said. "We have a few more people coming, but we might as well get started."

I watched them form a line in front of the assortment of goodies. Cory and Shirley stood back, letting the others go first. Cory's right arm was in a sling held tight against her side. I walked over to them.

"Cory, I'll get you some food when the line clears."

"Thanks, Sam. Go easy on the cookies."

I turned to Shirley and gestured to the three people who rode with her. "Who are your guests?" The man had thinning, gray hair and I guessed he was close to fifty. The two slender women looked like they were in their early forties.

"The blonde's Molly Staton and the brunette's Lenore Carpenter. They're fellow members of Asheville Apparitions. The guy's Jerry Wofford. He heard about the event and called the office. He owns the new craft brewery in town."

"Which one? We're being overrun with them."

Asheville boasted so many craft breweries that it had been designated Beer City, USA, four years in a row. National brewers were now moving in.

"Crystal Stream Beers."

"Never heard of them."

Shirley grabbed my arm. "Don't tell him that. He's not only making a cash donation, but he's supplying beer for the event. It's a good way to get his brand known."

"I wouldn't drink anything but Crystal Stream. What are some of the labels?"

"Labels?"

"Yeah. Does he have an ale or a porter? Most breweries offer a variety."

Shirley stepped in front of me and turned her back to her guests. "Damn it, Sam. I didn't think to ask."

"Don't worry. I'm sure he won't keep them a secret."

Shirley moved on to welcome other guests. The two women she'd pointed out came toward me, broad smiles on their faces.

With her bright blue eyes and short fair hair, Molly Staton looked more like a member of a neighborhood book club. The only hint of the hereafter was the slogan on her T-shirt: "I read dead people."

"Mr. Blackman, thank you so much for hosting. I'm Molly Staton, a friend of Shirley's." Molly turned to her dark-haired companion. "And this is Lenore Carpenter."

"Mr. Blackman, we can't thank you enough. Your participation means so much. I know the whole idea must seem a little odd, but we really do believe the Atwood twins will benefit in so many ways from the fundraiser."

Shirley must have told everyone about my hesitation to be involved. I didn't want to be tagged as Doubting Thomas.

"Please call me Sam. And it's a terrific idea. Loved it the minute I heard it."

They nodded, fully aware I was spouting a load of crap, but they were too polite to call me out.

People began to take their seats. Hewitt arrived in a vintage Hawaiian shirt and broad-brimmed straw hat, Asheville's version of Jimmy Buffett. A few chairs remained empty, either awaiting latecomers or marking the no-shows.

I set Cory's plate in the vacant chair to her right and then took a seat beside Nakayla.

Cory remained standing. "Shirley and I want to thank all of you for being here this evening and for your willingness to help the Atwood twins."

Her comment drew enthusiastic nods.

Jerry Wofford raised his hand. "Will anyone from the Atwood or Wilson families be helping?"

"No," Cory said. "We're taking this on without their involvement."

"But the twins are their grandchildren," Wofford argued.

Cory and Shirley both looked to Hewitt seated beside Wofford. Hewitt took off his hat and set it under his chair. He straightened up and took a deep breath. I knew we were in for one of Hewitt's legal lectures.

"Helen Wilson and the Atwoods are locked in a messy custody battle that won't be settled till this event is over."

Hewitt's mouth had opened and stayed open, but the words came from behind me. I twisted in my chair to see Tom Peterson coming through the door from the lobby. Cory picked up her plate and indicated for him to sit beside her.

"Sorry I'm late." He nodded to Hewitt. "I'm sure Mr. Donaldson and I agree that having the two families involved in this admirable cause would be a disaster."

"That's what I was about to say," Hewitt remarked stiffly.

Peterson swept his gaze around the circle like he was measuring the reactions of a jury. "And I hope you all appreciate that as selfless as Mr. Donaldson and his staff are with their time, they do represent Helen Wilson's interests. Since I represent the Atwoods, I'm happy to also volunteer and bring the necessary balance."

Everyone looked at Hewitt. He eyed the young attorney with undisguised suspicion. I knew he was calculating what impact if any the man's posturing could have on Helen Wilson's case.

Hewitt stood, crossed the circle, and offered his hand. "The best way to project neutrality is to leave the legal issues outside the activities of this committee."

Peterson gripped Hewitt's hand. "Counselor, I couldn't agree with you more."

Chapter Three

Jerry Wofford cleared his throat. "Do you think we could have some introductions? I have no idea who's who and what's going on."

The dueling attorneys and Cory sat. She retook control of the meeting.

"I'm Cory DeMille. I'm a paralegal for Hewitt Donaldson and I became involved because I met the twins during the preparation for Heather Atwood's divorce." She glanced at her right arm. "I was wounded when the shooting occurred. And, I don't know, I guess I feel a kinship to those boys. My wounds will heal, but theirs may never." Cory turned to her left and smiled at Shirley seated beside her. "Shirley came to me with the idea for the ghost tour and I agreed to help."

Shirley picked up the cue. "I'm Shirley. I work with Cory and Hewitt and I'm a founding member of Asheville Apparitions." She smiled at Molly and Lenore who were seated on the other side of Hewitt. "Several of us are here tonight. We not only want to raise money for Jimmy and Johnny Atwood, but also work to bring comfort to the spirit of Heather Atwood who must be grieving for her children."

I took a quick glance at the volunteers whom I suspected were not members of the spiritualist organization. In addition to Peterson and Wofford, a woman and man had arrived together and stood by themselves until we were seated. They were casually dressed and appeared to be in their mid-twenties. When Shirley mentioned consoling Heather's spirit, they looked at each other. The man rolled his eyes, but the woman gave him a sharp scowl. He mouthed, "Sorry."

As if sensing the skepticism in the room, Shirley said, "Now we know everyone here doesn't believe in the spiritual dimension that surrounds us." Instead of looking at the eye-roller, Shirley zeroed in on me. "But that's Okay. We're all working for the same cause and I want to join Cory in offering my thanks."

Shirley nodded to Nakayla.

"I'm Nakayla Robertson. Sam and I work in the same building with Shirley and Cory. When we heard about the fundraiser, we knew we wanted to help. I plan to work on ticket sales and sponsorships, and I'll be hosting one of the buses the night of the event."

Jerry Wofford leaned forward to see around Hewitt. "Are you the detectives?"

"Yes," Nakayla said. "The Blackman and Robertson Agency. We were also involved in the Atwood case, and although I'm not sure that the grieving spirit of Heather walks among us, I do want to do right by her. I hope that some semblance of justice will be done for her children."

Nakayla spoke with such conviction that everyone sat quietly for a moment.

"Sam," Cory prompted.

"Sorry," I said. "I'm Sam Blackman, Nakayla's partner. I'm all for the fundraiser, but uncertain I'll make the best host."

"Are you on a bus too?" Tom Peterson asked.

"No. I'm telling Helen's story up at the bridge on Beaucatcher Mountain."

The young couple across from me leaned closer.

"Helen's Bridge?" the man asked.

"Yes. But I won't be playing Helen."

His companion turned in her seat. "What's Helen's Bridge?" she asked him.

"We can discuss that later," Cory said. "Hewitt?"

The lawyer stood to speak, an unalterable trait of his professional style. "I'm Hewitt Donaldson. Outside of this fundraiser, I am the lawyer for Heather Atwood's mother. I'm not gracious enough to be a host, but I'm told I'm persuasive enough to strong-arm some sponsorships and block ticket sales. I plan to stay in the background and let you creative, more energetic people take charge."

"Really?" Shirley asked. "Stay in the background? I think the only time that happened was when you thought the people in front of you were part of the press corps."

Everyone laughed.

Hewitt sat and said in a stage whisper, "So much for Asheville's unemployment numbers declining."

Shirley bowed. "And that's why my boss, Mr. Donaldson, always gets the last word."

"Your turn, Mr. Wofford," Cory said.

The gray-haired man shrugged. "I'm afraid there's not much to tell. I moved here from Denver about nine months ago and traded the Rockies for the Appalachians. I worked for Coors and decided to open my own craft brewery. This is the hottest spot in the country for new beers and I take it as a challenge to compete with the best. When I heard about the tragedy in the courtroom and the fundraiser, I saw an opportunity to do some good and also publicize my brewery. I'm pleased to be a main sponsor."

"And we thank you for your generosity," Cory said.

Molly Staton spoke next. "I'm Helen," she said directly to me. "Your ghost of the bridge." She glanced around the circle and smiled. "Actually I'm Molly Staton. I work at the Pack Library and I've always been interested in the paranormal and supernatural. In addition to playing Helen for the event, I'll be coordinating volunteers with Lenore."

"And I'm Lenore Carpenter. I'm also a member of the Asheville Apparitions and in addition to helping Molly, I'll be lining up logistical support for the night of the ghost tour. I'm a professional event planner and happy to use my experience to help the twins." She turned to the young man on her right, signaling she had finished.

He reached behind his chair and held up a small backpack. I hadn't noticed it before.

"My name is Collin McPhillips. I'm a freelance photographer and this is my camera to prove it. Actually, I'm a photojournalist." He nodded to the young woman beside him. "But, I'm happy to shoot pictures and let someone else write the story. I was covering the courthouse the day Clyde Atwood went crazy. That's when I met Angela. We stayed in touch and when we heard about the fundraiser, we thought it might make an interesting article."

The woman tagged onto his comments. "We're happy to help with pre-publicity as well. We could write press releases, and I hope our article can bring in donations after the event."

"You are?" Cory questioned.

"Sorry. I'm Angela Douglas. I'm new to Asheville, but as a freelance writer, I can live anywhere. In addition to magazine articles, I've written scripts for some of those reality shows like 'Ghost Hunters' and 'Psychic Detective.'"

Hewitt laughed. "If you ever need to cast '*Psycho* Detective,' Sam's your man."

Lenore reached across Collin to shake Angela's hand. "Molly and I love those shows," she gushed. "How exciting to have you part of the team."

Cory DeMille's smooth brow creased with a trace of annoyance. I could tell she wasn't completely comfortable with someone exploiting the event for an article that could wind up in some weirdo publication. "Yes, Angela," Cory said, "welcome to Asheville. Perhaps we can talk later about the best way to use your talents. I want to make sure the twins remain the focus of everything we're doing."

"Absolutely," Angela agreed. "Someday I want them to read the story and to be proud of how this community rallied around them."

Cory relaxed. "Good. Now last but not least, it's Tom's turn to introduce himself."

I leaned forward, keen to learn how Hewitt's opposing counsel wound up sitting beside his trusted paralegal.

Like Hewitt, Peterson rose to his feet. "I'm Tom Peterson. I'd been part of the public defender's office for about six months. The Atwood trial was my first assignment and although it was trial by fire for me, the horrific outcome is something that will haunt me forever. I got to know Cory visiting her in the hospital."

I glanced at Nakayla. If this was news to her, she masked her surprise.

"I keep thinking I could have done something." Peterson's voice choked. "Talked to Atwood a few minutes. Calmed him down."

"Bullshit."

Hewitt's expletive snapped the young attorney's head around.

"Are you calling me a liar?" Now Peterson's voice was choked with anger.

"No, sir, I'm not." Hewitt spoke softly, even managing to smile. "You believe what you're saying. It's admirable but it's still bullshit. You couldn't have done anything. Atwood was a man who beat his wife. In my opinion, that's one of the most despicable acts a man can commit. If he wouldn't listen to her pleas, he certainly wouldn't listen to you. I suggest you learn from this case and then put it behind you. That means working on the fundraiser for the boys' future, not as some atonement for your imagined failure. You did the best you could with the hand you were dealt."

The rest of us sat motionless, waiting to see if the two lawyers launched into a full blown debate.

Peterson held his breath and took a ten count. "Thank you, counselor." He sat.

Hewitt extended his hand as if it held an invisible olive branch. "I apologize for interrupting. Sometimes I forget every room isn't a courtroom. Please share a little more as to how you came to Asheville."

Peterson looked at Cory.

"Please do, Tom. I know Sam will find it interesting."

He looked at me. "After law school, I went to work for another Sam. My Uncle Sam. I served four years active service in the JAG Corps. I'm in the reserves, but I can live anywhere. I chose Asheville and fortunately passed the North Carolina bar exam."

A military lawyer. As a chief warrant officer, I'd worked with the prosecutorial side in hundreds of investigations. Most of the JAGs were good guys, but some thought they were God's gift to military justice.

"Were you stateside?" I asked.

"In between two tours of Afghanistan."

"You should find Asheville less dangerous."

Tom Peterson's eyes narrowed as he gave me a hard look. "Clyde Atwood proved otherwise."

I said nothing. The quick reaction of a deputy was the only thing that had stopped Atwood from shooting me at point blank range.

"And Clyde Atwood isn't having the last word," Hewitt said. "At least that's why I'm here."

A murmur of approval rippled around the circle.

"What about security?" Angela asked. "It will be dark and it sounds like we'll have people stretched out all over Asheville."

"They'll be with guides," Cory assured.

"Angela's right," I said. "People tend to wander or trip in the dark. And buses can break down."

"Excellent points, Sam." Shirley had a devilish gleam in her eye. "You'll make a fine head of security planning. Does everyone agree?"

I won my first election by a landslide.

Chapter Four

"Nathan, do you copy?" I released the transmit button of the handheld, two-way walkie-talkie and waited for Nathan Armitage's response.

"Yes. Loud and clear. Any problems?"

"I haven't seen Molly yet. I thought she'd check in with me." I stood under the arch of the stone bridge spanning College Street. The steep slopes on either side of the road made climbing up to the top of the bridge impossible.

"Well, she didn't check in at the base," Nathan said. "Maybe she went straight to your site and parked above the bridge. That's where she's supposed to appear, right?"

"No. She's going to walk up to me out of the woods, but it's getting foggy up here."

Dusk deepened the shadows into impenetrable darkness, and clouds began dropping onto the high crest of Beaucatcher Mountain. The first busload of ghost tour patrons was scheduled to arrive in less than thirty minutes. They would disembark and gather under the bridge around the old storyteller, who was I wearing bib-overalls and a floppy, leather hat, looking like I'd just walked down from my still.

The fundraiser promised to be a huge success. We'd scheduled the ghost tour for the second Friday night in October when leaf colors brought a spike in tourists and yet the evenings weren't bitter cold. Nakayla, Cory, and Shirley sold out all the tickets;

Hewitt Donaldson and Jerry Wofford landed as many sponsors as the event could handle; Angela Douglas and Collin McPhillips delivered on their promise of media promotion; Molly Staton and Lenore Carpenter booked buses and coordinated volunteers; and Tom Peterson worked city hall to get the necessary permits.

I hit up my friend, Nathan Armitage, for communications equipment and some off-duty guards from his company. Nathan owned Armitage Security Services and provided radios of law-enforcement caliber for all transportation vehicles and guides. Nathan agreed to man our base at Pack Square while Hewitt and Tom Peterson drove backup vans that circulated along the route.

Peterson joined the conversation. "I didn't see Molly before I went mobile."

"Does she have a cell phone?" Hewitt Donaldson's question boomed from the receiver with surprising clarity.

"She should," Peterson said. "Her friend Lenore must have the number. But Lenore's in costume. I doubt if she'll have her phone with her."

Lenore Carpenter was stationed at the Grove Park Inn, one of Asheville's most famous and distinctive resorts with a history of guests including Harry Houdini, F. Scott Fitzgerald, and presidents from Woodrow Wilson to Barack Obama. One unknown guest had long overstayed. Known only as The Pink Lady, she roams the inn as a misty, spectral shape, the ghost of a young woman who plunged to her death in the Palm Court Atrium in the nineteen twenties. Her identity remains a mystery, but her eerie presence has been sighted for over ninety years. Whenever she does check out, she's going to have a hell of a hotel bill.

"I'm parked in the Grove Park lot. I'll see if I can find Lenore in the hotel," Peterson said.

"Okay," I said. "Meanwhile, if the first bus shows up before I hear from you, I'll tell my tale and summon whomever or whatever I can from beneath the bridge."

"Maybe you'll get the real Helen, Sam," Peterson said. "That would create terrific publicity for the cause."

"Nathan, who's on the first bus?" I asked.

"Nakayla's the host. Angela and Collin are riding along to get some photographs of Helen's first appearance for Angela's article. If Molly hasn't arrived, they can stick around until she gets there. I'm not sure how successful you're going to be with this first group anyway."

"Why's that?"

Nathan's voice tightened as he tried to stifle a laugh. "They don't speak English."

"What?"

"Hewitt sold a block of tickets to UNC-Asheville and so you've got a university mini-coach heading your way with twenty Japanese students on a cultural exchange program. But, they have an interpreter and I'm sure he can translate 'Helen, come forth!' with the same dramatic zeal you proclaim it." Nathan clicked off his transmit button but not before his laugh was broadcast to everyone on the team.

I shouted up to the bridge, "Molly! Molly, come forth!" No answer. Molly could have parked her car farther up the mountain where I wouldn't have seen her, but the plan was for her to check in with me at the base of the bridge.

I directed my flashlight beam over my head. Mist descended from under the arch high above me. I felt the dampness penetrate my overalls and I feared the rain predicted for after midnight might be moving in early. The deteriorating weather might add to the spooky atmosphere, but a downpour would be a disaster for the walking tour through Asheville and the food and beverage vendors along the route.

There was no sense waiting out in the open when I could be warm and dry in the car. I walked thirty yards down the slope to the turnout spot where Nakayla and her group would meet me. I started the Honda CR-V's engine and set the heater on high. Then I rehearsed my speech.

Twenty minutes later, the fog on the crest of the road beneath the arch brightened. The glow concentrated into two headlights and the oncoming vehicle swung wide to park on the turnout behind me. I grabbed the floppy leather hat off the seat, plopped it on my head, and stepped out of the car to face what I thought would be a mystified group of Japanese intellectuals who wondered what kind of culture I represented.

Nakayla's voice crackled from the walkie-talkie on the passenger's seat. "Arrived at Helen's Bridge. Sam is waiting."

"Okay from base," Nathan replied.

I closed the car door, walked back to the small bus, and stood in front of the headlights.

Nakayla alighted first, wearing an orange slicker and carrying her walkie-talkie in her right hand. A thin Asian man followed her into the pool of light.

"Sam, this is Mr. Tanaka. He'll be your translator, although everyone in the group has at least a rudimentary knowledge of English."

"A pleasure to meet you," I said. I wasn't sure whether I should nod, bow, or offer my hand.

Mr. Tanaka did all three. His grip was firm. "Thank you, Mr. Blackman. Miss Robertson has informed me as to what will transpire. I ask that you pause every few sentences so that I might translate and make sure no one misses a word of your marvelous story."

"Then stop me anytime if I'm going too fast."

Mr. Tanaka turned to the bus and waved. I didn't realize it was a signal for The Charge of the Light Brigade. The Japanese riders cascaded out like a bomb on the bus was seconds away from detonation. The light of Light Brigade became an explosion of camera flashes as they encircled me. Had they meant me harm, there would have been no escape.

I removed my hat, vainly thinking the bare-headed look might not appear as stupid when my picture was posted back to Japan.

Mr. Tanaka waved his hand again and the photo frenzy instantly ceased. He raised his voice and made a short statement. I recognized two words, "Sam Blackman." Several members of the group repeated my name in reverent whispers I fantasized might have been the awestruck tone women used when they said, "George Clooney."

More flashes came from behind me. I turned to see Collin McPhillips, camera close to his eye, documenting this international encounter. Angela stood beside him jotting notes in a small journal.

"Sam, you can begin now," Nakayla prompted.

What the hell. I pulled the hat down to my ears. "Follow me to the base of the bridge."

They jumped in line like a platoon called to move out and we marched up the rise to the looming arch. As soon as I stopped, they fanned into a perfect semi-circle with Mr. Tanaka and me at the center point of its radius.

I cleared my throat and then spoke with as much solemnity as I could muster. "The bridge over us was built in 1909 as a carriage way to the mansion on top of this ridge."

I paused and Tanaka delivered unintelligible, rapid-fire syllables while heads bobbed in unison.

When he finished, I picked up my story and we continued this verbal leapfrogging as I went through the history of the Pennsylvanian John Evans Brown making his fortune in New Zealand, returning to his native country, and settling in Asheville, where in 1889 he constructed the mansion he called Zealandia. I told of a small, nearby cottage that mountain lore claims housed a beautiful woman named Helen and her young daughter. Then, with dramatic intensity, I described the young girl trapped in the burning mansion and the mother's vain efforts to brave a barricade of flames and rescue her. I wandered off script in the enthusiasm of the moment, feeling myself swept up by the currents of my imagination.

"And in her grief and desperation, Helen dragged a rope from her cottage to this very bridge. Blinded by tears, she tied one end through a chink in the stone work and then pulled the knotted noose over her head. Calling out to the daughter whose name has been lost to time, she flung herself from the center of the bridge and hanged herself."

Mr. Tanaka nudged me and I realized I'd gotten so carried away, I'd forgotten to wait for his translation.

Although I couldn't understand his words, I felt the emotion with which he infused the tale. His listeners' mouths opened and their eyes danced back and forth from Mr. Tanaka to the top of the bridge above us.

"Now, the ghost of that poor woman walks forever searching for her daughter. Maybe Helen will come to us tonight, asking if we have seen her child." I turned around and stared at the bridge while Mr. Tanaka translated.

When he finished, I let the silence build for a moment, and then stretched both arms up to the sky. "Helen, come forth! Helen, come forth! Helen, come forth."

Mr. Tanaka mimicked my gestures and started speaking.

A blur of pale fabric appeared on top of the bridge's stone wall, hung for only a second on its edge, and then tumbled down toward us. A collective gasp rose from the crowd as we all jumped clear of the falling object. But it never struck the pavement. A thick rope snapped taut, jerking the object to a halt with a distinct crack. Then, swinging in the night breeze, the blur became the recognizable shape of a woman, her neck crooked at an impossible angle, her bare feet dangling six feet above the ground.

The Japanese group broke into spontaneous applause. Camera flashes fired like strobe lights making the gowned woman seem to twitch as the wind blew stronger.

"Oh, my God!" Nakayla ran to my side and clutched my arm.

Above us hung neither an apparition nor a theatrical specter, but Molly Staton in the flesh, and very dead.

Chapter Five

"Sam Blackman, you're as contagious as a medieval peasant with the plague." Homicide Detective Curt Newland made the accusation as he, Nakayla, and I watched the second ambulance roll down the mountain bound for Mission Hospital.

Two of the Japanese students had fainted when they realized a real body dangled from the bridge. Nakayla and Angela had tended to them while Collin and Mr. Tanaka herded the others back on the bus. I radioed Nathan Armitage to set both police and medical responders into action. Then I personally collected every camera and cell phone, insisting that they were evidence that would be returned as soon as any photographs were transferred to the police. I didn't want Molly's body posted on Twitter and Facebook. The Japanese were most cooperative and understanding.

"First, Heather Atwood and now Molly Staton." Newland turned and looked up at the body still suspended above us. "It doesn't pay to stand too close to you."

"I don't think I was close to her. At least not when she died."

"You touched her?"

"Just her foot. Body temperature was much lower than if the hanging killed her."

Newland shook his head. "Poor woman. When was the last time you saw her alive?"

"I didn't see her at all today. We were to meet up here about thirty minutes before that first bus arrived."

Newland looked at Nakayla. "You see her?"

"No. She never came by our headquarters at Pack Square."

"Was she expected to?"

"We all had our assignments and costumes. Most people checked in but it wasn't mandatory."

"Uncle Newly, there's no sign of anyone." The voice came out of the mist masking the top of the bridge.

Either Ted or Al Newland must have been manning the scene. The two uniformed Asheville policemen were the nephews of the old detective. Even if I could have seen the speaker, I wouldn't have known who he was. Ted and Al were identical twins, and they only called Newland "Uncle Newly" when they were excited. However, once they'd revealed the family nickname, Curt Newland had become "Newly" to his police colleagues as well.

"What's Efird say?" Newly asked.

Tuck Efird was Newly's partner and he'd gone to the upper level with the mobile crime lab. Newly had immediately requested the forensics team when Armitage told him the nature of the crime. Heavy fog and rain would erase too much critical evidence if Newly first waited to assess the scene.

"Efird's walking up Windswept Drive looking for any tire marks where a vehicle might have been parked on the side."

"Good luck with that," I told Newly. "The roads up here have no shoulders."

"Let's see for ourselves," Newly said. "I've got officers stopping traffic from all directions. And I want to release the scene as soon as I can so we can lower the body. I'm not waiting for the damned ME."

"Thank you," Nakayla whispered.

I knew from her subdued manner that Molly's grisly murder had shaken Nakayla to the core. Having to stand beneath the corpse of her friend was surely agonizing.

"We'll have her down as soon as we can," Newly promised.

With our flashlights crisscrossing the terrain, he led us under the arch and over the brow of the hill to where on the left Windswept Drive dead ended at College. The narrow road rose steeply up the grade of the highest ridge in a series of tight switchbacks, passing by the top of the bridge and up to a mountain peak community of homes with spectacular views.

The brittle blue lights of police vehicles flashed above and below us, showing where the roadblocks quarantined the crime scene. Those cars coming over Beaucatcher Mountain would have a detour route available, but the homeowners above us would have to take Windswept in the other direction until Newly cleared all access.

A brilliant white light cut through the darkness as the crime lab techs turned on powerful halogen beams to illuminate the top of the bridge. We left the road at a severe switchback and followed a short path to where one of Newly's nephews guarded the perimeter. The backwash of the halogens lit his name badge.

"Hi, Ted," I said in a flat, solemn voice. No one was glad to see anyone under these circumstances.

"Sam. Nakayla." He turned to his uncle. "The techs are just getting started. I've got these for you." He handed Newly a pair of shoe covers and latex gloves.

Newly took them, looked at me, and shook his head. He knew I was anxious to investigate. "Sorry, Sam. This is as far as I can let you go. When Tuck comes back, give him your statement. I'll not only need it for the record, but to rule you out as a suspect."

"Me?"

"You were alone up here before the bus arrived. The fact that you were under the bridge when Molly was thrown over should eliminate you, but I have to do my due diligence. You understand."

I did. I would have done the same thing. At this point we didn't know if the murder was committed by a single killer or a team, a team that could include me.

"Uncle Newly, Hawkins radioed that Nathan Armitage and Tom Peterson want to come up. They say they're part of the organizing group."

"Is that right?" Newly asked me.

"Yes. But Nathan was at Pack Square and Tom Peterson was working near Grove Park Inn."

"Peterson is that new lawyer, isn't he?"

"Yes," I said.

"Just what Asheville needs. Another goddamned ambulance chaser." He turned to his nephew. "Tell Hawkins to keep them at the roadblock. We'll get statements later."

"You want a list of everyone who knew Molly would be at the bridge?" Nakayla asked.

"Most definitely." He yelled over his shoulder. "Al, I need you here."

Within a few seconds, Ted's doppelgänger materialized out of the mist. A light drizzle seemed to accompany him.

"What is it, Uncle Newly?"

"Take Nakayla to your patrol car and write down the list of names she gives you."

"I was helping the techs," he complained, clearly wanting to stay at the scene.

"I can help the techs. These names are a priority."

"Okay." Al Newland pulled out his flashlight and flipped it on. "I'm parked down at the lower roadblock on College."

"Al Newland, can you come here?" The voice came from the glow of the bridge lights.

"He's doing something for me," Newly shouted.

"Then have him check his shoe covers," the bodiless voice demanded. "We found a ripped fragment and none of us has a tear."

Al played his flashlight over first one foot and then the other. The booties were intact.

"I'd better get over there," Newly said. "Take Nakayla, Al. Ted, wait with Sam till Tuck returns."

Ten minutes later, Tuck Efird and a couple of uniforms walked from the road to the small clearing where we stood on the fringe of the woods under an oak whose few remaining leaves offered a little shelter.

"Newly wants me to give you a statement," I said.

"Whatever gets me out of the rain." Efird shifted his weight from side to side with nervous energy.

Wiry and twenty pounds lighter and twenty years younger than Newly Newland, Efird reminded me of a feral cat anxious to pounce on anything that came within range. And, like a cat, he apparently didn't like water.

"Let's go to your car," he said. "It's closer."

When we reached the underside of the bridge's arch, Efird quickened his pace and stepped away from me, hugging the edge of the road so that he could put as much distance as possible between himself and Molly's body. He got in the passenger side of my CR-V, leaned across the seat and pushed the driver's door open. As I slid in, I saw the rain on Efird's cheeks wasn't as heavy as the tears around his eyes. He pulled a note pad and pen from his jacket pocket.

Without looking at me, he said, "You know what I need to know."

I gave him a concise summary of events from the time I checked in with Nathan Armitage, picked up my walkie-talkie, and drove to the bridge. I told him that I'd seen Hewitt Donaldson and Tom Peterson who were also getting their communications equipment. Tom was headed for the Grove Park Inn and Hewitt's area was near a haunted B & B on the Hendersonville Highway. Neither had a storytelling role like me, but were simply on standby should some problem develop along the bus routes.

"Didn't you wonder why Molly didn't show?" he asked.

"Yes. I radioed that she hadn't arrived."

"Did you walk up the road to see if her car was parked above?"

"No. Our instructions were to meet under the bridge. There was no reason to go to the upper level. Did you find any tire tracks?"

Efird ignored my question. "So, Molly was supposed to appear under the bridge?"

"Yes. But when the first bus arrived, I went through my 'Helen, come forth!' routine, thinking maybe she'd improvised and decided to appear at the top."

"Was that rope part of the props?"

"No. Molly was going to walk out of the dark asking if anyone had seen her daughter. That's the way Helen's sightings have been reported."

Efird drummed his pen on the note pad. "Well, did you see anything at all?"

"The occasional car came by while I was waiting. I saw headlights of a few going up to the houses, but if someone cut their lights, I wouldn't have known they stopped atop the bridge."

"So, you didn't hear anything?"

"Nothing that caught my attention."

Efird continued to stare at his note pad, yet to write a single word. For all his experience, the death had really shaken him.

"When Molly..." he paused a second and started again. "When the victim came over the bridge wall, did you see a flash of someone else? A hand? A sleeve?"

"No. I'm sorry. It happened so fast. And then camera flashes bounced off the mist like blinding lightning."

"Newly sent the tour bus to the station," Efird said. "Maybe we'll get lucky with the photos. That was quick thinking confiscating the phones and cameras. Thank you."

"I didn't know Molly very well," I said. "Do you have any idea why someone would kill her?"

Efird shook his head. "No. Probably some psycho who saw an opportunity to create a spectacle. Or some religious nut who considers the spiritualists to be devil worshipers. We've got plenty of backwoods preachers who see Satan at work behind every bush."

A sharp rap sounded on the driver's window. I turned to face Nakayla through beads of raindrops.

"Newly's ready to lower the body," she said. "He wants to know if Detective Efird's finished."

Efird closed his note pad and opened his door. "You can observe." He hurried away without waiting.

I pulled an umbrella from the backseat and shared its shelter with Nakayla.

"Learn anything?" she asked as we walked to the bridge.

"Not really. Just that Efird's upset. I've been with him at other crime scenes, but he's never been this distraught."

"You don't know about him and Molly?"

I stopped, forcing Nakayla to halt under the umbrella beside me. "No. What?"

"They were a couple. She and Efird dated for several years."

"Jeez, no wonder Newly sent him up the hill away from the body. Had they broken up?"

"About four months ago. Right before we started planning the ghost tour. Molly said it wasn't pleasant."

"She broke up with him?"

"Yes. She got into this spiritualist stuff and went to some psychic who claimed she was in a doomed relationship. You know Efird's been divorced twice."

I didn't, but I wasn't surprised. Law enforcement takes a tough toll on marriages. "What did Molly mean by wasn't pleasant?"

"I guess he took it hard. She didn't say he was violent or anything like that. Shirley or Lenore know more. They were all good friends."

"That's going to be touchy."

"Yes. Former boyfriends make prime suspects. Efird needs an alibi." Nakayla grabbed my hand holding the umbrella. "Come on, let's go. They've got another ambulance in position."

We stopped by the rear bumper and watched the EMTs wheel out a gurney. They maneuvered it directly under the dangling corpse so that the body could be lowered faceup.

"You ready?" Newly asked.

One of the techs nodded. The rope had been anchored by a grappling hook lodged in a crevice in the stone wall. Someone had chiseled it in advance so that the hook could be securely wedged.

"Okay, Al, Ted," Newly shouted. "Extract the hook and let the rope down slowly."

Newly and the two techs gently guided Molly onto the gurney with as much dignity as they could. Efird stood apart, almost at attention. One of the techs retrieved a folded sheet from the ambulance while his partner and Newly secured safety straps across Molly's torso.

As the tech with the sheet started toward the body, Nakayla stepped from under the umbrella.

"Wait a minute."

I followed behind her.

"What?" Newly asked.

"Her gown. It's not the costume she was supposed to wear."

"It looks old-fashioned to me," Newly said.

"It is. But I borrowed one from the North Carolina Stage Company and it was a dingy white. This is ivory and in much better condition."

"It's not Lenore's?" I asked.

"Who's Lenore?" Newly asked.

"Lenore Carpenter," Nakayla said. "She's playing the role of the Pink Lady at Grove Park."

"We should make sure they didn't switch and forget to tell you," Newly said.

"That didn't happen," Nakayla insisted. "The Grove Park Inn's ghost is dressed in pink. That's how she got her name."

We stared at the vintage gown in silence, wondering what significance it might have.

"Cover her," Newly said. "There's nothing more to be learned here." He searched the perimeter for his partner. "Tuck. Contact the morgue and leave word for the ME to treat that dress as critical evidence." He turned to the EMTs. "And leave that sheet with the body. If we find fibers, I'll want to rule it out."

Nakayla and I stood under the arch and watched the ambulance disappear into the rain. There was no siren. There was no need.

Chapter Six

Nakayla spent the night with me at my apartment. Neither of us wanted to talk about the horror we'd witnessed, yet both of us were unable to put the tragedy out of our mind. Nakayla finally went to bed around four in the morning while I sat up in the living room, my good leg propped on an ottoman and my prosthesis lying on the floor beside me.

Although Detective Newland had clearly indicated Molly Staton's death wasn't my case, the fact that a murderer had been lurking on the bridge right under my nose or, more accurately, right over my nose, entangled me with the crime as much as any investigation I'd ever been assigned in the U.S. Army. The sheer arrogance and bravado of the killer made it impossible for me to let go.

Shortly before six, the gray of dawn seeped between the slats of the wooden blinds and I knew any attempt at sleep was futile. I fitted the prosthesis on my left stump and moved as silently as I could to the bedroom. Nakayla lay curled on the right side of the mattress, her face turned away from the window. I closed the curtains, grabbed clean clothes from the closet, and retreated to the kitchen to dress.

I left three words printed on a paper napkin. "Gone to office." No work awaited me there. The urge to do something simply became an urge to do anything. The office created the illusion I had a plan that would bring Molly's killer to justice.

Early Saturday morning traffic in Asheville consisted of the occasional delivery truck and a change of shift at the hospital. I made it to my reserved parking space in under ten minutes and walked up Biltmore Avenue, stopping briefly to smell the aroma of baking bread emanating from City Bakery Café. Alas, they wouldn't open for another ninety minutes.

The coin-operated newspaper rack by the main entrance to our office building seemed jammed full of extra copies. The macabre murder must have dramatically increased the press run. I dug enough quarters out of my pocket to buy one.

A color photo of Helen's Bridge filled the space between the middle fold and banner headline—"Ghost Tour Tragedy." The photographer framed the arch with blue police lights streaking through the fog underneath it. The image of Molly's hanging body appeared only in my mind. I was relieved none of the pictures from the Japanese group or Collin McPhillips had leaked to the press.

The headline wasn't as tawdry or sensational as it could have been. I scanned the front page as I rode the elevator to the third floor. The main article contained nothing beyond what I'd known when I left the scene last night. Newland was quoted with the perfunctory statement about the investigation being in its early stages and that any comment would be inappropriate speculation.

The sidebar articles proved less benign. One column rehashed the grisly courthouse shooting as the backdrop for the Atwood twins' fundraiser. There was another piece about the Asheville Apparitions and their steering committee organizing the event. Someone had told the reporter I was responsible for security, which made me look like an incompetent bozo, not the best image for a professional investigator to project.

My unflattering publicity was inconsequential compared with the story about the custody fight for Jimmy and Johnny Atwood. Hewitt Donaldson figured prominently as did Tom Peterson. Clyde Atwood's mother, Nelda Atwood, was quoted as saying the fundraiser had been planned by Helen Wilson in an effort to buy off the courts with the help of Satan worshipers.

Nelda claimed the death of Molly Staton was a sign that her grandsons needed to be raised in a God-fearing home and not with a person who made deals with the devil.

A preacher named Horace Brooks said the custody battle wasn't for the earthly lives of the twins but for their eternal souls. "Helen Wilson might have that hotshot Hewitt Donaldson but the Atwoods have Jesus," the preacher proclaimed. I wondered how Tom Peterson felt about having Jesus as his senior counsel.

The upshot of the clamor was that Helen Wilson and her grandsons were once again at the center of a storm not of their making. And, sadly, the other person neglected in all the name-calling and custody histrionics was Molly Staton. Hardly a word was printed about her.

I left the newspaper on Nakayla's desk and noticed the message light flashing frantically on her phone. Ignoring what I suspected were the calls of desperate reporters, I retrieved water from the sink in the men's restroom and started a pot of coffee in the small Cuisinart brewer Nakayla kept atop one of her filing cabinets.

Bolstered with a mug of java, I quickly sped through the voicemails that began at nine the night before and ended at one-thirty in the morning. Each message began with the man or woman touting journalistic credentials ranging from local radio stations to CNN and ended with a plea to return the call as soon as possible. I had no intention of speaking with any of them and each message was promptly deleted. Each message, that is, except the last one. A whispery male voice said, "Mr. Blackman. You have crossed Helen's Bridge into the valley of the shadow of death. You and your black harlot. Be warned that the scythe of justice is sweeping away all who are found guilty."

My first thought was who the hell uses the word harlot these days? My second thought was he made a threat against Nakayla and that wouldn't stand. I pulled my cell phone from my belt, activated the audio app, and recorded the man's voice. Then I e-mailed the file to Detective Newland with the short text—**Got this at the office at one-thirty this morning.** I knew he had bigger fish to fry, but I wanted him aware of everything that might have any connection to Molly's murder.

I pulled a clean legal pad from my desk drawer and started writing the names of those people who knew Molly Staton would be at Helen's Bridge. Our organizing committee had the most detailed information. They also had ironclad alibis. Nakayla and I were on the scene with a busload of Japanese witnesses. The same held true for Angela Douglas and Collin McPhillips. Hewitt Donaldson and Tom Peterson had been transmitting from their assigned locations and Lenore was in place for her role as The Pink Lady at the Grove Park Inn. Shirley and Cory were coordinating the entire event from their headquarters at Pack Square. Jerry Wofford had been checking in with the food and drink vendors positioned along the walking route downtown. The other person with in-depth knowledge was Nathan Armitage, but he was manning the communications network at the same site as Shirley and Cory.

We'd kept the identity of those playing ghosts a secret to add to the impact when family and friends saw them in costume. Discovering whether someone had shared the cast list would be a priority. But names were only starting points. Without a motive, there would be no link between being aware of Molly's location and being her murderer.

I jotted the word "motive" on the pad. A personal animosity to Molly seemed the most likely candidate, but the context of the ghost tour raised the possibility that someone was taking out their anger on the event's participants and Molly happened to be the most vulnerable. But why the costume change? Although the ME report probably wouldn't be ready for a day or two, I felt certain the autopsy would show that Molly was killed elsewhere, maybe even in the early afternoon or morning. Either the killer didn't have access to Molly's planned wardrobe or the gown bore some other significance.

And until it could be determined whether Molly was the specific target or a symbolic target, Newland's investigation would have to cast an extremely wide net. He needed a breakthrough lead to narrow the focus. I looked at the office phone. A lead like a threatening call. Or a disgruntled boyfriend who in this case happened to be Newland's partner.

I stared at the list of names for a few minutes before adding Clyde's parents, Nelda and Cletus Atwood. As an afterthought, I wrote down Horace Brooks, the preacher quoted in the newspaper. He was the type of person who might still throw around the word harlot, and the voicemail wasn't so whispery as to thwart identification completely.

A knock sounded from the outer door. I glanced at my wristwatch and realized at some point my fruitless thoughts had become dreamless sleep. It was eight-fifteen. I swiveled the chair toward the door, expecting to see Nakayla and maybe a bag of warm muffins.

Homicide Detective Newly Newland entered. He wore the same wrinkled suit from the night before. Gray stubble covered his unshaven face. Bags under his eyes looked like they were packed for a two-week vacation.

Before I could utter a word, he said, "Yeah, I know. I look like hell. But I take consolation knowing you look bad twenty-four/seven." He glanced over his shoulder to check Nakayla's empty office. "Where's your lovely partner?"

"Asleep, I hope. Someone's got to keep a clear head." I stood. "Want a cup of coffee?"

He waved the offer aside. "If I have any more caffeine, I'll induce a heart attack."

"Then have a seat while I get a refill."

Newly crossed the room and plopped on the leather sofa. Returning with a fresh mug, I found he'd laid his head back and closed his eyes. I thought he'd fallen asleep.

"Those Japanese sure take a lot of pictures in a short period of time." He made the pronouncement, too tired to move anything but his lips.

"Is that what you've been doing? Reviewing photographs?"

He leaned forward. "Yes. And then one of our technicians

pulled them off and saved them in a computer folder under the person's name. Tuck's been taking statements from each of them."

"Any protest that you're confiscating their pictures?"

"Not from the Japanese. I explained that they are evidence and I need to keep them in a chain of custody so that they're not altered or publicized."

"Collin McPhillips felt differently?"

"Of course, he did. When he learned he wasn't getting his photos, he started screaming freedom of the press. I told him he could either have his camera back with all the pictures except for Molly's body, or I'd log everything—camera, lenses, bag—into the evidence room and he'd see them after the trial, if there ever is one."

"He caved?"

Newly nodded. "With the encouragement of his writer friend."

"Angela Douglas?"

"Yes. She told McPhillips that having some of the pictures was better than none, and she could write her article without police restraint."

I took a sip of hot coffee and considered how far to press Newly. "You learn anything from the photographs?"

Newly shook his head. "You know I can't go there. And I know you're champing at the bit to get involved."

"Then just tell me if you think the case is solvable."

He smiled. "All cases are solvable. The question is when. This murder is so bizarre that I'm confident a solution is out there. A run-of-the-mill drive-by shooting, now that's another matter."

I understood and agreed with what Newly was saying. The more unusual the crime, the more likely the perpetrator will be discovered. That principle was expressed by none other than Sherlock Holmes. Although he's only fictional, the principle is not. "Is your when soon?" I asked.

"Our when depends upon the speed with which we can exercise the process of elimination. I think motive and opportunity will reveal our killer."

I stared at him.

"I know," he said. "Not much above a drive-by. So, I'm interested in your voicemail."

"That's why you're here?"

"I thought it would be best to listen to it straight from your machine. I could tell there was ambient room noise on what you recorded for me. I'd like to have one of our techs pull a copy from the line so the only ambient sound is from the caller's location."

I was pleased Newly was taking the threat seriously. "Okay."

"Does your system record caller ID?"

"It's stamped on the message readout. I didn't recognize the number."

Newly brightened. "Well, that's at least something. Can I hear it?"

He followed me into my office and we stood over the phone. I replayed the message.

"Again," he said as soon as the caller finished.

We listened a second time. I noticed how melodramatic and contrived the delivery sounded, as if read from a script. I thought of Clyde Atwood's cheering section, the men behind him that first day of the trial, and their tough-guy posturing when I took the stand. "Sounds like a bad impression of Marlon Brando's Godfather, doesn't it?"

"Maybe that's what it's supposed to sound like," Newly replied. "What someone believes a threat should be."

"What do you know about that preacher Horace Brooks?"

Newly's eyebrows arched. "You think it's him?"

"Well, the speech is either bad Hollywood or bad Old Testament. The guy's quoted in today's paper asserting Helen Wilson is in league with devil worshipers trying to steal the twins away from the Atwoods."

Newly thought a moment. "One of the guys at the police station said Brooks showed up on the eleven o'clock TV news last night. Maybe he made the same statement then that appeared in the morning paper."

"Does he have a history of calling press conferences?"

"He's not shy about sticking his face in front of a camera. Brooks came to Asheville about fifteen years ago as a tent preacher. He never left."

"Must be one hell of a tent."

"He got promoted to bricks and mortar. The Church of the Righteous. It's out off the old highway to Canton. Most people call it the Church of the Self-Righteous."

"Fire and brimstone?" I asked.

"That's my understanding. I'm not saying they keep rattlers under the pulpit, but I bet they take the Bible so literally they believe Jesus spoke King James English."

"The Atwoods must be part of his congregation," I said.

"Yeah, but I can't see him for something like this."

"Maybe not," I agreed. "But who's to say his fiery rhetoric didn't encourage someone else?"

Newly sighed. "All right. I'll get the tech over and we'll copy the message. Then I'll have a little chat with the good reverend."

"That's one way," I said with little enthusiasm. "Or I could just pick up the phone and call the number. The message is on my machine."

"Why not?" Newly said. "Can I listen from Nakayla's extension?"

"Yeah. Once I dial through, I'll wave for you to pick up the lit line."

I punched in the number and signaled Newly. A click sounded as he lifted the receiver but the phone was still ringing on the other end.

No one answered and I expected perhaps the best we would get was someone's voicemail. Then the ringing stopped as the connection was made. I heard a clunk as the phone struck a hard object like the floor or a table.

A groggy voice whispered, "Hello?"

It was only one word but I recognized the speaker immediately. Hewitt Donaldson.

Chapter Seven

"Hello?" Hewitt repeated.

Newly looked at me and frowned, expecting me to engage the mystery voice in conversation. He didn't recognize Hewitt.

Before I could somehow extricate myself from the awkward situation, Hewitt said, "Sam, is that you?"

We were done in by Hewitt reading his caller ID. I had his number stored under his name on my cell phone and had long forgotten the actual digits. That's why I didn't recognize them on the office system. The curse of making things too convenient.

"Yes, Hewitt," I confessed. "I'm here with Detective Newland." I put Hewitt on alert so he would choose his words carefully. I had no idea why he would have left so tasteless a message that was beyond even his dark humor, but I wanted to give him the benefit of the doubt.

"Good morning, gentlemen." His groggy voice instantly cleared. "How can I help you?"

Newly gave me a nod to start talking.

"Hewitt, did you leave me a voicemail on my office phone last night?"

"Your office?"

"Yes."

"You mean after we spoke at eleven?"

"Yes. After that."

"Why would I have called your office? I knew you weren't there."

I looked at Newly through the open doors and shrugged. I didn't know how much the detective wanted me to reveal about the message's content.

"Donaldson. This is Newland. Would you mind telling me where you were at one-thirty this morning?"

"Yes, I would mind. But I'll make an exception. I was with Nathan Armitage. We were closing down the Thirsty Monk till two."

The Thirsty Monk Pub was a popular watering hole around the corner from my office and just a few blocks from Pack Square.

"Did anyone borrow your phone?" Newly asked.

Hewitt paused a moment, analyzing the questions to deduce the reason for our call. "Someone left a message from my number, right?"

"Yes," I said, taking control of the conversation away from Newly. "A vague threat to me and a disparaging remark about Nakayla. Your name didn't show up on the office machine."

"Well, it wasn't me and no one used my phone. It was in my pocket the entire evening."

"And this is your number?" Newly rattled off ten digits.

"Yes."

"Is it unlisted?"

"No. You can find it on my business card. But, I have no idea how it appeared on Sam's office phone."

"Some sort of spoof device," Newly said.

I had no idea what he was talking about and I knew Hewitt was even less tech savvy than me. "You want to explain?" I asked.

"You buy a special computer card or a piece of hardware and it substitutes a bogus ID. You can make it read anything you want. There was a huge scam last year run out of India that impersonated the IRS. Those initials actually appeared as the caller. The crooks bilked millions out of intimidated taxpayers."

"Should I listen to the message?" Hewitt asked. "Maybe I'll recognize the son of a bitch."

"That's not a bad idea," Newly agreed. "Meanwhile I'll see if the phone company can break the spoof layer and reveal the actual number."

"Good. If there are any charges I can press, then, by God, I will. Sam, how long are you planning to be in the office?"

"I'll stay till you get here."

"I'll see you in an hour." Hewitt hung up.

Newly and I resettled in the middle room, he on the sofa and I in an opposite chair.

"So, what do you think about the call?" I asked. "Someone making trouble for me or for Hewitt?"

Newly rubbed a palm across his grizzled chin. "Hard to say. We know Donaldson's pissed off a lot of people. And you're no saint, especially in the eyes of the Atwoods. That call was a good way to spite both of you. And pretty chicken shit since it came when there was no way you'd be in the office."

"The phone number spoof seems sophisticated for a backwoods preacher."

Newly looked at me with disapproval. "Don't underestimate Horace Brooks, Mister Hotshot Detective. He plays that backwoods preacher role all the way to the bank."

"What's the benefit for him getting involved in Molly Staton's murder?" I asked.

"He's God's warrior going up against satanic forces. This whole ghost thing was an easy target. He's championing the Atwoods and fighting evil. He couldn't have scripted it any better."

"But Molly's the victim here?"

"Yes, and he'll skate over that. Probably claim he was only trying to warn people about the dangers of fooling with dark spirits. It was a tragedy brought on by Molly's own actions and not through anything he said."

"You going to check him out?"

Newly nodded. "Once I get a clean copy of the voice and a reliable trace on the call." He cocked his head, eyeing me carefully. "Why did Hewitt call you at eleven?"

"He was checking on us. He invited Nakayla and me to join him for a drink. He knew we'd been through an ordeal and thought we might want to unwind. Going to a bar was the last thing Nakayla and I wanted to do. We went straight back to my place."

"And apparently Hewitt found other company." Newly stood. "I've got to get back to the station. I'll send our tech over."

I got to my feet and escorted Newly to the door.

He stepped into the hall and then turned around. "Did you see Hewitt at all last night?"

"Yes. When we were picking up our radios from Nathan Armitage. They were more reliable than using our cell phones."

"Do you remember what he was wearing?"

Alarm bells rang in my head. Newly asked the question casually, but it wasn't a casual question. "A tan jacket and one of those Hawaiian shirts he likes. Why?"

"No particular reason. Just a little due diligence since his number popped up on that message."

I didn't believe him and I irrationally spoke out in defense of my friend. "Are you doing due diligence on your partner?"

Newly's face hardened. "What's Tuck have to do with it?"

"I understand he and Molly were an item until a few months ago. If that becomes well known and a former boyfriend isn't fully investigated, people might think due diligence was being selectively applied."

He reddened. "I would have expected more from you, Sam. I don't take shortcuts and I don't give passes."

I realized I'd overstepped and called his integrity into question. Newly deserved better from me. I threw up my hands. "I'm sorry. That was uncalled for. I guess I'm just upset and I know Hewitt had nothing to do with it. Please accept my apology."

Newly took a deep breath and let it out slowly. "Okay." He headed for the elevator.

As I stepped back into the office, I heard him say, "Tuck doesn't have an alibi. I've already checked."

The police tech arrived about twenty minutes later. He clipped two wires to the receiver in Nakayla's office, recorded the message, and left me alone with my list of names and no idea what to do next. I thought about calling Nakayla, but if she was able to sleep, I didn't want to wake her.

Shortly after nine, Hewitt stormed in without knocking. He looked far better than Newly had. The green-on-red Hawaiian shirt had been exchanged for a red-on-green pattern. His bright eyes and clean-shaven face belied that he'd been out past two in the morning.

"Let me hear it," were the first words out of his mouth.

"Well, good morning to you too, Hewitt."

"Yeah, good morning." He headed for my office without waiting for me to get up from the sofa.

I found him staring at the phone as if challenging the device to repeat the offensive message ascribed to him.

I pressed the speaker button.

"Mr. Blackman. You have crossed Helen's Bridge into the valley of the shadow of death. You and your black harlot. Be warned that the scythe of justice is sweeping away all who are found guilty."

"A self-righteous crank," Hewitt proclaimed. "Where does it show my number?"

I pointed to the LED readout displaying his number and the one-thirty time log.

"And this spoof device created it?"

"That's what Newland thinks. He hopes the phone company can determine the real source of the call."

"Spoof. This sure as hell isn't a joke."

"I know. You recognize the voice?"

"Play it again and crank the volume up as loud as it will go."

We listened again, both leaning closer to the vibrating speaker.

"Nah," Hewitt said. "I've got no idea. But the asshole's trying to sound melodramatic with that ominous whisper."

"And he also sounds like he's reading a script. You haven't had any run-ins with the preacher Horace Brooks, have you?"

Hewitt stepped away from the desk as if now wanting to distance himself from the caller. "Not personally. I've heard he's been bad-mouthing me since I took the custody case for the Atwood twins. But I don't know what he'd have to gain by making it look like I was threatening you."

"I mentioned Brooks to Newland so at least the preacher's name's in the pool." I remembered Newly's comment that Brooks had been on the late TV newscast. "Let's try something."

I sat at my computer and opened the Internet browser. One of my bookmarks was the local television station and I clicked on the homepage for their news. As I suspected, the murder at Helen's Bridge was the top story in the video-on-demand replay section. Hewitt bent over my shoulder and we saw a reporter with crime scene tape and a portion of the bridge framed behind him. After briefly describing the dramatic appearance of Molly Staton's body, he gave a brief background on the charity fundraiser and stated not everyone in the community supported the event.

The video cut to Horace Brooks, a lean-faced white man with dark, narrow-set eyes. He wore a crisp blue suit, white dress shirt, and red tie. Dapper for a backwoods preacher and for so late at night. Framed on either side of him stood the Atwoods. Cletus wore a gray suit and yellow tie; Nelda was in a Sunday dress and her only jewelry was a silver cross around her neck. Each held a framed photograph. Although the single boy in the pictures seemed to be the same, I knew the Atwoods clutched individual portraits of their twin grandsons, Johnny and Jimmy.

"Our hearts go out to the family of Miss Staton," Brooks began. I paused the video.

"I think they're wearing TV makeup," I said.

"Brooks is a slick son of a bitch," Hewitt said. "He's staged an appearance that parades Cletus and Nelda Atwood out as the most responsible child-rearers since June and Ward Cleaver. I know for a fact Cletus has been cited for numerous DUIs. The apple didn't fall far from the tree when it came to him and Clyde."

I clicked play. Brooks shook his head solemnly. "But as horrible as these events are, we will continue to pursue the Atwoods' rights to their grandchildren." He turned his gaze from the off-screen interviewer and peered straight into the camera. "Helen Wilson might have that hotshot Hewitt Donaldson but the Atwoods have Jesus." The coverage cut back to the reporter at the bridge who wrapped up stating that the investigation was just beginning and that the TV news team would be working around the clock to bring us all the latest developments.

Hewitt snorted. "I can smell a con man through the computer monitor."

"A con man, yes, but is he a murderer?"

"He is if his rhetoric drove someone to murder Molly. I wouldn't defend the bastard if he offered me the keys to the Pearly Gates."

"What do you think about his voice?" I asked.

"Kinda of preachy, but that's to be expected. The voice on your phone was deeper."

"Too deep for Brooks to mimic?"

Hewitt moved to the corner of my desk. "Play it again, Sam." A chuckle broke through his exasperation as he realized he'd uttered the oft-quoted line. "Actually Bogart said, 'Play it, Sam.'"

We listened again, this time for pitch. And I caught a sound between "your black harlot" and "be warned" that I'd not noticed before.

"I can't make a judgment since the voice is disguised," I said, "but did you hear a higher-pitched background sound?"

"All the way through it?" Hewitt asked.

"No."

I told him the spot where to concentrate and played the message again. Hewitt bent and put his ear next to the blaring speaker.

When the message ended, he said, "Glasses. I think it's the tinkle of glasses and some distant conversation."

"I agree. Which means Newly's more sophisticated audio equipment should be able to enhance the ambient sound."

Hewitt ran a palm over his gray hair and tugged at his ponytail as if trying to stimulate his brain. "What about Cletus? Do you know if Newland is looking at him for this phone call?"

"No. But frankly the call is a flea on the tail of the dog. His first priority is checking out everyone who knew Molly Staton would be at that bridge. It's unlikely Cletus Atwood had that information."

Hewitt stared out the window to Beaucatcher Mountain in the distance. "Maybe. You said you and Newly believe Molly was killed elsewhere."

"Yes."

"Then how do we know her murderer didn't force that information out of her? That could also explain why she wasn't in the dress she was supposed to be wearing."

As an investigator, my modus operandi sought to narrow the suspect pool. Hewitt's question came from the mind of a defense attorney; even though he had no client, his first line of action was to increase the number of possible perpetrators.

"That's a good point," I said. "I'll raise it with Newly."

He turned to face me. "On the other hand, we have evidence of careful planning. Do we know when Molly was last seen alive?"

"I'm sure Newly's running that down."

"The closer to her time of death, the less likely the Helen's Bridge spectacle was orchestrated after her killer extracted the information. Too much to do and too many props to collect."

"Assuming it was one killer," I said.

Hewitt's eyes narrowed. "And a conspiracy complicates motive. What was gained by her death and who, in the plural, would benefit?"

"How do you see this affecting the custody suit?"

"I'm hoping the good Reverend Horace Brooks keeps on with his media stunts. I haven't seen the final numbers, but we were on track to raise a sizable sum for the kids' educational fund. The judge might not look favorably on awarding custody to grandparents who are outspoken obstacles to the boys' opportunity for a college education."

Hewitt laid his broad hand on my phone. "And if Newly is able to trace this threat back to Brooks, his heavenly piety and testimony for the Atwoods will be shot to hell. We'll see who's spoofed in the end."

My cell phone buzzed where I'd laid it on the desk. I picked it up and saw the call was from Nakayla. Before I could answer, Hewitt's rang.

He looked at his caller ID. "It's Shirley. She never calls on Saturday. I'd better take it." He stepped into the other room.

"Hi," I said. "You're up."

"Have you heard from Lenore?" Her voice was tense and urgent.

"No. What's wrong?"

"Shirley just called. She's been trying to reach her, but she's getting no answer."

"Maybe Lenore's sleeping in."

"Shirley's been trying to reach her since Molly's body was found. Lenore sure wasn't asleep at eight last night."

"When was she last seen at the Grove Park?"

"She wasn't." The answer didn't come from Nakayla. Hewitt stood in the doorway, the phone still at his ear. "Shirley's at Lenore's. She wants us to come there now."

Chapter Eight

Hewitt pulled his Jaguar to the curb in front of a story-and-a-half, light blue home with white trim and a manicured yard enclosed by a white picket fence.

Located just a few miles north of town, the nineteen twenties neighborhood was enjoying a resurgence as proximity to Asheville's vibrant center made the older homes desirable. Lenore Carpenter's looked like it received tender loving care. The lawn, surprisingly green for October, was raked clear of leaves. A garden shed stood to the right with a greenhouse attached to the rear. Hanging baskets devoid of flowers were lined up on the concrete apron ready to be stored for winter.

Hewitt unlatched the front gate and gestured for me to precede him up the walk. When I reached the first step to the porch, a woman opened the door. I stopped and stared, trying to place the familiar face. Then I made a futile effort to hide my surprise.

"Yeah. It's me," Shirley said. "I didn't have time to dress properly."

"You look fine." I meant it. Without the severe white makeup and tar-black mascara and eyeliner, she looked cute. But I had the good sense not to utter that four-letter word to Shirley. Not if I wanted to retain all my teeth.

"Where's Nakayla?" she asked.

"Meeting us here. Hewitt and I didn't want to wait for her."

"Have you heard from Lenore?" Hewitt asked.

"No. But come look. Something's wrong."

We followed Shirley into the living room. I was aware of a hardwood floor and white brick fireplace, but furniture and artwork passed as indistinct blurs. She quickly led us to a rear bedroom.

A double bed with a white comforter and decorative apricot pillows ran lengthwise beneath a window overlooking the backyard. An antique nightstand and matching dresser were the only other furniture. On the narrow wall facing the foot of the bed was a full-length mirror. Two Japanese prints hung on either side.

The center of our attention lay crumpled atop the comforter. At first I thought it was a piece of the bedding; perhaps a satin sheet to be folded and stored. But even as fashion-ignorant as I was, I noticed a ruffled shoulder strap and realized the pastel pink color went with nothing else in the room. We were looking at the dress for The Pink Lady, the ghost Lenore played the previous night. At least the ghost she was assigned to play.

"Can you tell if the dress has been worn?" I asked.

Shirley pulled back a layer of fabric to reveal a yellowing tag. "The costume identification information is still pinned to the neckline. Maybe Lenore reattached it, but then why didn't she hang the dress in its protective bag?"

"Is the bag here?" Hewitt asked.

"Yes. I found it in the front coat closet."

"How about her car?" I asked.

Shirley shook her head. "Gone. And we'd also rented a pair of period shoes to go with the dress. They're not in the house. Why would she wear the shoes and not the dress?"

"Maybe the dress didn't fit," Hewitt suggested.

"We tried the dress on at the theatrical company. Lenore liked it so much she asked if she could buy it."

Hewitt looked at me and pursed his lips. He was thinking and didn't like where his thoughts were leading. "And as far as we know, no one saw or heard from her yesterday?"

"I didn't," Shirley said.

"Neither did I." Nakayla answered the question as she entered the bedroom. "And I don't know if anyone saw her at the Grove Park Inn last night. The first bus scheduled turned around when Molly's murder brought everything to a screeching halt."

I looked around the room. Other than the dress, nothing seemed out of place. I dropped to my knees, lifted the bed skirt, and peered under the box springs. Shoved just out of sight were a pair of gardening shoes, the kind with the rubber base and leather upper that goes only as high as the ankle. The small size suggested they belonged to a woman. Flecks of black soil clung to the rubber and a few larger clumps were scattered on the floor. Looking closer, I noticed the dirt protruded a few inches from underneath the bed. A gap of clean hardwood extended another foot and then soil traces appeared again, but now in eight discernible lines about an inch wide.

"Everyone move back against the nearest wall." I got to my feet and turned to Shirley. "Was Lenore a good housekeeper?"

"Totally. You could eat off the floor."

"Not this floor. It looks like someone wheeled a small cart or wagon in here. Probably from the garden given the richness of the soil. Her gardening shoes are under the bed."

"That's crazy," Shirley argued. "She keeps her shoes in the shed, and that shed is cleaner than my house."

"I suggest you all go back to the front porch," I said. "Watch where you step."

When they had cleared out, I walked along the baseboard following traces of soil. Four of the lines were darker and I wondered if some of the wheels had been more deeply embedded in one of the flowerbeds. The trail led down the hall, past a bathroom, and through the kitchen to stop at a side door. Through the windowpane, I saw the shed directly opposite.

Concerned that I was in the midst of a crime scene, I pulled a handkerchief from my pocket and lightly grasped the doorknob. The deadbolt was already withdrawn and the latch released easily.

A wide concrete walkway spanned about ten feet from the kitchen door to the shed. The outbuilding was constructed on a cement slab with a three-foot apron running along the front. The shed's roof extended overhead just enough to provide rain protection for several rakes and spades that hung from hooks on the exterior wall.

From this angle I saw the two flower baskets farthest from the street were knocked over. Their potting soil spilled across the concrete like a three-dimensional inkblot. Four wheel-tracks emerged from the dirt but vanished as soon as they left the shelter of the overhang. Directly in front of me, eight tracks, four darker and four fainter, ran from the kitchen door but disappeared after crossing the threshold. Rain, I thought. The tracks had been made before last night's rain cleaned the exposed surfaces. But why were there only four tracks coming from the shed and eight from the kitchen?

I realized the cart or wagon must have been left somewhere else. I walked into the backyard. The flowerbed next to the rear wall was partially dug up. A trowel and pair of gloves lay against a rock border. There was no other gardening equipment.

The overturned hanging baskets near the shed door looked like they'd been kicked aside. No one would intentionally dump dirt so haphazardly. I knelt down and examined where wheels had rolled through the loose soil. Two impressions were larger and displayed a definite tread pattern. The other two depressions were flat. At the edge of the dirt, the clear imprint of a shoe showed where someone had stepped after the spill. The size appeared consistent with the shoes I found under the bed.

I turned my attention to the shed door. The padlock hung open on the clasp. My chest tightened. Hinges squeaked in mild protest as I pushed my way inside. Morning light shining through the attached greenhouse illuminated the interior brighter than I expected. I exhaled with relief. Sam Blackman, the investigator, had been expecting a body. I was never so glad to see only a lawnmower, edger, and fertilizer spreader on the floor.

The shed had a work sink and counter. Pegboard lined one wall, and trowels, trimmers, and hedge clippers hung from small hooks. A broad push broom leaned against fertilizer bags stacked in the corner. The concrete floor was dry and swept clean.

I moved to the greenhouse. The plants appeared to be orchids spread along three rows of narrow wooden shelves. Overhead, a hose with a misting nozzle dangled from a retractable holder. Heating units were mounted on wooden support posts. Everything appeared to be in order. But two overturned plant holders and a dirt trail through a spotless house told me otherwise.

"Sam!" Hewitt called from outside.

"I'm coming. Stay in the front."

I heard footsteps approaching. "Keep off the walk!" I hustled out of the shed, angry that Hewitt wouldn't do what I asked.

"What are you doing?" Homicide Detective Newly Newland gave me the hard cop stare usually reserved for suspects.

"Are you here to talk to Lenore Carpenter?"

"I'm here now to find out why four of last night's ghost tour participants are at the home of a fifth who's absent."

"We're looking for Lenore Carpenter. Her friend called us this morning because no one's seen her."

"Since when?"

"I don't know for sure. Not since before yesterday." I was curious as to why Newly had arrived. "Are you here for her statement?"

Newly ignored my question. "Who called you?"

"Shirley. Hewitt's office manager. She and Lenore are good friends."

"Was she good friends with Molly Staton?"

"Yes. They're members of that Asheville Apparitions spiritualist group."

Newly rocked back and forth on his heels. "Is Shirley here?"

"She's on the front porch with Hewitt and Nakayla."

"What's her last name?"

"I don't know."

He gave me a look like I had to be kidding.

"Everyone just calls her Shirley."

Newly nodded to the open shed door. "What are you poking around in there for?"

I pointed to the dirt from the overturned flower baskets. "Following an odd set of tracks." Then I talked him through the discovery of the rented dress, the shoes under the bed, and Shirley's assertion that Lenore would never have brought her gardening shoes and a wagon into the house.

"That's why they're standing on the porch?" he asked.

"Yes. This could be a crime scene. I was about to call you."

He grunted. "That was good thinking."

"I hope I'm wrong."

"Don't kid yourself." With that comment, he pivoted and headed back to the front porch.

Nakayla, Shirley, and Hewitt stood close to the side banister, watching the detective approach. I stood next to Nakayla as Newly positioned himself in front of the door.

"Sam's given me the rundown on why you're here and in light of what you found, I think it's prudent to keep the house sealed." He turned to Shirley. "I don't believe we've met. I'm Curt Newland."

"Shirley. I work for Hewitt."

"What's your last name?"

Shirley shrugged. "Lee."

"Shirley Lee?" Newly asked.

"No. My legal name is Cheryl Lee, but everyone always runs the words together and I got tired of correcting them. So, Shirley is fine."

One mystery solved, I thought. Now if Lenore would just pull up her driveway.

"And you last saw Lenore Carpenter when?"

"Wednesday. Our planning team had a final meeting and then I talked to her Thursday night. She called to verify that the Grove Park Inn had approved moving her appearance from the grand lobby to the Palm Atrium."

Newly fumbled in his suit pocket and found a note pad and pen. "Was that a last minute change?"

"Not really. It had been an option we'd discussed with the hotel. When we saw how successfully tickets sales were going, we were afraid the lobby would be too chaotic. Our group would get mixed up with the hotel guests, and Lenore might have trouble getting them to concentrate on her story."

"There wasn't a storyteller like Sam was at Helen's Bridge?"

"No. We decided to have Lenore tell her own story."

Newly nodded as he wrote. "And the Palm Atrium would be more authentic anyway."

"You know the history then," Shirley said.

Newly stopped writing and gave Shirley a skeptical look. "I wouldn't call it history because there's no proof it actually happened. We get an inquiry or two every year from people wanting to search our police records to document the report of her death. Just like the inquiries regarding Helen's Bridge. No police reports exist. But I know the legend is a young woman in a pink gown fell to her death from the fifth floor in the Palm Atrium in the early days of the hotel. No one knows whether she jumped or was pushed."

"Many staff and guests have felt her presence," Shirley said. "And she's appeared to children."

Newly lifted the pad and pen in surrender. "I'm not saying it's not a good story. Now the Grove Park likes to perpetuate it. Good for business. But you think someone would have noticed Lenore Carpenter walking through the hotel last night, wouldn't you?"

"And that's why I'm worried." Shirley's voice quivered. "She wouldn't have gone there without the dress."

"Am I right that the Pink Lady was a guest at the hotel?" Newly asked.

"Yes," Shirley said.

"Was Lenore playing the part so true to the ghost tale that she actually checked into the Grove Park?"

"No," Shirley said. "She was only going to be there from six-thirty to ten-thirty."

"So, as far as you know, there's no reason she would have checked in as a guest."

"Not that I know of."

Newly's eyes narrowed as he angled toward Hewitt. "Mr. Donaldson, are you also familiar with the Pink Lady?"

"I am. I grew up here and the story was one of those campfire tales I heard as a boy."

"Did the version you heard claim the young woman was a hotel guest?"

"Yes. And that she was thrown to her death by a lover. What's your point?"

"Do you happen to remember her room number?"

"I believe it was 545, but, again, what's your point?"

Newly closed his note pad and took a deep breath. "I'm sorry to inform all of you that the body of Lenore Carpenter was found early this morning in room 545."

A numbness spread through my chest. Nakayla gasped.

Shirley whimpered a muffled cry and collapsed onto the porch swing.

Newly looked at me. "I got the call shortly after leaving your office this morning. I made a quick trip to the room and then came here to see if there was any sign of an abduction."

I looked at Hewitt. His face had gone white as cotton. "You'd better sit down."

He joined Shirley on the swing and his tough as nails office manager buried her face in his shoulder and sobbed.

Newly stepped closer to Nakayla. "Last night you said Molly Staton wasn't wearing the white dress she was supposed to."

"That's right," Nakayla whispered.

"Lenore Carpenter was found in a vintage white dress," Newly said. "Forensics is only starting, but I believe we're looking at a second homicide and a killer who dressed Lenore in Molly's dress. He's purposely linking his crimes. I need to make sure everyone, and I mean everyone, is accounted for who played a role in last night's fundraiser. Someone might be acting out Asheville's ghost tales and leaving a trail of bodies behind."

Chapter Nine

Homicide Detective Newland placed a call for the Buncombe County mobile crime lab to come to Lenore Carpenter's home as soon as they wrapped the scene at the Grove Park Inn. Between the previous night and today's discovery of the second victim, the forensics team had their work cut out for them. Trace evidence would be crucial if links were to be established. As an investigator, I believed any break in the case would come from something small and not from the obvious connections like the switched dresses.

"I don't want to chance any further contamination of the scene," Newly told us. "I want each of you to tell me where you went in the house."

Shirley wiped her eyes. "I found the front door unlocked. I called out and when no one answered, I walked across the living room to the hallway. I saw the dress on her bed and knew something bad had happened."

"Did you go anywhere else?" Newly asked.

"I made a quick check of the other rooms to make sure Lenore wasn't lying unconscious somewhere, and then I stayed by the front door. I guess I sensed things should be left untouched. I called Nakayla first and then Hewitt."

Newly glanced at the vehicles parked in the street. "Who rode together?"

"I came with Hewitt from my office," I said. "Shirley took us straight to the bedroom. I'm the only one who followed the dirt trail through the kitchen." I looked at Hewitt, expecting him to confirm my story, but he stared at the front door as if trying to remember the simple details of our entry.

"Is that correct, Mr. Donaldson?" Newly asked.

Hewitt eyed Nakayla and Shirley, and then nodded. "Yes. We came to the porch where you found us."

"I'll need prints from each of you for elimination purposes." Newly glanced back to the street. "I've got a kit in the car."

We all looked at Hewitt, expecting him to protest some violation of his constitutional rights. He only said, "Then let's go to your car."

After we were inked and printed, Newly gave Hewitt and Shirley a direct order. "It's of the utmost urgency that you contact everyone involved with the ghost tour. Let them know what happened and warn them that right now we're not sure of either motive or the extent to which this killing could go further. And if anyone is missing, call me immediately." He reached in his pocket and handed his card to each of them. "I need Sam and Nakayla to give me more information on the other ghost tour locations."

As Hewitt walked past me, he whispered, "My office."

Newly led us to the front porch. Nakayla and I sat on a slatted swing and the detective pulled a wicker chair closer to us. He rested his note pad on his knee and clicked his ballpoint. "Okay, run through the tour and what roles were played at each site."

"Not every site had an actor," Nakayla said. "Some were only covered by the tour guide's commentary."

"Better give them all to me."

Nakayla set the swing in motion and let the rhythm guide the pace of her story. "The walking tour started at the registration booth at the Splashville end of Pack Square."

Splashville was the name of the fountains located at the far side of the square from our office. The streams of water opened and closed in a variety of combinations and were designed to soak kids and adventuresome adults who played in their spray.

"The first stop was City Hall and the story of the financial manager's suicide. We didn't have an actor. Just a chalk outline where we imagined his body struck the sidewalk."

In 1929, the stock market crash took the value of Asheville's investments from over one hundred eighty-seven million dollars to eighty-eight million. The nearly hundred million-dollar loss plunged the city into debt, and the financial manager threw himself off the eight-story, magnificent Art Deco building in one of the more spectacular suicides of the era. Splashville indeed.

"So, your tour guides told that story," Newly said.

"Yes. We'd stay there about five minutes and talked about how the manager's ghost had been seen multiple times in the lobby or office hallways."

A faint smile broke Newly's serious expression. "The manager's ghost allegedly seen. I'm after a flesh and blood culprit."

"We conveyed the sightings as fact to enhance the mood. And then we added a little bit about the building's architecture."

"Did everyone start at City Hall?"

"No," Nakayla said. "We had a shotgun start. Groups headed to different locations but then followed a planned order. I got the busload of Japanese and our first stop was Helen's Bridge."

Newly jotted a note on his pad. "All right. What was after City Hall?"

"The tour headed toward Marjorie Street and the area where town hangings occurred. No actors were involved. We mainly got people clear of that end of the square to loop around and come up Spruce Street to the Jackson Building."

"More jumpers?" Newly asked.

"Yes. But in addition to chalk outlines we had actors positioned in the two windows. You know the tales. The woman on the fifth floor would yell 'Taxi!' out her window for each new group."

Detective Newland nodded. He probably knew the stories from his childhood. I'd only learned them from Nakayla after the Jackson Building, Asheville's first skyscraper, had been chosen as one of our tour stops.

The fifteen-story Spanish Renaissance building was an architectural jewel. Built in 1924 on the site of the monument shop of Thomas Wolfe's father, the Jackson Building was capped with an ornate tower that was used in the 1939 film, *The Hunchback of Notre Dame*. Leopard gargoyles leaped from each top corner, and when it first opened, the tower held a four-hundred-times telescope and a powerful searchlight.

In 1929, a businessman on the twelfth floor lost all his assets in the crash. Like the city manager, he jumped to his death rather than face the shame of bankruptcy. In 1942, a young woman leaned too far out of her fifth floor office window and fell to the sidewalk. Witnesses said they thought she was trying to hail a taxi that was cruising the square.

Our actors had been stationed on each of the two floors and their respective offices were the only ones whose lights were on. To add to the ghoulish reenactment, the chalk outlines on the sidewalk were drawn holding hands, even though the deaths were separated by thirteen years.

"Lenny Colbert played the man," Nakayla said. "He simply paced back and forth and was seen as a silhouette. Nicole Worthington was the young woman. We hit her with a spotlight as her cue to yell taxi."

Newly wrote down the names. "Was she leaning out the window?"

"No. We didn't want to take a chance."

"Have you seen either of them since last night?"

"I haven't," Nakayla said.

I shook my head. "I'm sure they'll be at the top of the call list."

"Let's move on," Newly said.

"The next stop was the Battery Park Hotel," Nakayla said.

Newly shifted in his chair. "That's a good little hike on foot."

"We went by way of Church Street where the cemeteries used to be. The guides spoke about spirits seen walking in the moonlight, searching for their graves that had been moved as the land-locked churches expanded. They also talked about some of the old legends for which there are no standing structures."

"No actors in sheets?"

"No. We made use of the distance by selling drinks and snack food along the route to Battery Park."

"Was Helen your ghost?"

"Helen and her murderer."

Newly knew his ghost stories. This Helen wasn't Helen of the bridge but a nineteen-year-old woman brutally shot and slashed in her hotel room. In the summer of 1936, Helen Clevenger came down from New York to visit her uncle and see Asheville. On the morning of July 17th, he became alarmed when she didn't answer his knocks. He found his niece lying in a pool of blood, shot through the chest and cut around the face and throat. Police arrested a twenty-two-year-old hotel employee and got a confession out of him. I say got because the rumor is the confession was forcibly coerced. His motive was robbery and the means was a thirty-two-caliber pistol discovered in his room. It was enough for his execution.

But on the night of Helen's death, an eyewitness saw a running man believed to be the murderer. The physical description didn't match the accused. It did match the build of the hotel manager's son. The son was never seen in Asheville again. Now the Battery Park Hotel exists as senior apartments, and the elderly residents claim to catch fleeting glimpses of a young girl walking the hall near room 224, the scene of the murder.

"We paid for the current resident of what had been Helen's room to spend the night in the Haywood Park Hotel," Nakayla said. "Then we used a gel to cast a red aura over the interior of the room. Catherine Bagley played Helen and Tyler Winston was the murderer. They staged a brief scuffle in front of the window, and then disappeared from view. We played the sound effect of a gunshot."

"And their whereabouts?" Newly asked.

Nakayla shrugged. "I don't know. When Sam and I left you last night, we went back to the Kenilworth. Shirley was the first and only person I spoke with before coming here."

Newly wrote what I assumed to be the names of Catherine and Tyler. Then he stared out over the front yard for a moment.

"Of the actors you've mentioned, which ones are members of Asheville Apparitions?"

"All of them. Since the group did so much of the organizational work, we agreed they should have first dibs on the ghost roles."

Newly cocked his head and eyed me with surprise. "You belong to these ghost hunters?"

"No. I was just a host in a costume."

"Was Battery Park the last stop?"

"The last walking stop. From there, shuttle buses transported people to three locations. Three buses left at the start, each going to a different spot. Then all the other shuttles went first to the Samuel Reed House, followed by the Grove Park, and finally Helen's Bridge before returning to Pack Square."

"The Reed House. That's now the Biltmore Village Inn, right?"

"The owners gave a tour of their B and B while dressed in Victorian formal wear. They served hot cider and crumpets."

"So, no actors," Newly said.

"No. We had a loop of Gay Nineties music with the occasional footsteps and sounds of a pool table."

Samuel Reed had been George Vanderbilt's attorney and he built his Victorian home in 1892 on a mountain overlooking Biltmore Village on the south side of Asheville. No murders occurred in the home, but of Reed's nine children, only four made it to adulthood. Residents of the house have heard footsteps on the back stairs and the crack of balls and children's voices in what had once been the billiard room.

For the first time, Newly flipped back through his note pad, searching for something he'd written earlier. He stopped and tapped his ballpoint on the center of a page. "Hewitt Donaldson was on the south side last night. Was he at the Reed House?"

"You'll have to ask him," Nakayla said. "He was mobile as a troubleshooter. With all the vans going back and forth, we wanted a quick response in case someone was left behind or a vehicle had mechanical trouble."

Newly pressed the point. "So, he could have been in the Reed House?"

"What are you driving at?" I asked.

He closed the note pad. "Nothing particular. Just getting a sense for where everyone was. Sounds like you planned for everything."

"We didn't plan for a double homicide."

"No." Newly stood. "But somebody did."

Nakayla and I took his cue and rose from the porch swing. I figured our conversation had ended.

"And you didn't see anything in the shed or yard that could have left those dirt tracks through the house?" Newly asked.

"No," I said. "But I have my suspicions."

"Care to share?"

"After you answer a question for me."

He crossed his arms against his chest. He didn't like negotiating over information. "What's that?"

"Why are you so interested in Hewitt?"

"I'm not. At this point, I'm interested in everyone." Newly was a good detective, but a terrible liar. "So, what's your suspicion?"

"Look for a wheelchair."

We left Newland waiting for forensics, but not before he admonished us not to mention anything about the scene or our conversation. What did he think we were going to do? Call the newspaper?

Nakayla dropped me at the office and headed to her home in West Asheville for a shower and change of clothes. She would check in later and we'd grab lunch somewhere in town.

I exited the elevator and passed by our door, heading straight for Hewitt's office down the hall. His whispered message had carried an urgency that he wanted to see me without delay.

I found him at Shirley's desk where he must have been waiting for me.

"Let's go to the conference room," he said.

"Where's Shirley?"

"I told her to make her calls from home. She knows those apparition people better than I do."

Hewitt's conference room was unlike any other lawyer's I've known. Instead of a long table, a circular one filled the middle of the floor. Even though he had a massive ego, Hewitt displayed his tenet that all are created equal in the eyes of the law. There was no head of the table.

The walls were empty of the obligatory shelves of leather-bound books or professional degrees and awards attorneys put on view to impress their clients. Hewitt's walls were covered in framed album covers from the 1960s. Dylan, Rolling Stones, Cream, Beatles, Byrds, and Iron Butterfly to name a few. I was surprised he didn't have tracks piped through overhead speakers like Muzak on speed.

He took a seat and gestured for me to sit across from him.

"What's up?" I asked.

He leaned forward. "I want you to work for me."

"We are working for you. The Atwood custody case is still going on and Nakayla and I are monitoring the behavior of Clyde's parents."

"No, Sam. I want you to work for me. Personally."

"I don't understand."

"You need to find who killed Lenore and Molly."

"The police are investigating. Newland's a good detective."

"Newland will zero in on one person. A person he and the department would like to see brought down."

"Who?"

"Me. My prints are all over Lenore's house. She was my lover."

Chapter Ten

I stared at Hewitt. My challenge to Detective Newland to investigate his own partner because of Tuck Efird's relationship to Molly Staton had just boomeranged on me. Hewitt warranted the same scrutiny.

"How long?" I asked.

"A couple of months. Since we started working on the fundraiser together. I've known Lenore for years, but this time when our paths crossed, the chemistry was different. It just sort of happened."

There was probably a twenty-year difference in their ages, I thought. But, such a relationship wasn't that uncommon. Hewitt kept his personal life private. I knew he was divorced, although I wasn't sure how many times. I'd never known him to date, and chalked that up to his obsession with his career.

"Who knew about it?" I asked.

"No one. We wanted to play it out a little longer. Less awkward in case things fell apart."

"You don't think Lenore told anyone?"

Hewitt smiled. "It was Lenore's idea. She particularly didn't want Molly or Shirley to know."

"You have no motive. She hadn't broken up with you. You'd been to her house so naturally your fingerprints are there. End of story."

Hewitt leaned forward and raked his fingers through his long hair so hard several silver strands drifted to the floor. "But

I wasn't as forthcoming with Newland as I should have been. I did see Lenore yesterday. I stayed over Thursday night and ran out yesterday morning to buy us juice and coffee for breakfast. Yes, I can say my fingerprints were there because I visited her house, but you can bet your ass they're going to find a receipt in Lenore's trash with a time stamp on it. It will be a little difficult to explain my fingerprints on a bottle purchased only a few hours before her murder."

Circumstantial, I thought, but the timing would look bad. And I sensed Detective Newland had something else at play. His question about whether I knew what Hewitt had been wearing last night wasn't as casual as he pretended it to be.

"Then you'd better get ahead of it," I advised. "If he thinks you're covering up, it will only make him more suspicious."

"I know. Newland played it cagey not telling us Lenore was dead when he asked when we'd last seen her. Otherwise, I wouldn't have tried to hide that I'd been there."

"You want to see how he reacts to your statement before Nakayla and I investigate?"

Hewitt stood so fast it was like the chair ejected him. "No, goddammit. My problems aside, I want you to find whoever killed Lenore." He paced back and forth around the curve of the table. "My gut tells me someone involved with the Atwood case is behind it."

"What would they have to gain by killing Molly and Lenore?"

He stopped and threw up his hands. "What would anyone have to gain? I don't think we're talking logic here. Someone wanted to disrupt the event. They're so ignorant they probably thought we'd have to give everyone their money back, and Helen Wilson would look irresponsible as the twins' guardian."

I kept my seat and looked up at the distraught lawyer. I'd never seen him in such a state. The master of the courtroom seemed to be falling apart in his own office. For once, he was the one not thinking logically.

Hewitt must have read the doubt on my face. "What? If you have a better idea, I'm all ears."

I motioned for him to sit in the chair beside me. "Let's step back a moment and review what we do know."

He took a deep breath and sat.

"First, no one knew about your relationship with Lenore," I said.

"That's right. If she said she was keeping it a secret, it was a secret."

"Then whoever killed her isn't doing this to hurt you or frame you."

"No," he agreed, "not because of her. But they could be trying to discredit me since I'm Helen's attorney."

I hadn't thought about Hewitt as a target. His fear more likely grew out of his sense of his own importance rather than any conspiratorial scheme. "Okay. But that undercuts your theory that they're stupid. Look how these murders were orchestrated. Not one but two complex maneuvers to get Molly dressed and positioned at the bridge and Lenore into that hotel room. Can you see Cletus Atwood pulling that off?"

"Don't ever think ignorance trumps cunning," Hewitt said. "I've defended some characters who couldn't spell their own names, but if they saw you as prey, they'd out maneuver you at every turn."

"Yes, maybe they would scurry like conniving rats in the dark at Helen's Bridge, but do you think they could waltz Lenore's body through the lobby of the Grove Park Inn?"

Hewitt's eyes flickered as the question brought his rant to a halt. "No. That was brazen. I can't see Cletus Atwood having the poise or confidence to take the risk." He drummed his fingers on the conference table. "How do you think they managed it?"

I thought back to the spilled flowerpot and the soil tracked through the house. "I believe Lenore was murdered in the shed. My bet is the killer used a wheelchair to get her to the bedroom where he changed her into the dress. That's why her dirty gardening shoes were under the bed."

"Then where were the rest of her clothes?"

"Good question. Maybe forensics will find them stuffed in a hamper or the washing machine. They'll surface."

"And how did Lenore wind up in room 545?"

I shrugged. "The same way. Wheeled right into the Grove Park. A broad-brimmed hat, a lap blanket to hide a restraint, friendly nod to any bellhop, and no one would give them a second thought. How many wheelchairs do you think go into the inn a day?"

Hewitt nodded. "You give Detective Newland your theory?"

"I floated it by him. I expect he'll start looking at makes and models for a tread match."

"And how many wheelchairs are in Asheville?"

"All we need is one connected to someone with a motive."

"Which brings us back to the Atwoods," Hewitt said. "Either they're smarter than we give them credit for, or they enlisted some help."

Now I stood, physically breaking away from Hewitt's reluctance to view any other possibility. I walked to the wall and stared at a young Bob Dylan with his girlfriend, walking down a New York street on the album cover *Freewheelin'*. We needed to get our own wheels free from Hewitt's Atwood rut and at least explore other roads.

I turned around. "If I run an investigation, I'm not doing so with preconceived notions, either yours or mine."

"So you have other suspects?"

"If we can find other motives. I don't know what connects Lenore and Molly other than the Atwood case, but what if one was the target and the other silenced for whatever she knew or saw?"

Hewitt's eyebrows arched as he considered the point. "The hanging at the bridge was certainly more elaborate. So you think Lenore's death might have been improvised out of necessity?"

"I'm trying not to think anything at this stage other than follow whatever evidence we can find. Like who booked the room at the Grove Park?"

Hewitt's ruddy complexion paled. "I did. I picked up two keys Thursday so we could have early access on Friday. I left one with Lenore. I asked her to spend Thursday night there with me, but she preferred staying at her home." His voice caught. "Friday night after the event was supposed to be our romantic getaway."

Fingerprints. Room access. Hewitt was stepping in it big-time.

"Get to Newland now," I insisted. "And in person rather than over the phone."

"What are you going to do?"

"I'm going to the Grove Park. And it won't be for the view."

◇◇◇

The mammoth inn and spa rested on the side of Sunset Mountain, so named for the spectacular view of the western sky and Appalachian ridge line. Nakayla and I frequently drove up in late afternoons for a glass of wine on the inn's Sunset Terrace. We hardly spoke, preferring to watch the kaleidoscopic array of golds, pinks, and purples diffuse across the wisps of clouds. Simply sharing the moment was enough.

E.W. Grove had constructed his lodge in 1913 so that the well-to-do could escape the stress of the times to a retreat cocooned in rejuvenating fresh air and undisturbed tranquility. The patent medicine tycoon enforced his restrictions with such decrees as no running of water or flushing of commodes after ten-thirty at night. If you were too loud in the Great Hall of the inn, a printed card was delivered to your room reprimanding you for the behavior. Children were discouraged, dogs strictly forbidden, and alcohol was not a part of the drink selections. Obviously, that rule changed before F. Scott Fitzgerald showed up with his beer and booze in the mid-1930s.

The entire complex had been recently sold to the OMNI hotel chain, but the modifications imposed were more enhancements of the Grove Park's rich heritage rather than some overblown contemporary renovation.

In working our first case as a detective team, Nakayla and I had become acquainted with key staffers when we investigated F. Scott Fitzgerald's ties to the inn. Our involvement culminated in a shootout on the premises that left one of our suspects dead. Since then, our visits to the Grove Park had been strictly for drinks and the occasional dinner. The managers with whom we dealt had retired or moved on to other enterprises. So, as I drove through the stone-gated entrance, I knew I had neither special access to information nor anyone predisposed to help me.

Trying to put myself inside the head of the killer, I passed the valet parking at the front of the inn and entered the deck on the far side. An elevator connected all parking levels to a wing off the Great Hall that provided a route avoiding the throng clustered around the registration desk where attending bellhops eyed each guest for tip-worthy luggage.

I rode the elevator alone and then followed the signs to the Great Hall, passing only a few people engaged in their own conversations. Several staff members acknowledged me with a smile, but no one gave me a second look.

The Great Hall boasted two huge fireplaces, one at each end with comfortable chairs and sofas arranged in multiple group-ings where guests could drink and talk. Opposite the main entrance, the hall opened on the Sunset Terrace with its unrivaled mountain vista. The positioning of the fireplaces, main entrance, and terrace meant the center of the room was relatively empty. Everyone was in motion to some other destination.

I stepped close to the hearth of the nearer fireplace and surveyed the room. During the next five minutes, I saw three wheelchairs navigate through the open space, two propelled by their occupants and one pushed by what appeared to be an elderly lady's dutiful son. Only one of the three drew attention, a young man with a lower leg cast who seemed uncertain as to where he was going.

I also eyed the far edge of the opposite fireplace. The floor-to-ceiling stonework encased a working elevator, E.W. Grove's attempt to insulate the motor and cable noise from disturbing his guests. When the area around the door appeared clear, I purposefully strode across the Great Hall and pressed the button to summon the lift. I entered as the sole rider and selected the fifth floor. The old elevator started with a slight jolt and then rose with all the speed of a snail climbing a branch.

In addition to being housed in a fireplace, the elevator had the distinction of making the list of *Ripley's Believe It Or Not* for having not one or two but three doors for entering and exiting. As I faced the main door, I remembered the Palm Atrium floors triggered the door to my left. I'd been startled on my first ride when what I thought was a wall opened beside me. I thought about the implications of a wheelchair being positioned to roll straight in and straight out and concluded that even though the interior of the elevator was small, a wheelchair could be turned for the right-angle exit.

With a clunk, the elevator halted and the door slid open. I stepped out onto the fifth-floor balcony and peered over the waist-high safety wall. Below, palm ferns in wooden planters lined the perimeter of the atrium's courtyard. Leather and wicker furniture clustered in conversational arrangements. Their earth tones projected a calming atmosphere while the mauve trim of the balconies and decorative wall stencils kept the decor interesting.

But no one was seated. A few people stood along the length of the right side of the courtyard looking up across its width. I followed their gaze. Garish yellow crime scene tape blocked the long corridor at either end. Techs wheeled a collapsible gurney out a door. The sheet-covered body of Lenore Carpenter was headed for the morgue.

"Newly said you'd probably turn up."

Tuck Efird stepped beside me. I'd been so focused on the activity at the room I hadn't seen him approach from the opposite side of the fifth floor balcony.

"I saw Newly at Lenore's house. He told me what happened."

The strain was readily apparent on Efird's face. Like Newland, he hadn't slept since Molly's body dropped from the bridge.

"Newly shared your wheelchair theory." Efird made the statement while staring across the atrium at the gurney now rolling to the far diagonal corner. His tone was neither sarcastic nor enthusiastic.

"It's just a theory. The tread marks in Lenore's house seem consistent with that tire size."

"It's a damn good theory." Efird turned to me. "We found similar impressions in the soil atop Helen's Bridge."

"Really?"

"Gives us an idea where the car was parked along the roadside. But the son of a bitch stayed on the pavement so there were no tire marks."

"He took a hell of a chance," I said. "There's traffic on that road."

Efird stepped forward and squeezed the top of the balcony so hard his knuckles turned white. "I think he hid her body up there a couple hours earlier. Probably stuffed her on the back floor of his car and covered her with a blanket or tarp. A wheel-chair would unfold in just a few seconds. After twenty feet he'd be out of sight. We'll know more after the autopsy."

"I'm really sorry," I said.

"Thanks." The word choked in his throat. He faced me and blinked back tears. "I guess you heard Molly and I used to be together."

"Nakayla mentioned it."

He stepped closer. "I'm going to be the one to get the bastard, Sam. It's my case."

The warning to me was clear. Efird took my presence at his crime scene as proof I was an intruder. He appreciated my theory, but not my involvement.

"You know who booked the room?" he asked.

His question was rhetorical. I knew he meant to surprise me with the answer.

"Hewitt Donaldson," I said.

A scowl eclipsed the dawning triumph on his face. "Who told you that?"

"Hewitt Donaldson." I stated it like everyone in Asheville knew.

"Did he say why? And don't give me any of his lawyerly bullshit."

I wasn't about to betray Hewitt before he could give his reasons to Newland. But, if I clammed up, Efird would shut me out of any information he might have.

"He negotiated with Grove Park to be one of the sponsors of the fundraiser. I guess it included a room for Lenore to change for her pink lady portrayal."

"For two nights?"

"Maybe the costume was supposed to be delivered earlier in the day. Maybe there were other props to be stored. You'll have to ask Hewitt."

"Oh, I'll ask him all right."

I looked across the open atrium to where the gurney disappeared around a corner. "How are they exiting?"

"The manager showed us a route to a service elevator. The inn is public enough without parading Lenore's body through the front door."

"Could the killer have used the service elevator?"

"Maybe. But it's keyed. That doesn't mean someone didn't have a duplicate. Firemen carry them to override control in an emergency."

"Video surveillance?"

"Some, but there are gaps in coverage areas. If our guy scouted the place, he could work around them. We did see the van that new lawyer Peterson drove parked in the lot last night so his alibi for Molly checks out. He didn't leave till after Molly's body appeared. The time matches to when he showed up trying to get to the bridge."

I remembered both he and Nathan Armitage came to the roadblock.

"Have you searched for any tire treads here?"

Efird nodded. "Yeah. The room's getting a thorough exam. The housekeeper backed out the door as soon as she saw Lenore. No one else entered until we came."

Getting answers from Efird was like pulling teeth. "So, did you find any?"

"No. But any loose dirt could have come off between the killer's vehicle and the room."

And gurney wheels could be confused with wheelchair wheels, I thought. "Where was the body?"

"She was face-up on the floor, arms and legs splayed." Efird looked over the balcony. "Like she'd fallen from a great height."

I stared at the courtyard below. "Like the Pink Lady."

"I wonder why he didn't throw her over for real?" Efird said. "Like he did Molly."

"Too dangerous. The atrium is well lit. Someone could unexpectedly come out of any room on any level or walk through the Palm Court no matter the hour."

"You think he's done?" Efird asked.

"I don't know. What do you think?"

Efird rubbed the back of his neck, trying to press out his exhaustion. Then his eyes bore into mine with unrelenting determination. "Sam, we'll know if he's done when we learn why he began."

Chapter Eleven

I usually spent Sunday mornings with coffee and the *New York Times*. Occasionally, when the Spirit and Nakayla moved me, I would join her for services at Mount Zion Missionary Baptist Church, one of the larger African-American churches in Asheville and where her family had been members for generations. But on the Sunday after the two murders, I suggested Nakayla accompany me to the Church of the Righteous to get a first-hand view of the preacher, Horace Brooks, and hear for myself if he could have been the mystery caller who left that offensive voicemail.

"We don't want to draw attention," I said. "So, when they pass the snakes, handle them like it's no more unusual than passing the offering plate."

Nakayla laughed. "If the snakes come out, the only fear I have is that you'll trample me running for the door. I think we'll draw more attention as an interracial couple than novice snake handlers. Some of these ultra-conservative churches consider us an abomination."

I exited off I-40 onto Highway 23, following the directions posted on the church's web page. The Internet site had been more sophisticated than I'd expected with links to prayer chains, daily devotions, and, of course, a donation icon.

"Do you know anybody who goes there?" I asked.

"When I worked insurance investigations, a couple tried to pull a scam with fake medical bills from a minor car wreck. I'd caught them dead-to-rights, but they didn't want us to press charges because they said they'd planned to give the money to their church, the Church of the Righteous."

A light rain started sprinkling. I flipped on the CR-V's wipers. "Sort of a reverse of the devil made me do it. The preacher made me do it."

"Yeah. That was the first time I'd heard of Horace Brooks."

"Was he implicated?" I asked.

"That's the funny thing. When I told them I'd check on any church collusion, they panicked. Made a full confession that they'd devised the fraud on their own."

"Were they scared of Brooks?"

"Maybe. More likely they didn't want the humiliation that would come with the expanded investigation."

"What happened to them?"

"They paid a fine and received suspended sentences. I never thought about them again until now."

I took my eyes from the road and saw a wry grin on her face.

"What do you bet we sit in the pew right beside them?" she asked.

"I'm not taking that wager. Think they'd recognize you?"

"Probably. But I'd bet my last dollar you'll be recognized. Your picture was in the paper for both the Atwood trial and Molly's death."

I hadn't thought about my sudden notoriety. In my mind, we'd slip into the church on a back pew or chairs, and then get an up-close look at Brooks after the service. I figured like most preachers, he'd glad-hand his congregants as they left through the front door.

"Maybe you ought to go in alone," I suggested.

"Oh, no, hotshot. This was your idea. You're seeing it through."

The rain intensified and I leaned closer to the windshield. "Then we'll hide under an umbrella."

"Slow down," Nakayla ordered. "The turn to the church is coming up. It's a left."

"What's the street name?"

"Heavenly Way."

I couldn't have missed the celestial road if I'd tried. Left lane traffic stopped as no fewer than ten cars lined up to make the turn across the highway.

"Maybe we're backed up because they charge for parking," I said. "Or Heavenly Way is a toll road."

"Don't be snide," Nakayla admonished. "Just because it's not our cup of tea doesn't mean there aren't good people coming here. Horace Brooks must be tapping a need."

"Yeah. And tapping their wallets at the same time."

Nakayla scowled at me.

"Okay. I'll be on good behavior. Let's just get inside without having to talk to anyone."

The cars suddenly moved forward. At the turn, an off-duty sheriff's deputy held up oncoming traffic.

"Better than a light," Nakayla said.

Heavenly Way appropriately ascended the side of a ridge for at least a quarter mile until the trees gave way to a clearing. In the center stood a large metal building that could have been a warehouse, a gymnasium, or an airplane hangar. Money had gone for maximum square footage and not for architectural design. The only clue that the structure was a church came from the stone facade framing double front doors and extending about twenty feet away from the main wall. This entry served as the base for a blood-red cross mounted to its roof. At least the cross wasn't neon.

Umbrellas populated the parking lot like mushrooms and flowed back and forth from the church to the arriving vehicles. I realized my low-key entrance would be impossible. Greeters weren't simply saying hello at the door. They were out in the rain escorting people from their cars.

"They get an A for customer service," Nakayla said.

"Let's park at the far end where it's more isolated," I said. "We can hide under our umbrellas before we're surrounded by good Samaritans."

I pulled next to a dumpster in the back corner. "There's an umbrella on the floor behind you." I scrambled out and retrieved the second umbrella on my side. The rain now blew at an angle and I cursed myself for not wearing a raincoat over my sport coat and tie. I clicked the release button and the umbrella sprang open.

"Sam, we can't use these." Nakayla tilted her umbrella toward me.

I'd forgotten Jerry Wofford had given out these complimentary umbrellas to the volunteers on Friday. His Crystal Stream logo and a pint of golden lager adorned the surface. Beneath the beer in bold, yellow lettering was the tag line: Divinely Devised, Devilishly Delicious. I looked over my shoulder and saw a man and woman headed for us.

"Too late. Angle it away and let's move."

The greeters quickened their stride to intercept us. To my surprise, the man was African-American and the woman, Latina.

"Good morning," the man said. "The Lord be with you." He appeared to be around thirty. The woman might have been ten years older.

I wasn't sure how to respond. Fortunately, Nakayla answered, "And also with you."

The woman looked at my CR-V. "You could have parked a little closer."

"We wanted to save plenty of spaces for those who might not be as able-bodied," Nakayla explained.

I had to admire how easily she handled the situation, all the while moving us closer to the door.

The man extended his hand, first to Nakayla and then to me. "Very considerate. My name is Earl and this is Roberta. Glad you are joining us on this," he looked up to the heavens, "day of aquatic rejuvenation."

"That's one way of putting it," I said, feeling like I should at least demonstrate that I had vocal cords. "We're glad to be here. Please don't let us keep you from others who need assistance."

Roberta nodded. "We just wanted to say, welcome. We're all

family here." They turned and headed for a van with a handicapped tag dangling from its rearview mirror.

More greeters lined the steps to the front door. It was like running a gauntlet of good wishes. As we walked into the sanctuary, I expected to be handed a bulletin and escorted to a seat. Instead, an elderly gentleman in a worn gray sport coat asked us if we needed hearing assistance.

"No," I said. "We can sit in the back."

"Sit where ere ya like," he drawled in a soft mountain twang. "I've got these if ya need 'em." He moved to one side and revealed a table piled with electronic over-the-ear headsets, the wireless kind I'd used for those self-guided museum exhibition tours. "Let me take those wet umbrellas," he insisted. "I'll put them in the draining rack just inside the door. Don't want any puddles the old-timers could slip in."

The guy had to be in his late eighties. His old-timers must have been one year younger than God.

"Come see me afterwards," he said. "I'll fetch 'em for ya."

Nakayla and I handed him the beer logo umbrellas, now collapsed into non-distinguishable colors, and looked for seats.

There were no pews. Instead, about five hundred cushioned, folding chairs were arced in a huge semicircle around a stage. Two main aisles split the rows into three sections. Nakayla and I moved to the left and found two seats at the far end of the last row. She let me sit on the outside where I could stretch my prosthetic leg for comfort. I already felt a little dampness from the rain that had seeped between the stump of my limb and the device.

Unlike the Presbyterian church in which I grew up, the seats were filling from the front. As the time neared eleven, it became apparent that no one else would probably sit in the three or even four last rows. So, instead of hiding in a crowd, Nakayla and I managed to catch the eye of everyone walking down our side of the sanctuary.

Most people smiled or nodded a welcome, understanding that we were visitors dipping our toe in their congregational pool.

If anyone recognized me, they masked their reaction well. That was until Cletus and Nelda Atwood arrived.

"Look away," Nakayla whispered.

Of course, I did the opposite and stared straight into their faces as they passed our row. Nelda paled while Cletus' cheeks burned red as hot coals. He took a step toward us, but his wife grabbed his arm.

At that moment, an electric guitar chord resounded through the room. The worshipers rose to their feet and I saw a band in place to the right of the stage. A choir filed in from both wings and met in the center. Purple curtains that framed the back wall and stage wings parted to reveal large projector screens. Lights dimmed as the screens brightened. Video of a brilliant blue sky and puffy white clouds filled all three screens. The point of view matched a pilot's perspective as a jet climbed swiftly. Then, in the distant heavens, a cross the color of the one over the church entrance, the same blood-red hue as the choir's robes, grew larger. When it filled the screen, gold rays bloomed behind it and the band struck the downbeat of a praise hymn I didn't recognize.

Words began rolling up the video screens and I understood why there were no bulletins or hymnals. What I'd assumed was a backwoods mountain church turned out to be a temple of technology.

People raised their hands over their heads and joined the choir. The lyrics were simple and the tune hypnotic—"Jesus is good to me, he wants good for me, if his I will always be, Jesus will take care of me." That was the chorus with the verses being only slight variations.

I'm not the most schooled in theological matters, but I am a theist and respectful of any faith devoted to a benevolent God. One of my closer friends in the military, Randy Moffit, had been a chaplain in Iraq. I attended his services sporadically, but really enjoyed one-on-one conversations over a couple of beers. Randy summed up this hymn, what I suspected to be this church, and what he called Prosperity Gospel in one sentence—"Jesus is my boyfriend and he's going to buy me presents."

The final chorus ended with a long, exuberant Amen. As the congregation sat, Horace Brooks strode on stage, his image magnified three-fold by the giant screens. There was neither podium nor pulpit. The preacher stood in the center wearing a dark blue suit, white shirt, and striped yellow tie. He smiled and stretched out his arms.

"God is in this place." His voice boomed through the speakers so loudly I wondered why anyone would ever need the headsets dispensed by the old gentleman. On the TV close-up, I noticed a wireless microphone clipped just below the knot in his tie. The earpiece in his right ear must have provided program feedback.

"Amen!" shouted the congregation.

"Jesus is in this place," Brooks proclaimed.

"Amen!" responded the congregation.

"And the Holy Spirit moves among us." Brooks made a rippling motion with his hands like the current of a mountain stream.

I offered a hearty "Amen!" But the congregation in unison said, "Open my heart to receive him." I decided to keep my mouth shut for the rest of the service.

"Then let us go to our God in prayer." Brooks bowed his head.

I closed my eyes and the preacher launched into a five-minute prayer that my friend Randy Moffit called a "just wanna." "Lord, we just wanna praise you." "Lord, we just wanna thank you." Randy wasn't mocking or belittling either the prayer or those who pray it. He was rebuking a fellow chaplain who made a disparaging remark about some of the more fundamentalist believers he encountered. Randy pointedly said at least they prayed and did so with a degree of humility often missing from those who simply mouthed words from a prayer book.

My mind snapped back from that Baghdad debate when I heard Brooks say, "And Lord, we just want you to deliver us from the demons in our midst. Those who would destroy marriages, those who would destroy families, those who would cause others to destroy themselves." I wanted to open my eyes and see if he was pointing at Nakayla and me. If everyone had turned around to gaze upon the two demons in their midst. Was Brooks pumping up his congregation for a good stoning?

"Drive out those demons of alcoholism, of adultery, of persecution, bullying, and poverty that destroy hope and nurture despair. We ask these things in the name of the one whose spilled blood demonstrates love and forgiveness. We who are unworthy yet valued in the Kingdom of Heaven pray, "Our Father …""

The congregation completed the Lord's Prayer with a jubilant "Amen."

Brooks seamlessly went into the recitation of scripture, quoting from the first chapter of the Gospel of Mark telling of Jesus' confrontation with demons possessing a man in the synagogue. How they sought to reveal his identity before the proper time. Brooks directed our attention to the screens where the Bible words appeared, some in black and some in red. We were instructed to read the ones in black aloud, the words of the demons. The ones in red, Jesus' words, were dramatically spoken by Brooks. It was a good technique, a creative way to engage everyone with the passage.

Brooks then wove the text into a sermon of how evil will recognize good first and then try to hide its true intentions. Satan is the master of lies, not fighting God's will but perverting it. And sometimes the innocent may not realize they are pawns of evil until it is too late. Until they have destroyed a family or hurled themselves from a high place and destroyed themselves.

Nakayla and I looked at each other. The not-so-subtle reference to Molly and Lenore and their ghost roles could have only been clearer if he mentioned them by name.

After the sermon, a young man and woman sang a duet while ushers passed offering plates along the rows. I dropped a twenty onto a mound of cash. Then the ushers returned to the aisles, this time carrying wireless hand microphones.

Brooks walked to the center of the stage. "And now we will spend a few minutes sharing our joys and concerns so that as a community of faith we can pray for each other during the coming week. Simply raise your hand and the usher nearest you will provide the microphone."

For a few seconds, no one moved. Then a few hands went up. An elderly lady asked for prayers for her unsaved loved ones. A young man told how God had gotten him a new job. A couple stood together, holding hands, and announced they were expecting their first child. Each statement of joy or concern was answered with a smattering of Amens. I was struck by the diversity of the speakers—black, white, Latino, young, old.

Nakayla's comment about Brooks tapping a need appeared to cross all demographic lines except one. I remembered the cars and pickups in the parking lot all had years and miles on them. Many with bald tires and rusted fenders appeared older than the church building. In a world measuring status by things possessed, these people lived on the margins. Gathered here, they found acceptance. I suspected it was equal parts faith and fellowship. A sanctuary, in multiple meanings of the word, and a social encounter for those whose only access to a country club would be through an entrance marked Employees Only.

A shadow fell over me. I looked up to see the old man from the headset table. He had a microphone in his right hand while waving his left over his head.

"Yes," Brooks said. "All the way in the back."

The septuagenarian spoke into the mike. "We have a visitor who'd like to share something." Then he stuck the mike in my face.

It pointed to my head like a gun. I wanted to bite the liver-spotted hand wrapped around it. People turned in their seats to stare at me.

"Don't be shy, my friend," Brooks prodded. "You are among family."

Nakayla leaned forward and snatched the mike away. She stood and every eye followed her rise.

"I just wanted to say that I will pray that all of us here will do what the Lord requires of us—to seek justice, and to love kindness, and to walk humbly with our God."

Heads nodded and a unified "Amen" filled the air. The congregation turned back to Brooks.

"Words of the prophet Micah," the preacher said. "An excellent prayer that I commend to be the close of every prayer we offer this coming week." He took a few steps closer to the edge of the stage. "Thank you. And welcome, Nakayla Robertson and Sam Blackman."

Heads snapped around, astonishment on faces, and none more so than mine.

The rest of the service passed in a blur of songs and hallelujahs. There was a tap on my shoulder and I looked up to see the old man who had ambushed me.

"Pastor Horace would like ya to see him for a few minutes if ya got the time."

I wanted to say, "Sorry, Nakayla has to get back to her coven," but instead I said, "Sure. Mind telling me how he knew we were here?"

"Junior told him through that intercom in his ear."

"Junior who?"

"Junior Atwood. Cletus' younger brother and Clyde's uncle. Junior told me you wanted to say something in the service. That's why I brought ya the mike." He smiled at Nakayla. "Nice prayer, little lady."

"And is Junior the one who also told you Pastor Horace wants to see us?"

"Yep. That Junior knows his sound stuff. Pastor Horace has a separate channel so he can speak just to Junior. Ya know, tell him if the level's too loud, or he's going to change the order of the service. Junior learned about all that technical machinery in the Army. He was a lifer, and now he runs our A/V equipment, plus we're buying our own radio station."

The old man led us up the side aisle against the flow of exiting church members. We were like salmon swimming upstream. Some people still smiled at us; others gave curious stares. None were outright hostile.

"What's your name?" I asked.

"Ya can call me Wheezer. Rhymes with geezer. My given name is Wally Feezor, but it got collapsed to one word years ago."

I should introduce Wally Feezor, aka Wheezer, to Cheryl Lee, aka Shirley, and they could start a collapsed name club.

"You been a member long?" I asked.

"Yep. Since that first night Pastor Horace showed up with his tent in Asheville. My dear wife, Libby, God rest her soul, dragged me to see him. And God used him to cast out my demon."

"Your demon?"

"I was a bad drunk. About to lose my wife and kids because the alcohol was working on me from the inside, where nobody could see and only I could hear its constant calling. God spoke and touched me there that night. Couldn't have done it by myself, as sure as I'm talking to ya."

We reached the left of the stage and Wheezer pushed open a door. We walked down a hallway, just the three of us, and then the old man suddenly stopped. "I never hit Libby, but I was afraid the drink would push me into something I'd never do sober." He lowered his voice to a warbley whisper. "I know that's what happened to Clyde Atwood. His momma tried to get him to church. So did his wife, Heather. But the demon had him." Wheezer started walking again. "Now what's done is done."

We turned a corner and I saw Horace Brooks talking to the couple who had sung the duet.

"Wait here by this door," Wheezer said. "It's the pastor's office. While you're talking to him, I'll bring your umbrellas and lay them along the edge of the hall. Nice to meet ya." He hurried away as fast as his old legs could carry him.

"You think we've been summoned to the principal's office?" Nakayla asked.

"I don't know. But if Brooks starts throwing Bible verses at us, I'm counting on you to defend me."

Brooks turned and swung his arm in an arc toward his office door. "Please go in. I appreciate your giving me a few minutes of your time."

We stepped inside. The office furniture was utilitarian: a tidy desk, three chairs around a coffee table, and a filing cabinet. Two of the four walls were covered by bookshelves holding what appeared to be Bibles, Bible commentaries, encyclopedias, and thick books by Bonhoeffer, Barth, and a few other familiar names in a host of tomes I suspected to be heavy-duty theological reading. The only window looked over a children's playground where rain bounced off the slide and swing seats.

On the walls with the window and the door were framed photographs of church activities. Kids were leading worship services and working in community food pantries. Adults were on field trips to nursing homes or tutoring kids in what looked like after-school programs. I saw no pictures of Brooks and no college or university degrees. Maybe he was self-educated or maybe he attached no importance to whatever formal training he might have received. But his library was far more extensive than what I expected.

"Have a seat," he said.

We sat. For a moment, we looked at him and he looked at us. He seemed older than he appeared in the news clip. Maybe it was that the harsh, head-on lights of the cameras had obliterated the furrows in his forehead and flattened the bags under his eyes. I searched for traces of makeup, the sign that his TV image held priority. He just looked like an ordinary guy in his mid-fifties who would disappear at a conference of bankers, insurance brokers, or lawyers. The man sitting across from me wasn't the man I'd expected, based on the TV and newspaper quotes.

Brooks crossed his legs and relaxed. "First, let me say you are welcome here. I'm going to take it at face value that you joined us for sincere worship and that you do seek justice, love kindness, and walk humbly with God."

I felt a tinge of color burn my cheeks. I'd come to judge him but he'd skillfully thrown the spotlight back on me.

I leaned forward and tried to match the intensity of his gaze. "Yes, I seek those things, but to speak truthfully, I came to take your measure." The phrase sounded nice and Biblical.

Brooks' dark eyes widened. "My measure? Why?"

"Two women are dead. Two women who were working to raise money for those orphaned twins. You were quoted as saying some things that I…" I looked at Nakayla…"that we took as inflammatory. If they were murdered because of their efforts for the Atwood boys, then your demonizing them and their actions might have led one of your flock astray big-time."

Brooks said nothing. He seemed to be pondering the possibility I'd thrown at him. He looked at Nakayla. "Do you feel this way?"

"You called them Satan worshipers," she said.

He raised his right hand like swearing an oath. "I didn't. Nelda Atwood made that statement and I disavowed it."

"When?" Nakayla asked.

"Friday night. The TV reporter tried to bait me for a response. Of course, that never made the air."

"What about your quote that Helen Wilson has that hotshot attorney Hewitt Donaldson but the Atwoods have Jesus?" I asked.

Brooks sighed. "Yes. I said it and I'd say it again. If you're speaking truthfully, would you say Donaldson isn't a hotshot?"

I thought about Hewitt's hubris and bigger than life style. His courtroom dramatics and calculated traps and strategies. I thought about his Jaguar and the license plate NOT-GIL-T.

"Hewitt has a persona that he uses for the benefit of his clients, many of whom have nowhere else to turn."

"Yes. The persona of a hotshot. I get it. But the Atwoods have their faith that the right thing will be done. And the rest of my sentence was left on the cutting room floor. I said that the Atwoods have Jesus and their faith will carry them through. I spoke those words for their benefit to try and keep them from lashing out or making unfortunate accusations like the Satan worshipers one."

"And why did you call out our names to the whole congregation?"

"Junior told me you were going to speak and should he keep the mike off."

"How did he even know we were there?"

"I guess he either saw you or Cletus told him. I told Junior if you wanted to speak, you should speak."

"I didn't want to speak. Wheezer just stuck the mike in my face."

Brooks uncrossed his legs and leaned forward. "What?"

"We never asked to speak."

The preacher shook his head. "I guess someone hoped to embarrass you." He nodded to Nakayla. "But you gave such a good prayer request, I wanted to publicly acknowledge you and defuse any unwarranted tension your visit might have created." Brooks looked at me. "Public embarrassment is a long way from murder, Mr. Blackman. And like all of us, Helen Wilson is a long way from being a saint."

"What's that suppose to mean?" I asked.

"Just that she never approved of her daughter's marriage to Clyde and worked every way to undercut it."

"Clyde was abusive. I saw it with my own eyes."

"I know. And I was trying to work with him. But I'm telling you what I heard directly from Heather Atwood's lips as she sat in the chair you're sitting in." He glanced around his office. "This isn't a confessional and she's no longer alive, so I feel a duty to ask you to look at the whole picture here. Helen Wilson is the one showing no interest in shared custody. Helen Wilson is the one who might be poisoning the twins' attitude to the Atwoods because she was doing the same thing to their relationship with Clyde. That's not me speaking, that's Heather.

"But, after Clyde shot the deputy, and I do believe it was accidental, Heather returned to her mother's house, the home she'd tried to escape by marrying Clyde right out of high school. To seek justice means for me that everyone receives a fair hearing regardless of whether they're well off or have the slickest lawyer in town."

His eyes glistened as he struggled to keep some emotion in check. "The deaths of Clyde and Heather and of Molly Staton and Lenore Carpenter are truly tragic. But I don't believe any actions or words by me or anyone in my congregation are to blame."

He stood. "That's all I can tell you."

Nakayla and I rose.

"Thank you for your time," I said.

He walked behind his desk, opened a drawer and retrieved a business card. "Take this and call me if there's anything I can do to help."

I dropped the card in my coat pocket.

Brooks shook my hand and then clutched Nakayla's with both of his. "One favor for you to consider. Share your prayer request with Mr. Donaldson to seek justice, love kindness, and walk humbly," he smiled and dropped his hands, "with anyone." Then his face turned grave. "Because if we don't humble ourselves, God will do it for us."

We picked up our beer umbrellas from the hall and left.

When we were in the CR-V, Nakayla asked, "What now?"

"We look more closely at Helen Wilson. And I want you to find out all you can about Horace Brooks. Hewitt might be slick, but Brooks could be in a league all his own."

I pulled out my phone before buckling my seatbelt and checked for messages. I'd turned it off completely so that even the vibrate mode wouldn't make a sound in the sanctuary. As it powered up, chimes announced two messages.

"Who is it?" Nakayla asked.

"One's from Newly's cell. The other number's familiar but I can't place it."

I retrieved Newly's first.

"Sam, give me a call when you get this message. I need to alert you to a new development."

"Sounds promising," Nakayla said. "Call him back."

"Let me check the other one first."

I pressed playback on the touch screen.

"Sam." Hewitt's voice was whispery and strained. "The fat's in the fire now. Newland's taken me into custody and I'm going to be arraigned on two counts of homicide. Consider yourself on the clock."

Chapter Twelve

Sunday afternoon at the Asheville police station is normally as exciting as watching grass grow. This Sunday, as Nakayla and I entered Pack Square, the parking spaces were full and two TV news trucks were angled against the curb with their microwave antennae extended skyward.

"Word must be out," Nakayla said.

I'd opted not to return Newly's phone call. Instead, I wanted to see him face-to-face. The homicide detective would probably stonewall any information behind the "I can't comment about an ongoing investigation" phrase, but at least I would be able to read his body language.

"I wonder if Hewitt will have a fool for a client," Nakayla said.

She referenced the old adage that an attorney who represents himself has a fool for a client. Hewitt considered himself a cut above the other defense lawyers in town. And would any of them even want a client as high-maintenance as I suspected Hewitt would be?

"Maybe I should call Cory," Nakayla suggested.

"She's only a paralegal."

"But Hewitt might listen to her. If not Cory, then certainly Shirley."

"Start with Shirley. She won't take any of Hewitt's crap."

"Then let me take your car back to the office," she said. "You can call me when you've got information or just meet me there."

I stopped in front of the station and left the CR-V running. Nakayla gave me a kiss as we passed in front of the bumper. "Good luck," she said. "I'll be anxious to hear."

I opened the door and stepped into a buzz of conversation. At least fifteen reporters jammed the small waiting area. Everyone turned to check out the new arrival, and the buzz ceased.

A woman I recognized as a field reporter for the FOX TV affiliate was first to come at me. "Sam, Sam, can you confirm that Hewitt Donaldson's been arrested?"

Her question spurred the others into action, and a chorus of variations on the same theme resounded through the room.

I smiled and said the first thing that popped in my mind. "The Lord be with you."

That halted the verbal onslaught for about a half a second.

I pushed through toward the officer on-duty who greeted the public from behind a glass window more like a movie ticket booth. "I'm just here to settle up some parking tickets. I didn't realize I was so news worthy."

The policeman, Ralph Cochran, knew me, and he was clearly amused by my predicament. "You're smart to turn yourself in, Sam." He spoke loud enough for everyone to hear. "The traffic division is waiting."

The reporters grumbled because they knew we were jerking them around. Ralph pressed a button and a click sounded as the security door deadbolt retracted.

"He's in the pen," Ralph said.

Someone outside the system overhearing that remark would assume the duty officer was talking about Hewitt being in a holding pen, or in a penitentiary. I knew Ralph told me where to find Detective Newland. He was in the bullpen, the area of shared desks where cops most commonly share information. I found Newly at its heart, the coffee machine.

Although he still looked whipped, Newly had at least shaved and changed clothes from yesterday.

He tipped his cup to me. "Did you dress up just for me?"

"No. For Pastor Brooks at the Church of the Righteous."

He turned toward the hall leading deeper into the complex. "Grab a mug of this rot gut and come to an interview room. You can tell me about the good preacher's sermon."

I surveyed the bullpen where at least five cops were either on the phone or a computer.

"Are they working the case?" I asked Newly.

"Yeah. At the request of the chief and Carter."

"D.A. Carter's involved already?"

Newly's eyes narrowed. "Let's talk in an interview room?"

"Where's Efird?"

"He's gone to talk with Molly's sister. I suggested someone a little more removed from Molly do it." Newly shrugged. "But Tuck's hardheaded."

I said nothing. If things had ended badly between Efird and Molly, then Newly's suggestion should have been more of an order. But, they were partners, and I understood why Newly wanted to avoid a confrontation this early in the game.

"Okay." I filled a chipped mug with their black poison and followed Newly down the hall to the first room on the left.

He went immediately to his customary side of the table, positioning himself between me and the door.

I slipped into the chair opposite him. "Do I need a lawyer?"

"Not yet. Especially since I'm going to deny we ever had this conversation."

I took a swallow of the bitter, scorched coffee to buy a few seconds as my mind raced to figure out where Newly was going. I set the mug on the table and leaned forward. "I'm working for Hewitt. He's hired Nakayla and me to find the murderer. If you think it's Hewitt, then we're already at cross purposes."

"Are you claiming attorney-client privileges with the attorney as the client?"

His question stumped me. Hewitt was my client and as a private investigator, I didn't enjoy the same legal status as a lawyer. He'd hired me. If he was representing himself and he drew the distinction of Hewitt the lawyer and Hewitt the defendant, then working for Hewitt the case attorney would stand a better chance of shielding me from a prosecutorial subpoena. Better still, Hewitt and I should communicate only verbally, and anything written would be done so by Hewitt as part of his attorney work for his client, Hewitt Donaldson. But since Hewitt and I hadn't spoken about the best way to keep our communication confidential, I was very leery of saying anything to Newly.

"I'm not claiming anything because all he's told me is that you've taken him into custody."

"And that's when he engaged you to find the killer?"

"No. That happened yesterday right after he learned Lenore had been murdered."

Newly cocked his head. "Before he was taken into custody?"

I knew I'd slipped up somehow. "Yes. But all he said was find who killed Lenore."

Newly took a sip of coffee and then puffed out his cheeks to cool his mouth. "Then you weren't working with him in his role as a defense attorney for a client. So, why didn't he trust the police to handle it?"

"Like me, he knew Tuck Efird had an emotional breakup with Molly Staton."

"Molly isn't Lenore. Why didn't he hire you then? You saw him earlier Saturday morning."

In trying to dance around my conversation with Hewitt, I'd managed to waltz myself right into a corner. Well, I guessed Newly had something substantial on Hewitt and the most likely culprit was the proliferation of Hewitt's fingerprints throughout Lenore's house.

"Look, Newly. I don't know what's going on. What Hewitt told me was that he'd been dating Lenore Carpenter. He was visibly shaken when he learned of her death. You were there. You saw him. He's convinced you'll look for evidence to tag him for the crimes and not vigorously pursue all leads. I don't think he's worried about being convicted, but he is worried that the real killer will get away."

"What did you tell him?"

"To see you immediately."

Newly visibly relaxed, as if my answer broke away some barrier between us. "He did. Yesterday afternoon."

"Now you know everything I know."

"No. I know more than you know." The homicide detective got up from the table. "Stay put." He walked to the door and slid a brass panel that changed the word "Vacant" to "Occupied" on the door's exterior. Then he turned off the lights.

The two-way mirror on the wall facing me became a window with enough transparency to see a few lights glowing on the other side. Newly cupped his hands around his eyes and leaned close to the glass to better scan the adjacent observation room. Then he turned around.

"Change seats with me so I can see if anyone comes in there."

I pushed my mug of coffee across the table and moved to the other side. "What's going on?"

Newly slid his chair so I wouldn't block his view of the now transparent mirror. "I told you yesterday I would follow the evidence wherever it leads, even if it's to my partner."

"I know. And I said I was sorry for doubting you."

He lowered his voice to a whisper. "Now the evidence is leading to Hewitt Donaldson, and where some of my colleagues might be reluctant to investigate a cop, there is no such reluctance when it comes to investigating a defense attorney who uses every trick in the book, and then some, to get his clients off."

"I know that too."

"Well, as much as I might be at odds with Mr. Donaldson, I'm not one to jump ahead of the process."

I listened between the words for what Newly was telling me. "You didn't want to take him into custody, did you?"

"No. Things are a little too pat for my taste. Too circumstantial. But Carter overrode me. And Tuck, well, my partner's too close to this one, and too ready to bring Donaldson down."

"D.A. Carter enjoys the headlines," I said.

"Especially when we're making national news with this one," Newly agreed. "Carter's become a politician first and a prosecutor second."

I wondered why Newly was telling me this. Maybe he wanted to make sure he held my respect. We'd had our differences, but when his former partner was murdered, Nakayla and I uncovered the killer. That earned us unofficial admittance as good guys in the police world, and the Asheville department extended us every courtesy they could.

I said nothing, waiting on him to explain why he was whispering to me in a darkened interview room.

"So, I don't want the murders of Molly Staton and Lenore Carpenter to become Carter's political agenda or Tuck's personal agenda."

"I don't either, but what can I do?"

Newly leaned across the table.

"Donaldson has hired you to investigate. His goal is two-fold—first, find the killer and second, clear his own name of what will likely be a double homicide indictment. I don't give a rat's ass about clearing Donaldson, but I do want to apprehend the real murderer. You can focus elsewhere while I'm ordered to concentrate on Donaldson."

Hewitt had been incorrect about the police becoming fixated on him as the sole suspect. It was the D.A. driving that agenda. Newly must be under a lot of pressure if he felt the need to confide in me.

"What about discovery?" I asked. "Is there funny business going on?"

"I don't think Carter will risk withholding exculpatory evidence, and so far I'm not aware of any. But he'll play tight with everything he can and try to surprise Donaldson whenever he can. You know as well as I do every piece of information is a possible connection to something else, something that could be exculpatory but will never come to light unless it's pursued."

"You're giving me access to your case file?"

"I'm giving you my trust in exchange for yours."

I laughed. "Newly, you know when someone says trust me, it's the first sign not to trust him."

Newly's expression remained grave. "Trust but verify was President Reagan's motto. He was before your time, but it's good advice. Trust me to share what information I can, and you can verify its authenticity and follow it wherever you want. I'm trusting you not to use this information in any way that blows back on me. And I'm trusting you to share any leads you uncover, especially as they relate to Tuck. I don't want any surprises."

Newly's motive became crystal clear. D.A. Carter and probably his police chief were boxing him into building the case against Hewitt. He knew Nakayla and I would be turning over every rock we could find in an effort to exonerate the lawyer. Newly was willing to give us some rocks to lift if we told him what we found beneath them. The last thing he wanted was to be blindsided by a partner who'd committed two murders. I didn't believe Tuck Efird was capable of such a crime, just as Newly had serious doubts about Hewitt Donaldson's guilt. Both of us were going out on a limb exchanging our information this way, but I was willing to go along.

"All right. It's a deal." I stuck out my hand and he gave it a firm squeeze. "Now, do you want to hear about my adventure at the Church of the Righteous?"

"In a moment. But first you need to know where things stand here. Hewitt is demanding a probable cause hearing. It's his right and he knows his rights. He'll be confronted with the evidence we've unearthed so far."

"Which is?"

"His fingerprints all over Lenore Carpenter's home and on items used within the time window of Lenore's murder."

"He told you that," I said.

"Yes, he did. We also found his prints on her washing machine. Her missing gardening clothes and clothes of a different size that we believe belonged to Molly Staton had been run through a wash cycle."

"Hewitt supposedly destroys DNA evidence while leaving his prints?"

Newly shrugged. "But we're not just talking about Lenore's house. We found a wheelchair in the back of his garage with soil samples that match Lenore's potting soil."

That hit me like a slap in the face. Especially since I was the one who told them to look for a wheelchair. Without trying to sound defensive, I said, "Again, he doesn't deny spending time at her house."

"Additional soil on the wheels that appears to match the mica-rich ground at Helen's Bridge."

I said nothing.

"And then there's the photograph."

"What photograph?" My stomach knotted because I knew I wasn't going to like the answer.

"That photographer who was on the scene when Molly's body was dropped from the bridge."

"Collin McPhillips," I said.

"Yes. He framed a vertical shot. The Japanese all had horizontal framing. As a result, his image includes the top of the bridge. One of the shots in his rapid-fire sequence shows the blur of Molly's body as it's being rolled over the bridge wall. It also shows the blur of a shoulder and a shirt. A Hawaiian shirt. A Hawaiian shirt in the same colors worn by Hewitt Donaldson on Friday night."

"Interesting," was all I could say.

"That's one reaction. The discovery enabled us to get a more extensive search warrant for his property grounds, and we're pursuing another search warrant for his office. The office is going to be a screaming nightmare because of confidential files and attorney-client privilege. We'll work with Hewitt and his staff as best we can, but Carter's confident he's got enough already for an indictment."

"But you're not."

"Oh, he'll get his indictment, and we'll explore every nook and cranny of Donaldson's life big enough to stick our nose in. But, like I said, it's too neat. My gut doesn't like it."

"Then I'll look into the wheelchair and shirt. Anything else?"

"No, but that could change hour to hour. The ME is expediting the autopsy on the two bodies. I should have a preliminary by tonight."

"When's the hearing?"

"Nine tomorrow morning." Newly stood. "Let's swap places and turn on the lights. Then you can tell me about the good Reverend Brooks."

◇◇◇

"What's the status of the voicemail?" Nakayla asked the question as soon as I finished telling her the details of my conversation with Detective Newland.

"He hasn't received an analysis. He's also submitted a request to the phone company for the call records for Hewitt's landline."

Nakayla slipped off her shoes and tucked her bare feet into the seam between the leather sofa cushions. We sat in our office. She nursed a cup of green tea. I sat in my customary chair across from her and sipped a glass of straight soda water in a futile attempt to purge cop coffee from my taste buds.

"I don't think he believes Horace Brooks is involved, and after meeting the preacher, I'm inclined to agree."

Nakayla nodded. "I did a little digging into his background. He's a graduate of Princeton Theological Seminary and was a promising young theologian at Union Theological Seminary in New York City. Until his wife and one-year-old son were killed by a hit and run driver on the Upper West Side. He was on the opposite side of the street watching them cross. He was meeting them for ice cream."

"Jesus. Did you get this from an Asheville source?"

"No. A national data search going back twenty years. Brooks doesn't wear his tragedy on his sleeve. Evidently he abruptly quit his professorship and went off the radar. He and his tent surfaced here in Asheville two years later."

"And I bet he hit rock bottom somewhere between New York and North Carolina," I said. "Sounds like he's rebuilt his faith on simplicity."

Nakayla pursed her lips. "Maybe it's more a case of simplify-ing his message. His office library looked pretty deep to me."

"More volumes than Hewitt's law office," I agreed. "I was impressed he didn't have any pictures of himself."

"Or his family."

"Yes, or his family." I thought how painful it must be to lose them right before your eyes. I'd seen men die in battle and I'd survived an attack targeted to kill me, but to witness your wife and child run down in front of you must have tested every conceivable theological tenet Brooks held dear.

"Did Newly say anything about Junior?" Nakayla asked.

"Junior Atwood? I didn't ask him. I was focused on linking Brooks to the voicemail."

"But Junior set you up with the microphone this morning. He's demonstrated he's not above playing a dirty trick."

"Maybe. Or if it wasn't Brooks, maybe Cletus did it on his own. Either way, I don't think the voicemail's going to lead us anywhere that connects to the murders. Our priority is to learn how Hewitt got tagged with the hard evidence—the wheelchair and the photograph with a lookalike shirt."

"Did you tell Hewitt that Newly's helping us?"

"No. I didn't speak to Hewitt. But Newly told me Hewitt's notifying Carter that he plans to be his own attorney, and that as the defense attorney, he's hired us as his investigators. I also think we should hire him."

Nakayla set down her tea and crossed her arms in obvious disapproval. "Hire him for what?"

"For a dollar. We're seeking his legal counsel on whether we have any liability as organizers of the fundraiser. It's my idea to build an extra wall of attorney-client confidentiality." I leaned back in the chair with self-satisfaction. "I'm not as dumb as I look."

"I wouldn't test that in court, hotshot, unless justice really is blind. Should we look for an explanation for the shirt?"

"Not yet. There's nothing we can do between now and his hearing. Why risk Newly's confidence? If Carter's playing his cards close, he'll know any leak about the shirt came from inside. I'll confide in Hewitt once he's out on bail."

"You think he'll get it?"

"It'll be stiff, but Hewitt's a lifelong resident, and I doubt if the judge will see him as a flight risk. Hewitt can argue that imprisonment would cripple his abilities to act as his own attorney."

Nakayla nodded. "Okay. And in the meantime we do what?"

"I want to talk to Collin McPhillips and learn if he remembers anything about his photographs. And I'd like to see Hewitt's garage where they found the wheelchair. Any sign of forced entry will help his defense."

"I still think the voicemail is important. Someone tried to link Hewitt to the call, and that's exactly what's happening with the other evidence."

Nakayla had a point. Just because we'd eased off Horace Brooks didn't mean the phone threat was less relevant.

My cell rang. I pulled it from my belt and recognized the number. "It's Newly. I'll mention Junior."

I pressed the green accept icon. "Yeah?"

"Can you talk?" Newly's voice was low.

"Yeah."

"Here's a heads up. You know that voicemail you got at one-thirty?"

"Nakayla and I were just talking about it."

"Well, our audio techs isolated and amplified the background. It's a bar. You definitely hear snatches of conversation and glasses clinking."

Hewitt's alibi suddenly evaporated. "Was it from the Thirsty Monk?"

"We haven't been able to penetrate beyond Donaldson's number."

"That doesn't make any sense. Why spoof your own phone?"

"Why, indeed? I can only think of one reason. To build the defense case that someone was framing you. To confuse a jury. No one does that better than Hewitt Donaldson."

Nakayla looked at me, trying to follow the conversation from my side alone.

I shook my head. "I don't know about a jury, Newly, but it sure as hell is confusing me."

Chapter Thirteen

Nakayla and I replayed the voice message five more times. I could hear the murmur of conversation and the clinks of glasses, although nothing clear enough to identify the exact location.

"The voice doesn't sound like Hewitt," Nakayla said.

"Newly's techs reported it had been filtered and modulated more than once."

"Why so many times?"

"If the voice were run through a single effect, a reverse process could bring it closer to the original. Multiple filters make it difficult to reconstruct the initial sound frequencies."

"So, the D.A. can't prove the call's from Hewitt?"

"No, but he can introduce the number from which it was placed."

Nakayla frowned. "I thought Hewitt's number was spoofed."

"There's no definitive proof yet. Newly says if it's a spoof, it's damned sophisticated. And Hewitt was in the bar till two. Nathan Armitage will confirm that. Odds are either Nathan or Hewitt went to the restroom and left the other alone at some point. I doubt if they can swear they were together at precisely the time the call was made."

"Has Newly accessed the records of Hewitt's cell phone?" Nakayla asked.

"In the process. But Carter's not waiting. He thinks he's got enough for his indictment and he's pressing ahead full throttle."

Nakayla swung her feet off the sofa and planted them squarely on the Persian carpet. "Then we'd better get moving. I'll contact Shirley and let her know what's going on. She'll have a number for Collin McPhillips. I guess we should see him as soon as we can."

I stood. "Ask Shirley if Hewitt ever had a wheelchair. And we need to look at his garage to see how secure it was." I reached into the pocket of my sport coat. "Now I'm going to make a phone call of my own." I held Pastor Brooks' card in front of Nakayla's face. "He offered his help and I'm taking him up on it."

"Why?"

"Somebody went to great lengths to mask the voice on that message. You're the one who pointed out his dirty tricks."

"Junior Atwood?"

"He's the resident audio expert at the Church of the Righteous. I'd like Brooks to arrange a little meeting, and then we'll replay the message for both of them. Their reactions could prove interesting."

I reached Brooks and told him I'd like to speak with Junior and him. I said Junior's experience with audio equipment could be very helpful to an investigation. Since I understood there might be some hard feelings because of my role in Clyde Atwood's trial, I told Brooks I'd appreciate if he would sit in. I wouldn't need much time.

The preacher said Junior hauled farm-raised mountain trout from Asheville to Nashville every Monday and Tuesday where he delivered fresh fish to Tennessee wholesalers. But he'd be back for the Wednesday evening service. Brooks suggested we meet at the church at six o'clock.

"Can I tell Junior what you're looking for?" Brooks asked.

"I've got some recorded sound that's garbled. It's for another case, not the custody dispute." That was true. The case would be Hewitt's murder trial. "Wheezer told me Junior had been an audio specialist in the military."

"Okay," Brooks agreed. "We can meet in my office. You know the way."

When I hung up, Nakayla was still talking to Shirley. Rather than eavesdrop, I stretched out on the sofa to think.

"Wake up, Sam."

"I was just resting my eyes."

"From the drool on your chin, I'd say you were also resting your lips."

She took my customary chair. "So, tell me about your talk with Pastor Brooks."

I sat up and took a deep breath to clear my foggy brain. "We're set for six o'clock Wednesday evening. By then Newly should have confirmation on whether it was Hewitt's phone that made the call. How's Shirley?"

"In a word, subdued. I think the charges against Hewitt stunned her."

Quiet retreat wasn't the reaction I expected from Shirley. "Did she know Hewitt was seeing Lenore?" I asked.

"No. That blindsided her. Lenore, Molly, and Shirley were tight and Shirley can't believe Lenore held back her affair with Hewitt."

"Maybe Lenore took Molly into her confidence but excluded Shirley. Both Lenore and Molly were a good fifteen years older, and Hewitt is Shirley's boss."

"That's what I told her." Nakayla looked out the window toward Beaucatcher Mountain. I knew she was reliving that horrible scene at Helen's Bridge. Her eyes teared. "It's just the avalanche of everything that's come tumbling down in the last few days."

"Did you ask her about the wheelchair?"

Nakayla wiped her eyes and smiled. "At least that got a chuckle out of her."

"Why?"

"Shirley says Hewitt keeps it as a prop."

"A prop?"

"Sometimes he'll put his defendant in it. He claims it racks up sympathy points with the jury."

Even for Hewitt, the audacity rose off the chart. "But if there's no medical need—"

She interrupted me. "Shirley said he always finds a way. A sprained knee is his favorite."

"What's Shirley doing next?"

Nakayla shrugged. "Waiting. She and Cory talked and decided nothing should be done until after tomorrow's hearing. Then, assuming Hewitt's released on bail, they anticipate he'll call a strategy session. They don't want to second-guess what that strategy might be."

"Well, Hewitt made it clear we're on the clock so I'm not waiting." I stood. "Get your coat. We're going to Hewitt's house."

"All right." Nakayla brushed her hand across her chin. "But you might want to wipe that drool off your face first, Sherlock."

◇◇◇

I slowed the CR-V as we neared Hewitt's. A police car was parked broadside across the driveway. The late afternoon sun had already dipped behind the back ridge and the deep shadows made the glow of the house's windows appear all the brighter.

The mobile crime lab sat diagonally on the apron of the concrete between the detached garage and front porch. Newly had gotten his expanded search warrant. I drove around the bend until I was out of sight and eased to a stop on the narrow shoulder.

Nakayla unsnapped her seatbelt. "What are the odds we'll get in?"

"Zip on the house. Fifty-fifty on the garage."

"What makes the garage a better prospect?"

I reached up and clicked off the overhead courtesy lights to keep the interior dark when we opened the doors. "Because there are two of us, and you're going to chat up the officer in the car while I circle around him."

"You're going to break into the garage?" she whispered.

"No. But I'm going to see if someone else did. Go work that irresistible Robertson charm. I'll give you a minute to get him engaged."

We got out and synchronized closing the doors so there was only one sound. Nakayla took a note pad and pen from her jacket and walked back along the road toward the house. I pulled a small flashlight from my pocket and waited.

In a few moments, Nakayla's voice rose above the breeze. "Officer, may I ask you a few questions?"

With that cue, I crossed the drainage ditch and entered the woods separating Hewitt from his neighbor. Fortunately, the ground was still damp from Friday night's rain. The wet leaves muffled my footsteps and I could see low hanging branches well enough that the flashlight wasn't necessary.

I looped up the hill where I could descend behind the single-car garage. The voices of Nakayla and the officer grew louder. I hoped she had stationed herself to keep his back turned away from my approach. Technically, I didn't cross under any crime scene tape so I wasn't violating a marked police line.

I'd been to Hewitt's house before but I'd never paid attention to his garage. As I drew nearer, I could see there was no rear window. I opted to stay along the side farthest from the house, walking close to the garage wall where the shadows were deepest.

"I'm not authorized to disclose anything that might have been found." The officer speaking to Nakayla sounded annoyed.

I turned the corner and saw him standing on the far side of his patrol car. Nakayla faced me. She was flashing her most ingratiating smile.

"But surely the warrant specifies what the search is seeking," she said. "That's practically public information. Tuck Efird would have no problem with you sharing that."

I stepped in front of the garage. Old-style double doors were latched in the center, but there was no padlock. The lax security meant anyone could have gained access. I looked down to see if perhaps a bolt on the bottom secured the doors to the concrete driveway. The lights from the house were bright enough to reflect off silver ends of a freshly severed lock. I knelt for closer examination.

The police wouldn't have hesitated to use bolt cutters to remove the tarnished padlock. I could only assume in their zeal they left the lock where it fell. If so, there had been no consideration that it might be evidence and no check for fingerprints.

"Who are you to tell me what Detective Efird agrees to share?" The cop was coming to the end of his fuse and would soon tell Nakayla to clear off.

I clicked the flashlight on and played the beam over the lock. The grime from years of enduring the elements dulled the metal except for the shiny ends where the cutter had sliced through the shackle. I bent closer, placing the light to within a few inches of the lock's base. Fine scratch lines radiated from the key slot. Someone had recently picked this lock. The silver marks were nearly as bright as the freshly cut ends. I pulled my phone from my belt, pressed the camera icon, and placed the lens on the concrete by the lock.

I managed to take three photographs before the flash caught the eye of the uniformed officer.

"Hey, what the hell do you think you're doing?"

I looked over my shoulder to see him running around his car with Nakayla close on his heels.

I stood. "I'm doing the job somebody else should have done."

"What's going on?" Tuck Efird shouted the question from the front porch, and then he jogged down the steps and across the driveway. "Why didn't you keep him back?" he yelled at the patrolman.

"Because he didn't see me," I said. "If he had, he would have stopped me." I pointed to the padlock lying between us. "Why'd you give up picking the lock? Now it's ruined."

Efird gave a cursory glance down. "What are you talking about? We didn't waste time picking Donaldson's goddamned lock. If he's too poor to buy a replacement, he can put on another fundraiser."

"Then you didn't take time to properly examine it. Someone picked this lock, and if you don't check for prints, I will."

Efird rolled on a pair of gloves and I handed him my flashlight. While he studied the scratches, I emailed the photos to Nakayla, insuring the images were safely in the Internet cloud.

"You could have made these yourself," Efird said.

"I could have. Is your theory I bent down and tried to pick a lock no longer securing anything?"

Efird didn't answer. Instead, he turned to the patrolman. "Has someone been stationed here since we found the wheelchair?"

"The wheelchair I told you to look for?" I couldn't resist reminding him I'd already contributed to the investigation.

"We've been on-site the whole time," the policeman said. "If anyone made scratches, it was before the lock was cut."

"And Nakayla and I just came to check on the house." I wasn't about to let Efird know I'd received advance information from his partner.

"By checking on the house, you mean sneaking up to the garage?" Efird reached in his pocket and retrieved an evidence bag.

"We saw the driveway blocked, I noticed the lock, and I wanted a closer look. I'd say it was a good thing I did." I reached out for my flashlight. "You don't have to thank me."

Efird snorted through his nose. "Don't push it, Sam. You might find you've crawled out on a limb with the wrong guy this time."

I'd accomplished the most I could hope for. Hewitt would argue someone picked his garage lock not once but twice, and used the wheelchair to frame him. But who? Without a credible suspect, we had no one to fit into that classic defense, "some other dude did it." No one but the detective standing in front of me.

Two dead women and their lovers—Hewitt's affair with Lenore kept private and Efird's relationship with Molly ending with emotional fireworks. What connections linked them together? And what drove someone to murder?

Chapter Fourteen

Asheville's premier defense attorney was so red in the face I was afraid he'd burst a blood vessel. No one dared interrupt while he vented his rage and frustration.

"Never in my life have I endured such nonsense!" Hewitt Donaldson spit out the words more than said them. "And, by God, when we find out who's behind this, I'll pour every resource I have into getting a conviction."

Nakayla, Shirley, Cory, and I sat at the round conference table while Hewitt circled us like we were playing some diabolical version of "Duck, Duck, Goose."

He halted his diatribe and a switch seemed to flip somewhere in his brain. He stopped pacing, closed his eyes and took several deep breaths. "I know, I know," he whispered. "Ranting is getting us nowhere." With that self-admonition, he sat next to Shirley and began stating the facts at hand.

We'd been called to his office Monday evening for a five o'clock strategy session. The day had been hectic, and everyone, especially Hewitt, was exhausted. D.A. Carter had bombarded the probable cause hearing with every scrap of accusatory evidence he could muster: the discovery of the wheelchair in Hewitt's garage and the corresponding tread marks and soil from the two murder scenes; the photograph of a blurry patch of a Hawaiian shirt just above the bridge wall as Molly's body was pushed over; fibers in the trunk of Hewitt's Jaguar that appeared to be from the vintage dresses worn by the victims; the threatening phone call placed to our office; hairs discovered at both murder scenes that matched Hewitt's color and were undergoing DNA analysis; and a sworn statement from Detective Tuck Efird that Molly Staton told him Lenore Carpenter planned to break off her relationship with Hewitt. Carter also made much of the fact that Hewitt was mobile during the Friday night fundraiser with no verification of his location at the time of the murders.

Hewitt offered no rebuttal but asked for an accelerated arraignment and a request for bail. Despite Carter's plea that Hewitt was a flight risk, bail was set at five hundred thousand dollars. Hewitt Donaldson the accused was now Hewitt Donaldson the lawyer and he jumped into action like a junkyard dog attacking a trespasser.

"What more can we learn from the padlock?" he asked me.

"The police lab should disassemble it. If the scratches appear on the interior tumblers, then we know it was more than a surface attempt. Odds are someone opened it."

"How would they know the wheelchair was in the garage?" Cory asked.

"They probably didn't," Hewitt said. "They might have been looking for anything to incriminate me and the wheelchair offered both a practical and a damning option."

"And the hairs and the trunk fibers?" Shirley asked.

"I don't lock the car and there's a trunk release under the dashboard. I'd prefer some thief open the door rather than break a window." He ran his fingers over his scalp. "As for the hair, I lose more strands each day than an oak loses leaves in October." He jotted a note on the legal pad in front of him. "Shirley, check the activity for my credit cards."

"For what?"

"Hell, I don't know. Surprises. We have to look where the police are looking. I don't want to be blindsided."

Nakayla shot me a glance and I knew something was on her mind. She was reluctant to interrupt Hewitt as he ran through his priorities. I nodded that she should jump in with whatever was bothering her.

"Hewitt, were you blindsided by Tuck Efird's statement about what Molly told him?"

Hewitt swallowed. Nakayla's question triggered some emotion he tried to repress. After a moment, he waved his hand dismissively. "Hearsay. I could have objected but it will never be admissible at trial." His eyes moistened. "I can't cross examine Molly or Lenore so no judge will allow it." His face hardened. "And if it is introduced, I'll testify that Lenore told me Molly was afraid of Tuck Efird. They did break up and I can call firsthand witnesses to that fact."

"Can you suggest any motive for the killings?" I asked.

Hewitt shook his head. "No. Other than some link to the Atwood trial, and you and Nakayla are following that trail through Brooks and Junior Atwood. We need to determine for sure where Junior and Cletus were Friday."

Cory raised her hand like a kid in elementary school asking permission to speak.

"What?" Hewitt demanded.

"Won't the police be searching for more connections than that? Shouldn't we be anticipating their looking beyond your relationship with Lenore?"

Hewitt drummed his fingers on the table while he weighed Cory's question. Before he could answer, a buzzer sounded from the hall.

"Someone's at the door," Shirley said. "I locked it before our meeting."

Cory stood. "It might be Tom Peterson."

Hewitt scowled. "Then tell him to pick you up later."

Cory hurried away.

"The Wilson-Atwood custody case is now a real burden," Hewitt said. "Especially if it gets entangled with my own legal problems. I'm inclined to press Helen Wilson to accept some form of shared custody and put that mess behind us."

Hewitt wasn't one to back down from a fight, but in this case, perhaps all parties would be better served by a settlement.

Cory returned, but she wasn't alone. Tom Peterson stepped into the conference room behind her. He wore a crisply pressed gray suit, white shirt, and muted burgundy tie and looked like he was headed for a TV interview.

"Tom has something he'd like to tell us," Cory said.

Peterson walked closer to Hewitt.

The older attorney remained in his seat. "Well, out with it."

Peterson swept his eyes across all of us, suddenly unsure whether his presence was such a good idea. He cleared his throat. "First, I want you to know Cory has told me nothing about the case against Mr. Donaldson or how he plans to defend himself against the ridiculous charges. And that's what they are. Ridiculous.

"Second, I plan to resign from the Atwood custody case."

Hewitt shifted in his chair. "But you have an obligation to your client."

"And that obligation entails mutual trust. The Atwoods are delighted that you find yourself in this current predicament. They haven't said anything to implicate themselves and I wouldn't tell you if they had, but to continue to represent them would prohibit my purpose for being here."

"Which is?" Hewitt prompted.

"As a professional courtesy, I'm offering to represent you."

I've seen Hewitt Donaldson shocked very few times. This proposal made the list. Hewitt's mouth dropped open and his eyes blinked like a swimmer emerging from beneath the water. Peterson said nothing further.

Hewitt looked at Cory. She shook her head, not to signal her boss to reject the offer, but with an expression conveying she had nothing to do with it.

"Well, sir," Hewitt said with measured formality. "I appreciate your offer, but I think I'll be fine with the assembled team. And I still represent Mrs. Wilson and I'd abhor even the slightest perception of possible collusion by either of us with respect to our clients' interests."

"And if I could get the Atwoods to settle immediately?"

Hewitt's bushy eyebrows arched. "On what terms?"

"Helen Wilson retains guardian status and makes all educational decisions for the twins. The Atwoods are allowed custody one weekend a month, beginning at four on Friday afternoons and ending at four on Sunday afternoons. That's only forty-eight hours out of an entire month."

Hewitt rubbed his palm across his chin as he digested the proposal. "They've agreed?"

"Not yet. I've only floated it as a possibility. Now I'll tell them I'm resigning the case, and with your current legal dilemma, there might not be a better time for terms. I'll remind them their son did shoot the twins' mother and it will be hard to keep that fact from tainting the merits of their case."

Hewitt cocked his head and studied the young lawyer more closely. "And you feel sure you can deliver these terms?"

Peterson smiled. "Not by myself. I've enlisted the aid of their pastor."

"Horace Brooks?" I jumped in, unable to restrain my curiosity on how such an alliance had been struck.

"Yes. I visited Pastor Brooks this afternoon. He agrees some relationship with the twins is better than none at all. He believes a public display of name-calling and spiteful recriminations serve no one, especially the boys." Peterson paused and gave Hewitt a sly smile. "Can you get Helen Wilson to agree to such a proposal?"

Hewitt looked across the table at me. I knew he was mulling what I'd told him earlier: how, according to Brooks, Helen Wilson had set out to undermine the relationship between her daughter and Clyde.

"I will be as persuasive as I can," Hewitt said. "But that's a separate issue from your involvement with my case."

Tom Peterson spread his hands, palms up. "Understood. But might I suggest that the presentation in the courtroom will suffer if you are the sole voice for your innocence. And if you take the stand, do you plan to question yourself and object during cross examination? A jury trial is part theater. A one-man show could carry the subtle implication that no one else will stand with you."

No one knew the power of courtroom theatrics better than Hewitt. He bit his lower lip as he contemplated what Peterson was saying.

"Besides," Peterson pressed, "I've been trained as a prosecutor." He looked at me. "Sam and I should work well together, especially as I approach any trial from a prosecutorial point of view."

The argument had merit. And there was another factor I figured Hewitt would weigh. Tom Peterson was new in town. Hewitt hadn't had the chance to piss him off like he had all his other colleagues of the bar.

"And what would be your first step?" Hewitt asked.

"Ensure there's no way a motive can be established. We don't want to link the victims to you. If D.A. Carter can't find something personal, then he'll look for something professional. I'd expect him to obtain a search warrant for your records and subpoena anything connecting the three of you."

Hewitt nodded. "And how would you prevent that?"

"Assuming no such relationship exists, we play client confidentiality to the max. Perhaps our fallback can be to offer them a client list and maybe billing records. Will either Molly or Lenore show up on them?"

"They will not."

"Great," Peterson said enthusiastically. "Then with no provable link, a double homicide charge falls apart."

Hewitt's relationship with Lenore had been presented in the probable cause hearing, but as far as I knew, no triangle existed involving Hewitt, Lenore, and Molly.

"What about a single relationship?" I asked, knowing full well I was calling out Hewitt's love affair with Lenore in front of Peterson. "Carter might pursue Lenore as the victim with Molly as collateral damage, or Molly with Lenore as someone who perhaps knew too much."

"Not a relationship that would provide a motive for murder," Hewitt said sharply.

"Whatever it is, wouldn't it be better to disclose it?" Peterson asked. "Otherwise it looks like you've got something to hide."

"Hewitt." Shirley called his name but said no more. The one word was enough to send a message.

Hewitt pointed to the empty chair across from him. "Sit down."

Tom Peterson took the place where Cory had been sitting between Shirley and Nakayla. Cory eased into the chair between Hewitt and me.

Hewitt continued. "I'll bring you up to speed, but it will be brief. Lenore and I were in a relationship, so my prints are all over her house. That's all I'm going to say about that. Sam can cover you later on what we learned at today's hearing."

"Whenever's convenient," I told Peterson.

He nodded but kept his eyes on Hewitt.

"I agree with your assessment, Mr. Peterson," Hewitt said. "My law practice will be a target in a search for links. There will be none to Molly, but my history with Lenore will be established by court records. It's just a matter of time before they uncover it."

"What history?" Peterson asked.

All of us except Shirley leaned closer.

"The trial of Kyle Duncan," Shirley whispered.

Hewitt raised a hand to silence her. "I met Lenore over twenty years ago when I defended a man named Kyle Duncan. He was accused of murdering a woman in a most brutal fashion. The prosecution said he broke into her home, thinking she was out. But, she'd called in sick to work. They claimed she'd surprised him and recognized him as one of the workmen doing restoration on her house in the Montford district. That's one of the historic areas of Asheville."

"I'm familiar with the neighborhood," Peterson said.

"Whoever she confronted beat her to death with a hammer. Lenore Carpenter was juror number seven. She was only in her early twenties at the time."

Tom Peterson shook his head. "But there were eleven other jurors. And what significance can the prosecution draw? You've addressed thousands of jurors over the years."

"But this case ended in a mistrial," Hewitt said. "A hung jury with one member holding out for an innocent verdict."

Peterson's eyes widened. "Lenore."

"Correct. But I had no personal involvement with her at the time of the trial. Absolutely nothing inappropriate. We became friends when she took a hell of a lot of heat for her courageous stand."

"Was Duncan retried?" Peterson asked.

"No. The D.A. at the time pushed for it, but then the Sheriff's Department had a colossal screw-up with the evidence. The murder weapon had been pivotal for both the prosecution and the defense. Duncan didn't deny that the hammer was his, but he insisted it was in the house along with the tools of the other workmen. His prints were on it, but blood splatter covered some of them. I argued that if Duncan had been the last person to hold the hammer, then his hand would have blocked the splatter from covering his prints. And the autopsy of the head trauma suggested the attacker was left-handed. Duncan was right-handed."

"And the prosecution's claim?"

"Duncan was a smug, crafty bastard. Other workers on the job testified he'd made lewd comments about the victim, Marie Roddey. One claimed Duncan pocketed a silver candy dish from her living room."

"Did he confront Duncan?" Peterson asked.

"No. He said you didn't confront Duncan unless you wanted a fight. Duncan wasn't supposed to be in that part of the house. The project was a den expansion and new screened porch. So, the second workman wasn't supposed to be there either. He was using an inside bathroom instead of the Porta-Jon in the backyard."

"Did the police find the silver dish?"

"Yes. In Duncan's room in a boardinghouse. Duncan claimed it had been planted. The worker testifying against him lived in the same house. I also challenged the jury to consider why a murderer would leave a murder weapon behind with his prints on it."

"Did you think he was guilty?" Peterson asked.

Hewitt waved the question aside. "Irrelevant. The salient point is Lenore had reasonable doubts. The second trial never happened because some idiot used the hammer to repair a broken shelf in the evidence storage room, and it was misplaced. That was just one of several incidents that compromised the chain of custody for multiple cases and pending appeals."

Peterson shook his head. "If this trial is the link, why wait twenty years to take your revenge? And where does Molly fit?"

His questions mirrored my own.

Hewitt jabbed his finger at the young lawyer. "Finding that answer, Mr. Peterson, is why I'm hiring you. Cory will give you the case files." He shifted his eyes first to Nakayla and then to me. "And I suggest the esteemed Blackman and Robertson Detective Agency begin tracking down Marie Roddey's relatives and closest friends." Hewitt stood and started for the door. He abruptly stopped and turned around. "And find the whereabouts of Kyle Duncan. If the murders are connected to the trial, then he might have already been the first victim."

"Where are you going?" Shirley asked.

"To convince Helen Wilson to accept the offer Mr. Peterson brought us."

Chapter Fifteen

The five of us sat at the conference table in silence until we heard the office door close and Hewitt's footsteps fade away.

Shirley rolled her dark eyes. "Welcome, Tom, to King Hewitt's Nuts of the Round Table. You have to be crazy to work here."

"I know. I'll try to stay out of his way."

"Good luck with that." Shirley stood. "Let's make this Command Central." She looked down at Peterson. "You're in the Jackson Building, right?"

"Yeah, but I can bring a laptop here if that's helpful."

Shirley grimaced. "Trust me. You'll get more done if you work elsewhere, and you're only a block away. I'll set up a secure Internet site to share files and documents. We can meet here every morning at seven-thirty and close out the end of the day with a drink downstairs. I know that will keep Hewitt happy."

Cory raised her hand. "Should Tom and I get the Duncan files?"

"No," Shirley said. "You and I can do that." She turned to Peterson. "They're in off-site storage near UNC–Asheville. It makes more sense for you to talk with Nakayla and Sam." She glanced at the oversize silver watch on her wrist. "Five-forty. Give me your office key and I'll have the files waiting for you in the morning."

"No," I said. "I want them kept in our office. There are two of us and we're going to do the tracking. Tom can pull whatever he needs. If Hewitt wants to see something, then the files are just down the hall."

Shirley raised her arms over her head. "Hallelujah. A useful suggestion. All right, Cory. Let's go, girl. It could take a while to find them."

"We'll help you bring them up in the morning," Nakayla offered.

Shirley pointed her finger at Nakayla. "Okay. But don't let these boneheads near the coffee machine. They couldn't make a decent pot if they poured it straight from Starbucks."

The Wicked Witch of the West was back. We were making progress.

Nakayla and I spent ten minutes briefing Peterson on the hearing. He scowled when I revealed that Hewitt's fingerprints were on items purchased close to the estimated time of Lenore's murder. D.A. Carter had made much of the preliminary autopsies indicating both women had been strangled, and that no one could account for Molly Staton's whereabouts after seven on Thursday night. Shirley had been the last person to speak to her. She claimed Molly told her she was going to bed early and would pick up her costume from Lenore Friday morning. Shirley had tried to phone Molly several times that day but only reached her voicemail.

"What's Hewitt's alibi for that time?" Peterson asked.

Nakayla picked up the story. "Shirley says he left the office around six on Thursday and was going home."

"But we know he went to Lenore's," Peterson said.

"But not when," Nakayla said. "The only time confirmation comes from his fingerprints on the breakfast food he purchased Friday morning. He could have gone home first, or to Molly's, or God only knows where, until that breakfast. Neither Lenore nor Molly are alive to verify his alibi."

"And Friday after breakfast?" Peterson asked.

Nakayla shrugged. "He picked up the passenger van from the rental company, checked in with sponsors, and bounced in and out of the office."

"Well, we'll need to build a timeline showing how Hewitt couldn't have been able to commit the murders."

"And failing that?" I asked.

Peterson looked grim. "We have to find another suspect and tell a damn good story."

◇◇◇

At seven-thirty the next morning, we re-assembled in the conference room. Nakayla and I had arrived twenty minutes earlier to help Shirley move the boxes of the Duncan files from her car to our office. Tom Peterson would review the transcripts of the case while Nakayla and I tracked down the key players. That was the plan unless Hewitt decided to send us off in another direction.

We took our same seats, as if yesterday's meeting had prescribed a permanent placement at the table. Hewitt was five minutes late, so we sat in silence, no one wanting to initiate chitchat while our leader was missing.

When he did appear, he looked like a man returning from a rejuvenating vacation—clean shaven, hair tied back in a ponytail, eyes clear, and a sparkling smile as wide as his round face.

"Good morning, people." He dropped in his chair and set a fresh legal pad in front of him. "I trust everyone got a good night's rest."

"You trust wrong," Shirley said. "Some of us are concerned about a friend being tried on capital murder charges."

"I'm concerned for your friend as well. But it's my job to be upbeat and encouraging. I expect the same from you."

Nakayla and I looked at each other. Hewitt was demonstrating compartmentalization to an extreme degree. Hewitt the attorney v. Hewitt the client. Whatever wall he'd constructed between the two couldn't be psychologically healthy. Behind that wall had to lurk grief, anger, and a certain amount of fear. I understood what Hewitt was attempting to do and why. The question was how long could he play this charade before the wall came tumbling down.

Two vertical frown lines creased Shirley's forehead. "Then before I do my Mary Poppins impersonation, let me tell the euphoric counselor that his client's credit card was used to buy things from Past Presents and Online-Ontime Hardware."

"What the hell are they?" Hewitt asked.

"An online shop specializing in vintage clothing and another in general hardware."

"Molly's dress from one," Nakayla said.

It took me a second to make the connection. Three dresses were at play: Lenore's original dress left on her bed at home, Molly's dress that Lenore's body was discovered wearing in the Grove Park Inn, and the third dress clothing Molly at Helen's Bridge.

Hewitt's mouth dropped. "I bought it?"

"Bought it Thursday and overnighted it from Chicago to Asheville."

"Where was it shipped?" I asked.

Shirley shook her head. "All I've seen is the charge on the company credit card. I did a quick Internet search and placed a phone call, but the shop's on Central Time so I'll try again later."

"Then you don't know for sure if it's a dress," Hewitt said.

Shirley stared at him for a few seconds before turning to Cory. "Did you buy a prom dress on the company card?"

"All right," Hewitt conceded. "It has to be the third dress. But why such a complicated arrangement? Molly and Lenore had dresses already."

"Not tied to you," Peterson said. "And I think Lenore picked up both from the theater company. Molly might have been the first target and the killer wanted to make sure the staging would be correct. This way you're interjected into the middle."

Hewitt turned back to Shirley. "Follow up, especially where it was shipped because I sure as hell didn't receive it. What about that hardware store?"

Shirley looked even more despondent. "Two grappling hooks and a hundred feet of rope. The billing went to Louisville, Kentucky."

"Jesus," Hewitt groaned. "Well, check them out as well." He forced a smile. "One bit of good news. Helen Wilson agreed to the custody arrangement. Cory, I want you to draft the document outlining the basic terms Tom offered last night."

I noticed Hewitt had dropped "Mr. Peterson." Tom was on the team.

"Do you want me to notify the court we've reached a settlement?" Peterson asked.

"Yes. And then start reading the transcripts and other materials from the Duncan trial."

"What am I looking for?"

"Not what but who. The witnesses plus any depositions or interview notes regarding anyone who appeared to have a zealous compulsion to see Duncan convicted."

"You mean the prosecution's case," Peterson said.

Hewitt nodded. "In a nutshell, that's your target."

We broke up with a meeting set for five that evening in Rhubarb's bar downstairs. Nakayla and Peterson started sorting through the boxes of files. I was anxious to pursue more immediate leads, namely how Hewitt's Hawaiian shirt came to be in the photograph at Helen's Bridge. I didn't doubt what Newly had told me about it, but I was more interested in learning what the photographer knew about his incriminating picture.

Although it was only a little after eight in the morning, I called Collin McPhillips, and he agreed to meet me at the Over Easy Cafe, a popular breakfast spot a few blocks off Pack Square. When I arrived, he was already at a back table.

"You got here fast," I said.

He lifted his camera case from the chair across from him so that I could sit down. "I was shooting some scenics for the chamber of commerce. The light is better in the early morning."

"An article with Angela?"

"Nah. Just some seasonal stuff to freshen their website."

A waitress stopped at the edge of the table. "You need menus?" McPhillips looked to me.

"No," I said. "Give me two over-easy and black coffee."

"The same," McPhillips said. As soon as she left, he leaned forward and whispered, "So what's all this about Donaldson? Did he really kill Molly and Lenore?"

"A set-up. We don't know who or why. The evidence is all circumstantial."

"You know the cops kept my card."

"Your card?" I tried to look like I had no idea what he was talking about.

"The card from my camera with all the photographs on it."

"Probably some chain of custody concern."

"Custody of what?" he asked. "I mean I can see them not wanting the pictures of a dangling body going public, but they could wipe the card. Those things aren't cheap."

"Maybe your photos showed something special they're investigating."

McPhillips leaned back. "Like what, man? I didn't see anything those Japanese didn't."

"The police kept all their pictures too."

He said nothing.

"Did you see anything on top of the bridge?" I asked.

"Like what?"

"Like the body coming over."

He studied me for a moment. "Have you been talking to the police?"

"We all did."

"But they called me in a second time Sunday afternoon with that same question."

So, McPhillips didn't know one of his shots had captured the blur of a shirt. And he must not have heard about the evidence introduced at the probable cause hearing. I decided I needed to proceed as if McPhillips didn't have a clue as to how his photographs boosted the prosecutor's case.

I glanced around the restaurant. No one paid us any attention. "I need you to promise not to say where you heard this."

Again, he leaned over the table until we were less than a foot apart. "I'm a journalist. I protect my sources."

I nodded as if I actually believed him. My personal philosophy was never tell a journalist anything you don't want spread across the front page the next day.

"Here's what I know," I said. "One of the photos shows the blur of a Hawaiian shirt as Molly's body rolls over the wall of the bridge."

His eyes widened. "Donaldson wears Hawaiian shirts."

"Yeah. But so do a lot of people."

"In Asheville? In October?"

"He had a jacket over it. Does it make sense he would take the jacket off out in the rain?"

McPhillips thought a moment. "Yes, if he didn't want to get his jacket dirty and wet. Then he could zip the clean, dry jacket up over his damp shirt without anyone noticing."

Probably the argument D.A. Carter would make, I thought. "But you don't remember seeing a shirt in your frame?"

"No. But I wasn't looking at the top of the bridge. I was expecting Molly to walk out of the darkness from underneath."

"Well, the word I heard was the photo was yours. It was the only one taken vertically. All the others were horizontal shots and didn't include the top of the bridge."

McPhillips opened his mouth to say something but then stopped.

"What?" I prompted.

"Nothing." He paused a moment. "Did the police talk to Angela again?"

"Not that I know. Should they?"

"Just that she was right behind me and had the same angle."

"Are you still collaborating?"

"On what? I've got no pictures. She claims she's going to write some magazine article. If there's a trial, I'm sure she'll wait for that."

"A trial means photographs outside the courthouse, doesn't it?"

He couldn't restrain a smile. "I guess it does."

Our order came and the conversation shifted to McPhillips asking me about some of my more interesting cases, both in the military and the agency. Breakfast ended with a pitch.

We stood and McPhillips picked up his camera case. "You

know, I take damn good photographs under any conditions. I wouldn't turn down a little surveillance work now and then."

"Give me a card," I said. "In my business, you never know."

I walked back to our office thinking how McPhillips had good instincts. Of all the photographers shooting Helen's Bridge, he'd been the only one to frame for its full height.

Chapter Sixteen

"Did you learn anything?" Nakayla asked the question from the floor where she sat still sifting through the files from the Duncan trial.

I held up Collin McPhillips' business card. "A source to use when I don't want an all-night stakeout at a sleazy motel."

"McPhillips couldn't add anything about the shirt photo?"

"He didn't even know it was in the frame. Claimed it was a lucky shot because he held his camera vertically." I gave a quick glance around. "Where's Peterson?"

"He took transcripts back to the Jackson Building." Nakayla nimbly rose, clutching a few folders in her right hand. "I've got some bio info on Kyle Duncan that might help me locate him. Social security number, last known Asheville address, that kind of thing."

"What do you think about Peterson?" I asked.

"As a suspect? Well, he certainly knew all the plans. But I thought you said Efird saw video of his van at the Grove Park when Molly's body dropped from the bridge."

"He did. Newly also interviewed him. Peterson had gone into the Grove Park looking for Lenore when we were trying to reach Molly or he would have left sooner. The bartender at the Sunset Terrace remembered him. I meant is Peterson up to the task?"

She carried the files to the sofa and sat. I took the chair opposite.

"Well, based solely on his performance as Clyde Atwood's lawyer, I'd say no. He was easily lured into the D.A.'s traps."

"Hewitt's traps," I reminded her.

"Okay, but so far he's been insightful in working Hewitt's case. Maybe he's just hardwired to think like a prosecutor. In that sense, he could prove to be a real asset."

"I was thinking the same thing, particularly since Hewitt told him to focus on the prosecution."

"I think he's a good guy," Nakayla said. "And I think he's good for Cory."

"You think they're serious?"

"Cory doesn't take relationships lightly. They seem to click, both personally and professionally."

I knew Cory had broken up with her FBI boyfriend about six months ago. He'd been transferred to San Francisco and romance couldn't endure the distance. "Who knows? Maybe Cory gets a new partner and Hewitt gets a new partner. Stranger things have happened."

Nakayla laughed. "Oh, yeah? Name one. But I asked Peterson to put together a list of possible persons of interest. Meanwhile I'll go with the obvious ones like Marie Roddey's relatives and the status of Kyle Duncan himself."

"Give me his bio. I'll run him down. Then I'll check with Newly to see if the lab has determined whether the garage lock was picked."

She handed me a single sheet of paper, yellowed with age, that was little more than a list of vital statistics. Kyle Duncan was twenty-seven at the time of his arrest. He'd be close to fifty now. As a detective agency, we subscribed to databases with more extensive resources than Google or the various people locators populating the Internet.

I entered as much specific data as I could—full name, age, race, social security number, birthplace, and the option for living and deceased. I removed all filters so that categories of news, websites, still images, and videos would be included in the search pool.

The first hit was a newspaper article with the headline, "Kyle Duncan Trial Goes To Jury." I expected to see an *Asheville Citizen-Times* byline. Instead, the article appeared in the *Durango Herald*. Why would a town in Colorado be interested in an Asheville murder trial? Then I looked more closely.

"Nakayla. Come here." I rolled my desk chair to one side to give her room. "Check the date on this story."

She leaned over my shoulder. "October 21, 2000. Nearly fifteen years ago."

Two photographs accompanied the news story. One featured a pretty dark-haired white woman who looked to be in her late thirties. The picture had been snapped outside with a portion of the Rocky Mountains behind her. Beneath, the caption read, "Sandra Pendleton, murder victim." The second photo was the head-on mug shot of a wide-eyed Kyle Duncan. His face was leaner and more feral than the pictures in Hewitt's files. Although the caption stated Duncan was the alleged murderer, the sneer on his lips shouted guilty.

Nakayla and I spent the next thirty minutes going through the *Herald's* archives. The story was all too familiar. Sandra Pendleton was a widow with two children—Eileen, eleven, and Timothy, fourteen. Her husband, P.D. Pendleton, had been killed in Iraq in the First Gulf War. She'd returned to Durango from Denver to care for her ailing mother and to raise her children in a small town environment.

A few months before the murder, Sandra's mother passed away and she inherited the house. There were no other living relatives.

The prosecution claimed Kyle Duncan offered to do some remodeling work. He'd come to Durango six months earlier and worked construction in the area. He was a loner. Sandra advanced him money for materials and he'd started replacing some rotten wood on the back porch. On the second afternoon, the children had gotten off their school bus and discovered their mother's body on the kitchen floor. She'd been struck in the temple with a blunt instrument. Forensics identified a crowbar as the most likely weapon.

The police picked Duncan up at his rooming house where he claimed to have spent the day in bed with a stomach bug. His tools were still at Sandra's house, but there was no crowbar. Duncan claimed it had been there with the rest of his tools.

His public defender followed the same arguments Hewitt had used in the Asheville trial five years earlier. However, this time the prosecution had two additional pieces of evidence. A postman was half a block away and saw a man run from behind the Pendleton house and drive away in an old blue pickup. Although he couldn't make out the man's features, his general physique matched Duncan's. The truck was also similar to Duncan's Ford F-150. Unfortunately, the postman hadn't been able to read the plate number or identify the state. Kyle Duncan had Idaho tags.

The second piece of evidence came from Sandra herself. She kept a handwritten diary. The night before her death, she recorded that the receipts from Kyle Duncan didn't match the amount of money he claimed to have spent on materials. She dreaded a confrontation with him, but wouldn't let the discrepancy go unchallenged. One of the receipts was found under her body.

The fact that the postman hadn't seen the man carrying a crowbar led the police to conduct a more thorough search of the house. They found the murder weapon tossed twenty feet under the crawlspace. Traces of the victim's blood and hair adhered to the metal. Like Hewitt, the public defender tried to make much of the fact that the crowbar struck Sandra Pendleton on the right side, an impact spot more likely to indicate a left-handed attacker. But this time, the prosecution demonstrated that Sandra's standing position by the refrigerator would have made a swing from the right impossible. A backhanded blow could have more than enough power to crush the skull. And the blood splatter supported a backhanded grip.

The jury was out for three hours before returning a guilty verdict. Kyle Duncan was sentenced to death by lethal injection.

And there the stories stopped.

"Do you think he's still on death row?" Nakayla asked.

"I did a quick search of an anti-capital punishment site, but Kyle Duncan's name didn't appear."

"And nothing shows up in the Asheville papers?" Nakayla asked.

"Not after Duncan's mistrial. A murder charge half a continent and five years away might not have surfaced on the radar. If the Durango prosecutor knew about the prior trial, he probably couldn't use it. He had enough evidence without risking a tainted jury pool. And it sounds like Duncan could have been in Idaho for several years if he left Asheville right after his release. Their local paper might not have dug beyond that."

Nakayla backed away from the computer. "So, Hewitt and Lenore let a guilty man go free."

"Yeah. And the consequences went far beyond Asheville."

"Jerry Wofford," Nakayla whispered.

"The beer entrepreneur from Colorado," I said. "Check him out."

"What are you going to do?"

I looked at my watch. "Not too early to call Durango. I want to find out what happened to Kyle Duncan."

Nakayla retreated to her office and I heard her fingers flying across the keyboard. I closed my door and did an online search for the number for the Durango police department.

The switchboard routed me to a Detective Tonnisen. When I told him I was interested in speaking with someone familiar with the Kyle Duncan murder case of 2000, he put me on hold. I listened to a string of police and community PR announcements that must have gone on for ten minutes.

Then a gruff voice grunted, "Detective Archer."

He sounded old enough to have been around for the investigation and experienced enough to smell a bullshit story if I tried to spin one. I wished I thought through my play before placing the call.

"Detective Archer. My name's Sam Blackman and I'm calling from Asheville, North Carolina."

"Tonnisen said you're asking about the Duncan case."

"Yes, sir. There might be a connection to a cold case I'm working."

"A cold case in Asheville?" He sounded skeptical.

"Yes. Let me say upfront I'm private. And I know what you're thinking. That I'm running down unrelated cases to inflate my bill. I'm on my own time and I'm a former CID chief warrant officer. This is personal."

"I'm listening."

I grabbed a pen and flipped open my note pad. "There was a murder here twenty years back. The circumstances were similar to what I've read regarding your case. Kyle Duncan was in North Carolina at the time."

"And went through a mistrial," he said sharply. "I know all that so don't play games with me."

"I'm not. I just didn't know about your case till today. You got a conviction and I'm hoping Kyle Duncan will own up to what he did here."

"Sorry to tell you, but you're wasting your time. Kyle Duncan's six-feet-under."

"Then the execution was carried out?"

"The son of a bitch cheated the needle and died of acute leukemia. Guess you could say he was bad blood through and through."

"And he never said anything about the murder back here?"

"The D.A. had us sit tight on that info. Didn't want to chance prejudicial evidence. And we had him dead to rights as it was."

"Do you know if there were any relatives or friends of the victim threatening to take matters into their own hands if there wasn't a conviction?"

Archer paused, probably pondering why I asked the question. "Sandra Pendleton was a sweet woman whose husband paid the ultimate price for his country. I'd say the entire population of Durango would have taken matters into their own hands. Fortunately, a jury gave a fair and deliberate verdict."

"What about the kids?" I asked.

He sighed. "That's another tragedy. They had to go into foster care. I think Denver where they could be placed together in a home. The Pendleton house was sold and the proceeds put in trust for their education. They've never been seen since."

I looked at my notes. Three words. Leukemia and foster care. There was nothing else I could ask.

"Thank you, Detective Archer. You've been most gracious with your time."

"Wish I could bring some closure for your family, Mr. Blackman. For what it's worth, I'm sure Duncan was your man. He had dead eyes, you know what I mean?"

"I do. Thanks again."

Warmth now replaced the brusque tone of his voice. "Yeah. I wish I could help. You weren't the first to call looking for Duncan as a cold case solution. You won't be the last."

He hung up, and I was left debating with myself. Had I been working on my own, I would have acted immediately. But I owed it to Hewitt to run things by him.

Shirley looked up from her desk as I entered. She appeared to be cross-checking a calendar with information on her computer screen.

"Hewitt in?" I asked.

"He's with Cory in the conference room. They're reviewing client names in case they're subpoenaed."

"What are you doing?"

"Writing the acceptance speech for my Nobel Prize. What do you think I'm doing? I'm searching our credit card records for irregularities or vendors who might have appropriated the card number."

"Did you find out the shipping information for those two orders?"

"Yes. Cory's house."

"Cory's?"

"FedEx overnighted both with a ten thirty-delivery. No signature required. Cory was at work and both FedEx and UPS know to leave packages in her carport. We figure someone watched for the truck and then took them."

"No one knew Cory's schedule better than Hewitt," I said.

"So, are you turning witness for the prosecution?"

"Too crowded." I walked past her. "I need a few moments alone with him."

"Be my guest. I'll buzz him to meet you in his office."

Hewitt's door was unlocked so I didn't wait for him. Where the conference room looked like a tribute to sixties rock bands, Hewitt's inner sanctum resembled something from a hundred years ago. His desk was an old partners' style, the design with drawers either side of a large surface where partners could sit facing each other. There were law books on ceiling high shelves that Hewitt actually used. I could see bookmarks protruding above their spines. Two walls displayed framed black-and-white photographs of Asheville in the late eighteen hundreds and early nineteen hundreds. Pack Square was populated with horse-drawn wagons. There was an iconic shot of the W.O. Wolfe monument shop where Thomas Wolfe's father dealt in cemetery markers, the most famous of which became the starring title for *Look Homeward, Angel*.

I looked out the window at Pack Square and the Jackson Building now towering on that very spot Thomas Wolfe spent much of his childhood. In a few more years, it would be a hundred years old. Time. The irresistible force with no immoveable object to stop it. Twenty years ago, Kyle Duncan had gotten away with murder. Fifteen years ago, justice caught up with him, but another woman died in the process. How fast would time pass for someone seeking revenge for either of Duncan's murders? If revenge is a dish best served cold, the execution of Lenore Carpenter certainly occurred with chilling precision. But how long ago could such a plan have been devised? Who could have foreseen the events set in motion by Clyde Atwood's courtroom rampage? Why was Molly murdered? Did she just happen to be at the wrong place at the wrong time? Shirley said

Molly was going by Lenore's for her costume. Maybe she caught the murderer in the act.

"Shirley said we need to talk?" Hewitt motioned me to take the only guest chair and he sat behind his desk.

I got right to the point. "Kyle Duncan is dead. He died in prison of leukemia ten years ago."

"Serving time for what?"

"A murder in Durango, Colorado. A young widow with two children. He used a crowbar. This time." I punched the last two words.

His face colored. "Are you lecturing me?"

"Should I?"

"I do my job. I provide the best defense I can. My clients have a constitutional right to be represented in court. I have to let the chips fall where they may."

"You didn't know Kyle Duncan committed another murder?"

"Not another murder. A murder. And maybe I did. Sometimes I get calls from lawyers in other regions defending a former client. I can't be expected to remember them all."

Compartmentalization, I thought. Hewitt got Kyle Duncan off and consequences be damned.

"What's Colorado have to do with Asheville, anyway?" he asked.

"Jerry Wofford, for one."

His face went blank for a second, and then the light bulb switched on. "Does he have ties to the victim?"

"Not that we know. I came to you immediately to see how you want to play it."

Hewitt laced his fingers together and tucked them under his chin. I waited.

"Could be coincidence," he said. "The beer phenomenon in Asheville has lured big and small brewers from all over the country. Colorado is also a big beer producer."

"I agree."

"What do you think?" Hewitt asked.

"I have been thinking. My recommendation is to turn the information over to Detective Newland."

Hewitt puffed up like a blowfish. "The prosecutor's lead investigator? Why don't we just schedule a meeting with Carter so I can tell him my strategy?"

I slid the chair to the desk where I could reach out and shake him if I needed to. "He's not Carter's bag boy. You're not to repeat this, but Newland has serious doubts about your guilt and thinks Carter is running half cocked."

"Well, at least someone over there has a brain."

"So, goddammit, let him use it."

Hewitt jerked back like I'd slapped him. "Don't talk to me like that."

"Or what? You'll fire me?" I stood, forcing him to look up at me. "Newland can talk to the Durango police cop-to-cop. He'll get further than I can because I'm not in their club. We play fair with Newland on this backdoor channel and he'll play fair with me. Yes, he's no fan of yours by a long shot, but he does want to solve the case, not just get a conviction."

"All right. Sit down, you're giving me a crick in my neck." He waved me into the chair. "That means you'll have to tell him about Lenore being on the Duncan jury. And that gives him another connection to me."

"A connection we want established if it defines you as a possible victim."

Hewitt nodded. "Okay. But I don't want any word leaking out about my feeding the police information. Carter would disregard anything that even smells like it came from me."

"I won't tell Newland we've spoken. As far as he knows, I'm doing this behind your back."

Hewitt managed a smile. "Which means if it comes to light, I'll have to fire you."

"So, what's the downside?"

I was joking, but Hewitt considered the question.

"The downside is we're putting too many eggs in a policeman's basket. You and Nakayla work on Wofford's background."

"She's already on it."

"What about the Durango woman's children?"

"They went into foster care. There were no relatives."

"Then bring Tom Peterson in on it. Foster care and adoption records are usually sealed. Let's see if he can find out what happened to those kids. He might have to seek a court order."

"Then I hope we'll have something to report tonight at the bar."

"Yeah. But instead of downstairs, let's move it to the Thirsty Monk for tonight. I want to see how I supposedly made this threatening phone call to you, especially since I don't even know your damn office number."

I stood and headed for the door.

"Sam," Hewitt said softly.

I turned. "Yeah."

"What was the woman's name? The woman in Durango."

"Sandra. Sandra Pendleton. Her children were fourteen and eleven."

Hewitt looked away. "I'm sorry about that."

I left and closed the door behind me. Hewitt's wall had its first crack.

Chapter Seventeen

"God, that was a bloody mess of a crime scene. One of those that haunts your memory." Detective Newland made the comment and then popped a ketchup-drenched french fry into his mouth.

He and I sat in a back booth in Luella's Bar-B-Que on the north side of Asheville. We both had platters of chopped pork, fries, and cornbread in front of us and could talk grisly murders without diminishing our appetite one bite.

"I figured you were involved," I said. "Even if it was twenty years ago."

"One of my first assignments after I made detective. I'd forgotten Lenore was on that jury." He wiped sauce from his chin. "Boy, that sure backfired."

"What do you mean?"

"The D.A. at the time, Lloyd Whitmire, thought she would identify with the victim. He thought he had her in his pocket."

"What happened?"

"Hewitt Donaldson happened. One of his impassioned closing arguments pleading for the jurors not to compound one tragedy with another and convict an innocent man. Whitmire didn't count on Lenore being quite so young and impressionable. Donaldson harped on the forensics report that the fatal blow was most likely struck by the left hand. He even had Duncan wear his left arm in a sling during the trial as if he had some chronic sprain."

"Did he put him in a wheelchair?"

Newly laughed, and then choked a little on a mouthful of meat. He took a swig of sweet tea to clear his throat. "No, but if Marie Roddey had died from a kick to the head, I'm sure he would have."

"And Lenore was afraid of sending an innocent man to death row because of Hewitt's theatrics?"

"This trial was right after the O.J. Simpson verdict. Donaldson actually used the line 'if the wound doesn't fit, you must acquit.' He was shameless."

"Anyone stand out who would carry a grudge for twenty years?"

Newly set down his silverware. "You think this goes back to the Duncan trial? I thought you were just giving me background on how Lenore and Donaldson met."

"That's how they met but it in no way provides a shred of a motive. If anything, it makes the two allies."

"Against whom? Who would wait twenty years for revenge? And what about Molly Staton?"

"I don't know. That's why I'm asking."

Newly picked up his fork and heaped it with a mound of barbecue. I waited, letting him chew in silence.

After another gulp of tea, he pointed the empty fork at my chest. "Look, I've been around long enough to know anything is possible. But really, Sam, a twenty-year hatred that just happens to culminate now?"

"Then how about a fifteen-year hatred targeting the people who let a killer go free to kill again?"

Newly lowered the fork. "What are you talking about?"

I shared what I'd learned from the Durango homicide detective.

"And why is someone from Durango more likely to be involved than from Duncan's trial in Asheville?"

It was a fair question and I had a possible if not improbable answer.

"Because in Asheville, Hewitt and Lenore enabled a killer to go free. In Durango, they enabled him to murder. They bear responsibility for Sandra Pendleton's death, not Marie Roddey's."

Newly pondered the distinction. He wiped his lips and laid his napkin by his empty plate. "All right. I'll give this Detective Archer a call and see where it leads. You're trying to track the children?"

"Tom Peterson is working that angle."

"So they'd be mid-to-late twenties now?"

"Yes, if what Archer told me about their ages is accurate." A thought flashed through my mind. Mid-to-late twenties. The age of Collin McPhillips, the photographer who said he just happened to frame the shot that captured Molly's body tumbling from the bridge and the blur of a Hawaiian shirt.

Newly craned his neck as he peered over my shoulder. "Where's our waitress? I need my check so I can get back."

"I'm buying today."

Newly eyed me suspiciously. "Not trying to bribe a police officer, are you?"

"Since when is encouraging a police detective to find the truth a bribe?"

Newly grinned and settled back in the booth. "You're right. In that case, I'll have dessert."

◇◇◇

It was nearly two when I returned to the office. Nakayla had sorted the box of files into separate stacks beside her desk, each with a note card on top identifying a specific category such as evidence, witness testimony, or personal history.

"Any luck with Wofford?" I asked.

She looked up from her computer screen. "Don't tell me. Barbecue."

I glanced down and saw the red stain below the third button of my shirt. "Yes, but can you tell from where?"

"An overloaded fork is my guess. It must be nice to get lunch."

"I was working hard. Newly's going to call Durango. And…" I'd kept my right hand behind my back and now dangled a Luella's takeout bag in front of her.

Nakayla grinned and snatched it away. "Thanks, partner."

I swept my arm across the stacks of files. "A thank you for organizing all of this. Anything come to light?"

"Kyle Duncan appears to have been a loner. No military service. A couple of DUIs and two aggravated assault charges in Raleigh before moving to Asheville."

"Domestic?"

"No, but arguments on construction sites. One with a co-worker and another with a foreman. The guy was a hothead. And basically a drifter who lived off the grid."

"Wonder why he went to Idaho?" I asked.

"Probably a good place to stay farther off the grid," Nakayla conjectured. "As for his victim, Marie Roddey, she has a surviving mother in a retirement community in Charlotte. Her father is deceased. There's one sister, also in Charlotte. She's married with two kids in high school. Both she and her husband work for Wells Fargo. I called her at work but was told she's been out of the country for two weeks. She's a video producer and involved in some project highlighting their offices in Asia."

"That's a damn good alibi."

Nakayla cleared some papers from the corner of her desk and unwrapped her sandwich. "I don't see her or her family as suspects. There was a boyfriend. Tony Martin, a high school English teacher."

"Did Hewitt go after him?"

"No. He was chaperoning a field trip to Washington D.C. I tracked him down through Facebook. He's married and a high school principal in Wilmington, North Carolina."

"About as far away as you can get and still be in the state."

Nakayla picked up her sandwich. "Do you mind?"

"Not at all. You're much prettier with a mouthful of food than Newly was."

"Thanks. You really know how to make a girl feel special."

"Then you haven't had a chance to background Wofford."

She held up one finger while she took a bite. I don't know how women manage it. Not a crumb fell.

"Just a quick online check," she said. "He joined Coors in 1983 as a production manager in Golden, Colorado."

"Where's Golden?"

"About twenty miles west of Denver. Coors has a huge brewery there. In 2004, he went from the production side to marketing strategy. This coincided with the merger with the Canadian brewer Molson. He moved from Golden to Denver."

"How long was he there?"

"Until February. He had over thirty years with the company. Then he moved to Asheville."

"Wife? Children?"

"His wife died of ALS in 2013."

I let out a breath. "Lou Gehrig's Disease. That's tough. And hard on the caregiver. Maybe Wofford just wanted a fresh start."

"There are no children I can find. His background of production and marketing makes a great combination for starting a craft beer."

"Investors?"

Nakayla shrugged. "I haven't gotten that far."

"Do you mind checking?" I eyed her partially eaten sandwich. "After lunch, of course."

"Maybe. Since you asked nicely. What's your plan?"

"Nothing goes better with barbecue than a beer."

Nakayla waved me out of her office. "The sacrifices you make."

I turned at the door. "Oh, and check if Wofford and his wife ever kept foster children. Even temporarily."

Wofford's Crystal Stream Brewery was near Bruxton and Coxe Avenues, the core site for Asheville's exploding beer industry. Like most afternoons, my damaged left leg was beginning to chafe against the sleeve of my prosthesis. I was tempted to drive, but the walk to the car wasn't that much shorter than the distance to Wofford's tasting room and company office.

Technically, the Crystal Stream Tasting Room was more of a pub with a simplified menu of sandwiches, cheeseboards, and boiled peanuts. Unlike a pub, they were only open till nine, and it was all about the beer. Order a chardonnay and you'd find yourself out on the sidewalk.

Nakayla and I had been a few times, most recently for a planning meeting for the ghost tour. The place had become so jammed with people and dogs that we had to cram into Wofford's office.

The building was industrial grade, little more than a weatherized warehouse. Pickups and deliveries came to a roll-up garage door right on the sidewalk. In warmer months, the door was left open to accommodate more tables. But, on this Tuesday in October, the crowd would be reduced to a few tourists and those regulars who tasted their Crystal Stream by the pint.

I heard nothing from within. The room wouldn't open for another twenty minutes, and I guessed Wofford's staff was in the back where they brewed the beer. I walked around the corner to a side door that bore the words Employees Only. A buzzer was mounted on the jamb next to the knob. Above, a small security camera angled down. I pressed the button and smiled up at the lens. A click sounded as someone opened an electronic lock and I entered a short hallway. Jerry Wofford stepped out of the first office on the left, his expression morphing from curiosity to concern.

"Sam. What's up?"

"You've heard about Hewitt?"

"Of course. The police spoke with me yesterday. I said I didn't know anything." He glanced over his shoulder to check if anyone was behind him. "He didn't do it, did he?"

"No. But I want to go over a few things. We're doing our own investigation."

If Wofford was curious as to the "we," he didn't ask.

"Okay. But I have to check on the staff first. They were cleaning one of the kettles and we open to the public in a few minutes. Some of them have to shift over to the tasting room." He motioned to his office. "Do you mind waiting in here? I'll only be a few minutes."

"No problem. Take your time."

He turned and disappeared through a door at the opposite end of the hall. I got a glimpse of large stainless steel tanks with rows of gauges. Two people wearing protective clothing were flushing out one of them. The room looked as clean and cared for as a surgical operating room.

Wofford must have put his money in the brewing equipment because his office looked like it belonged on a WWII battleship. Gray steel desk, gray metal filing cabinets, and a dented credenza with a state-of-the-art computer. The screen saver appeared to be a close-up of a glass of lager with bubbles rising to an unseen surface.

Nicely framed photographs of Rocky Mountain vistas hung on the walls. I guessed they were favorite pictures Wofford transported from his Coors days. I walked between the desk and credenza. Various invoices were spread across the blotter. None of them appeared overdue. Two four-by-five photographs in hinged frames were on the desk. One showed a young Wofford and a beautiful woman emerging from a church in wedding attire. The second featured the same woman at least thirty years older seated in a wheelchair with a man and woman standing behind her. The couple had to be in their early twenties, and their resemblance suggested they were siblings. Wofford's ailing wife and children?

Not wanting to be caught prying, I moved to one of three straight-back chairs lined against the wall and waited. He returned in less than five minutes with a bottle of beer in each hand.

"This counts as work," he said, offering me one. "I love my job."

Instead of sitting behind his desk, Wofford grabbed the chair beside me and swung it around to face me. He sat with our knees only a foot apart, closer than what I considered normal. The close proximity heightened my awareness of the ache in my stump. I stretched my left leg out beside his chair.

"Sorry. I'm a little sore after the walk."

He looked down at my knee. "Your war wound. I'm amazed at how well you get around."

"It's a loss I've learned to live with. We all have losses of one kind or another."

He'd started to take a drink, but returned the bottle to his lap. "You know I lost my wife."

I nodded. "Nakayla told me. That's losing a part of yourself. Even more so than my leg."

"There's not a day goes by when she's not in my thoughts. What can we do, Sam, but live on and hopefully do a little good along the way?"

"Do you have children?"

"No. We tried. Margaret did a lot of volunteer work with the children's hospital in Denver. I guess you could say she had a lot of children." His voice caught. "Many came to her funeral." He took a long drink of beer and then set the bottle on the floor beside him. "But you didn't come here to talk about me."

Actually I did, I thought. "No, but I hope perhaps you can help. The prosecutor has circumstantial evidence that points at Hewitt. I believe someone has gone to great lengths to create that evidence."

"Why? Is someone else in line for top suspect?"

"We have no motive. Makes it hard to find suspects."

Wofford leaned his chair back on two legs. He wore blue jeans and a red flannel shirt, and it struck me all we needed was a potbelly stove to make this a true mountain conversation.

"Well, I'm too new here," he said. "I don't know the ins and outs of the local feuds."

"Sometimes new folks see things the rest of us blur over."

Wofford rocked forward. "Sorry. Other than our meetings, I wasn't around Hewitt, Molly, or Lenore. I told the police that."

"Do you mind sharing what else they asked?"

"Did I see Hewitt last Friday. I told them no. I was here."

"Here? I thought you were at Pack Square."

Wofford bent down and held up his bottle. "Here's where the beer is. If any of our vendors ran short, I could resupply them. And they could reach me by phone. I didn't need Armitage's radio gear."

"How'd you learn about Molly?"

"Armitage called. I drove immediately to Pack Square to find out what was going on."

I was running out of questions so I made a pretense of admiring the scenic photographs on the wall. "You miss Colorado?"

He turned and followed my gaze. "I miss the Rockies. The Appalachians are pretty but out West we'd call them foothills."

"I went there a long time ago to see a friend in Golden."

His face brightened. "That's where I worked. What's your friend's name?"

"Sandra Pendleton," I lied.

If Wofford recognized the murder victim's name, he did a hell of a job masking it. "Nope. Doesn't ring a bell."

I finished the beer and stood. "Thanks for your time. Sounds like you were out of the loop last Friday."

He rose and offered his hand. "Sorry I couldn't be more helpful."

"No problem. I enjoyed talking. And I'm very sorry about your wife." I motioned to the back of the double-framed pictures on his desk. "I noticed those photographs while I was waiting. She was a beautiful woman."

He swallowed hard. "We'd have been married thirty-five years last June."

"And the young man and woman?"

"Her sister's children. Our only niece and nephew. We went on a little outing. Margaret had ALS and could no longer speak. But she smiled the whole day." He took a deep breath. "No disrespect to your sacrifice, Sam, but I would rather have lost my leg."

"I understand." The insight suddenly hit me. If I hadn't lost my leg, I would never have found Nakayla.

I walked back to my office, the ache of each step a reminder of my good fortune.

And I had a second realization. Jerry Wofford had no alibi.

Chapter Eighteen

At five that evening, we crowded around the cellar bar at the Thirsty Monk. The pub had three floors: the cellar that specialized in Belgian beers and where we gathered because of Hewitt's fondness for the wheaty brews, the ground floor that offered a wide range of craft beers, and a second-floor bar patterned after a Jazz Age speakeasy flowing with whiskey and gin.

The two beer floors were each manned by a bartender who took everyone's order. Our bartender pulled a Snowplow Wit for Hewitt as he saw us walking toward him.

"Your usual, Mr. Donaldson." He turned his attention to the rest of us. "And Mr. Peterson, would you like to try a Belgian or will you want your Bells Amber Ale from upstairs?"

Cory laughed and punched her boyfriend's arm. "Wow, you waste no time getting known."

"I'm a lawyer who has trouble passing any bar." He nudged Hewitt. "I'll try what my friend's having."

The bartender took our orders without writing anything down. Hewitt told him we'd be ready for a second round in a few minutes. I was sure his excellent memory for names and faces increased his tips. How could you stiff a guy who remembers you?

We carried glasses and bottles to a table at the front and sat down.

"So," Hewitt said, "what did we learn today?"

Shirley reported first on the credit card check and said nothing seemed unusual over the past months. She reviewed all charges since the Atwood shooting because we figured that must have been the catalyst that set the killer in motion.

Cory had spent the day keeping Hewitt's other clients on track and negotiating with the prosecution on discovery procedures.

We were all anxious to hear from Tom Peterson since he had been reading through the trial transcripts.

"I'm afraid I didn't have a particularly productive day," he said. "The trial came down to a battle of stories." He looked across Cory to Hewitt. "Your emphasis on the wound obviously carried the day with Lenore. The prosecutor had no witnesses other than Duncan's co-worker who claimed Duncan had stolen the silver dish. No one else saw those men in the victim's house so it was one man's word against another's that their confrontation even occurred. Personally, I think the prosecution had a stronger case with the weapon and fingerprints, and the D.A should have made more of the possibility of a backhanded blow like the case in Colorado. The blood splatter supported that interpretation."

"And he could have gone for a re-trial if the evidence hadn't been screwed up," Hewitt said. "Because it was a mistrial, there wasn't the same hue and cry as an outright acquittal. I think the public assumed the prosecutor would take another shot at it and change his strategy."

"So, any anger was mitigated?" Peterson asked.

"Nobody shot us on the street." Hewitt spun his beer glass between his palms. "I just don't get it. The Duncan trial was so long ago, and if it's the Atwood case, why Molly and Lenore?"

"I don't know," Peterson said. "I'm at a dead end. But I'm more inclined to an Atwood connection. At least Molly and Lenore were both involved in the fundraiser."

Hewitt looked to Nakayla. "Give me some good news."

"When we learned about the Colorado murder, I looked for any links. Jerry Wofford is the only one in our planning circle with a Colorado connection."

"That we know of," Peterson interjected. He swept his gaze around the table. "Anyone else?"

No one responded.

"It's probably just coincidence," Nakayla continued. "He did work for Coors and experienced beer people have been flocking to Asheville." She swiveled to me. "But Sam made a call on him."

Before I could answer, the waiter returned with another round of beers. Without fail, he placed the proper brand before each of us.

Hewitt raised his glass. "To justice."

We repeated the word like an oath of allegiance.

I took a swallow and cleared my throat. "Nakayla learned Wofford was in Golden at the time of the Durango trial. He and his wife moved to Denver in 2004. I made up a story about having a friend in Colorado named Sandra Pendleton. He didn't bite."

"So, he's out," Hewitt said.

"Not necessarily. We know Sandra's children went into foster care in Denver. They could have overlapped. Wofford's wife was active in children's causes."

"Did they have children?" Shirley asked.

"No. But I saw a picture of his wife with a young couple matching the age the Pendleton kids should have been. Wofford says it was taken when his wife's ALS was far along. He claimed they were a niece and nephew. And I learned he was supposedly by himself at the brewery when Molly's body appeared."

Hewitt leaned forward in his chair to see around Cory. "Tom, weren't you checking on those kids?"

Peterson lowered his glass from his mouth. A mustache of foam coated his clean-shaven upper lip. "Sorry. I forgot to mention it. No luck. As I feared, the foster care records are sealed. I said the information was for a criminal proceeding, and all I wanted was a current address. I even took it to the departmental supervisor, but it's a no go. Evidently, there was some kind of scandal involving pedophiles who got into the foster care program. The agency's super-sensitive about revealing the children's names."

"Any pictures of the kids?" Nakayla asked.

"Not that I can find online," Peterson said. "You're welcome to look. Maybe you'll have better luck."

"We need to focus, people," Hewitt said. "Put Colorado on the back burner for now. Cory and I are pushing for discovery materials. I want to see the casts made from the wheelchair impressions, the analysis of my garage padlock, and anything else Carter is throwing at us. Are there any other angles we can pursue?"

I gave a quick glance around the bar to make sure no one was paying us close attention. I leaned forward and lowered my voice. "I spoke with Collin McPhillips today. He's the only one who caught the blur of that shirt on top of the bridge. He said he was just lucky to be framing vertically rather than horizontally."

"So?" Peterson asked.

"He knew Molly was supposed to walk out from behind the bridge's footing. Seems to me he would have shot to highlight that area."

"Have we done a background on him?" Hewitt asked.

"No," Shirley said. "Since he was clearly at the scene, the police ruled him out."

Hewitt frowned. "I don't care what the police are doing. Nakayla, you and Sam run him tomorrow." He paused a second. "See if he's got any ties to Colorado." The lawyer drained his beer and brought the glass down on the table like a gavel. "Shirley will cover the drinks. Anything else before I go?"

"You mentioned the Atwoods," I said. "Nakayla and I are talking with Cletus' brother Junior tomorrow evening."

"Good." Hewitt stood. "Then this court's adjourned until tomorrow morning."

Shirley and Cory left soon after, both headed back to the office for a few more hours. Tom Peterson stayed and offered to buy another round. I wanted to pass, but Nakayla accepted before I could speak. I guessed she was interested to learn a little more about Cory's new boyfriend.

"Is helping Hewitt causing a time crunch with your other clients?" Nakayla asked Peterson.

He laughed. "What other clients? I call myself just to make sure my phone's still working."

"So, this case helps with your visibility," I said.

"I took it because this has got to be one of the biggest and most controversial trials in Asheville's history. I want to be part of it."

"You mind if I ask what you're doing for money?"

Peterson lifted his beer. "Afraid I can't pay the bar tab?"

"No, just curious. Professional hazard."

"I didn't spend much in the Army. What are you going to buy in Afghanistan? I came here straight from discharge with enough to set up shop." He paused. "I guess you're right if I'm honest. The case isn't only a great challenge but it will definitely raise my profile. For good or bad."

Nakayla took a drink of pale ale and then stared into the glass. "Right now it doesn't look too good."

Peterson shrugged. "We'll see. He has a lot of confidence in you two."

Neither Nakayla nor I said anything.

After a few awkward seconds, Nakayla asked, "How do you like working the other side?"

"You mean working with Hewitt?"

"No. Working defense. I take it you were a JAG prosecutor."

Peterson shook his head. "I worked some defense on second tour, but I was primarily a TC. That's trial counsel, Army speak for prosecutor. I enjoyed working with investigators like Sam." He bounced the question to me. "You're the one who exclusively worked the prosecutorial side. How do you fit with someone like Hewitt?"

The question carried the distinct tone of disapproval. "I don't know what you mean by fit," I said. "My job's always been to find the facts and present them objectively."

"Oh, come on," Peterson pressed. "You've got to admit Hewitt distorts the facts any way he can to get his client off. I just don't understand how he can be indifferent to that murder in Durango."

I understood where Peterson was coming from, but in my military experience, Hewitt's histrionics wouldn't have happened at a court-martial. "What can I say? He plays within the system and stretches it as far as he can."

"And damn the consequences." Peterson finished his beer with a series of quick swallows and pushed the glass away. "Sorry to have talked myself into a bad mood. I might be more comfortable as a prosecutor, but that doesn't mean I don't believe Hewitt's innocent." He patted me on the back. "Find the facts and I'll distort away." He looked at Nakayla. "And I really care for Cory and she adores Hewitt. So, I know he can't be the devil." He turned and walked off.

"Well, that was interesting," Nakayla said. "What do you think was really going on?"

"I don't know. Could be several things."

"He might be concerned about your respect. All he knows is you were a military investigator and you testified at the Atwood trial for the prosecution. He didn't want to be tainted with any unfavorable opinion you have of Hewitt."

I mulled that point. I hadn't considered Peterson wanting my approval. "Maybe. Or maybe it's preparatory posturing."

"For what?"

"For if the trial starts to go south. A victory tags him as the man who contributed to Hewitt's acquittal. If that looks impossible, he can bail, citing a disagreement over tactics. He shouldn't say anything more because of attorney-client confidentiality."

Nakayla frowned. "You think he's that calculating?"

"You asked me what I thought was going on. It's a possibility."

"Yeah, I guess. But you're overlooking one important factor."

As she could tell from my expression, I was clueless.

"His statement about Cory, dummy. If he bails on Hewitt, Cory turns into the ice queen."

Nakayla had a point, and as a typical guy, I missed it. "Exactly what I was about to say."

"Yeah. Tell me another one and feel the temperature drop."

I wasn't an idiot. "Treat you to dinner?"

She stood. "And I choose. Let's go vegan at The Laughing Seed. Maybe no meat will make you a little more sensitive to affairs of the heart."

I downed the rest of my beer and started to get up when I remembered where I was. "Wait. Sit down a moment." I pulled my cell phone free. "I want to record the room. Hewitt supposedly made the call to our office from here, and I want a sound comparison."

Nakayla slid back in the chair. "Good idea. Won't it make a difference where he was seated?"

She was right. I got up and walked to the bar.

"Mr. Peterson settled the bill," the bartender said. "Would you like something else?"

"No. You've got such a great memory, I'm embarrassed to ask your name."

"It's Hank. Hank Ingalls."

"Hank, do you remember when Hewitt Donaldson was in here late last Friday night?"

His smile disappeared. "I sure do. The night that woman was killed. He and Mr. Armitage closed the place."

"Are we at his regular table or did he sit someplace else?"

"They sat there to start because he thought some others would join them. I noticed he made a call, and then he told me it would just be Mr. Armitage and him. They moved farther back to a smaller table."

"Was Mr. Armitage with him when he made the call?"

"I'm pretty sure. Later, Mr. Armitage ordered another round when Mr. Donaldson was in the restroom."

"Did Mr. Armitage go to the men's room?"

Hank gave me a look that told me I was moving into the weird category.

"Like you said, Mr. Donaldson was very upset. I just want to know if he seemed all right when he was alone."

If Hank thought the explanation was lame, he didn't show it. "Probably he did. They were here for three hours, but I can't say when."

"At two? Right before closing?"

"I don't know. I was busy ringing out."

I pulled a ten from my wallet.

Hank waved it away. "That's not necessary."

"I know it's not. That's why I'm giving it to you."

The smile returned and he took the bill. "Thank you, Mr. Blackman. Ms. Robertson. Sure I can't get you anything?"

"We're fine," Nakayla said. "But we'll be back."

When he'd turned away, Nakayla said, "So, you need to record from the rear of the bar and in the restroom."

"Yeah. Just to be sure."

Fortunately, the men's room was empty and I stood inside the door until I had a good minute of ambience recorded. An elderly couple sat at the rear small table Hank had indicated. I stood near them and pretended to be listening to a cell phone call.

"Mission accomplished?" Nakayla asked when I returned.

"Yeah. Let's go graze."

She started to rise and then stopped. "Shouldn't we stop upstairs?"

"Hank didn't say Hewitt went upstairs."

"I think you ought to check it out as well," she said. "Someone else could have placed the call from there, and Hewitt and Nathan wouldn't have seen them."

"The prosecution will argue Hewitt went upstairs," I argued.

"And Nathan and Hank can say otherwise."

"Damn it. That's a good idea. I guess I'm going to have to buy you a bottle of wine as well."

Chapter Nineteen

When we gathered the next morning, we traded beer for coffee and the Thirsty Monk for Hewitt's conference table. Not much progress had occurred. Shirley and Cory spent the previous evening drafting a statement that Hewitt planned to turn over to Detective Newland. It detailed how Hewitt first met Lenore during the Duncan trial and that neither she nor Molly had ever been a client.

With a separate memorandum, Hewitt threw down the gauntlet that he considered his client list as confidential and would fight any subpoena demanding its release.

"All right," Hewitt said. "Let's move on to some fresh thinking. What can we be doing that we're not?"

Tom Peterson spoke first. "Well, I think we have to look closer at Molly and Lenore. Did either of them have enemies we don't know about?" He looked at Hewitt. "Maybe Lenore had an old boyfriend who didn't like your becoming part of her life. Or Molly had a run-in with someone at work. The police might have skimmed over some of these possibilities because they made up their mind you're good for it."

Hewitt nodded. "Treat them singly and assume the other was collateral damage."

"Exactly. Lenore might have been the intended victim and Molly happened to be in the house."

Hewitt turned to Shirley beside him. "You knew them the best. Can you ask around?"

"Yes. But don't hold out much hope. Neither mentioned any conflicts or unwanted attention."

"Did you know I was seeing Lenore?"

Shirley's white makeup took on a tinge of red. "I get your point."

"Good. Cory, you concentrate on our clients and keep cases moving. Bring me only what's absolutely necessary." Hewitt looked across the table to Nakayla and me. "What are your priorities?"

"We've got the interview with Junior Atwood at six," Nakayla said. "I'm going to search as much background on him as I can. I'll also check out Wofford's wife. Maybe somehow her death triggered him into action."

"Why?" Peterson asked.

"Well, we won't know that till I collect more information."

"Okay," Hewitt said. "Sam, what about you?"

Nakayla and I had discussed our options the night before. She possessed superior computer skills. Our plan was to have me do the legwork during the day and then we would meet Junior Atwood and Pastor Brooks together. But Nakayla also had great people insights and I decided Collin McPhillips warranted a closer examination.

"Two things," I said. "Taking a fresh look means not only the evidence against us or for us, but also the missing evidence."

"Like what?" Hewitt and Peterson asked in unison.

"No tire tracks at the bridge. The police are probably theorizing that you got Molly's body up there ahead of time. Otherwise you were cutting it close from when you picked up the passenger van to when I cried, 'Helen, come forth.' It would make sense to pull farther out of sight to dump the body and rope. The ground was dry and hard earlier in the afternoon."

"But there were wheelchair marks," Peterson said.

"Yeah, but only on the level approach to the bridge. That means the body was hidden earlier off the path and then wheeled into position after the rain moistened the ground."

Hewitt shook his head. "That doesn't do me any good. I have no alibi for Friday afternoon."

"But we know how narrow that road is heading up to the housing complex. The van would have to pull off on the shoulder and leave a mark. Otherwise, it would block the road. Drivers would remember that. But a smaller car, maybe parked that night in the mountaintop neighborhood, wouldn't be noticed. He could walk down to where he hid the body and wheelchair."

"Why not park the van in the housing lot?" Peterson asked.

"The same reason not to block the road. A passenger van would stand out in a lot full of sedans and SUVs. Again, we have missing evidence—no trace of soil either from Lenore's garden or the bridge were found in the van or in the trunk of your Jaguar. And neither had been vacuumed afterwards."

Hewitt straightened in his chair. I could see him grabbing onto these points for his closing argument.

"What about the footprints?" Cory asked. "There's nothing in discovery yet."

It was an excellent question and one I should have asked.

"The police stripped my closets bare." Hewitt lifted his leg and showed us a shiny, patent-leather dress shoe. "They let me keep this pair because it was packed away with my tuxedo."

Despite the circumstances, I had to laugh. "It's not in discovery because there's probably no soil match or identifying heel mark to show they were your shoes."

"Damn right there isn't," Hewitt said. "I was never on that bridge."

I turned to Peterson. "You might want to focus on what evidence they don't have. Anything that creates holes in the prosecution's case."

"I will," he said.

"What else?" Hewitt demanded.

"I have some more questions for Collin McPhillips," I said. "But before circling back to him, Nakayla and I need to talk to Angela Douglas."

"Why her?" Peterson asked. "Wasn't she with you at the bridge?"

"Yes, and the police cleared her almost immediately. But if I'm looking at McPhillips, I need to look at her. Nakayla can read women far better than I can, so we'll interview her together. Shirley, will you give us a contact number?"

"As soon as we break," she promised.

"Good. Sounds like a full day." Hewitt picked up his legal pad and pointed the corner at me. "Call when you finish with Junior Atwood. I don't want to wait till tomorrow morning." He stood. "The rest of us will meet downstairs at five-thirty."

Nakayla and I went with Shirley and she gave us Angela Douglas' cell number.

"This is all I have," she said. "Never got a home or office address."

As Nakayla and I walked the hallway to our own suite, she said, "I haven't run a background on Angela yet."

"Do that before we go." I glanced at my watch. Five till eight. "I won't call before nine. Meanwhile, I'll check in with Newly."

I'd just picked up the phone to call the detective when Tom Peterson came in.

"Can I talk to you both a few minutes?" he asked.

"Sure," Nakayla said. "I put on a pot of fresh coffee. It'll be ready in five minutes." She gestured toward the sofa. "Sit down."

He raised his hand. "No, thanks. I won't be that long. I just wanted to apologize for last night. One too many beers and frustration that I'm not bringing much to the game."

"Think nothing of it," I said. "You're the one who had to get immersed in the Duncan trial and then Durango."

"Well, I'm really glad to be working with you. I'm there one hundred percent."

"We know," Nakayla said.

He turned to me. "Those were good suggestions. I wish I'd had you on my team when we both worked for Uncle Sam."

He backed out the door and closed it.

"Told you," Nakayla said.

"Told me what?"

"He wants your respect. He's doing this for you, not Hewitt."

◇◇◇

Nakayla spotted Angela Douglas at a back table where she sat nursing a cup of tea and reading through a notebook. I'd reached her at nine and arranged to meet at The Green Sage, a tea and coffee spot just a few blocks from the office.

"You go ahead," I told Nakayla. "What would you like?"

"Jasmine Green and a scone," she answered.

"You got it. Now go soften her up for my interrogation."

Nakayla laughed. "You? The guy who admits he can't read women? Are we playing good cop, dumb cop?"

When I joined them at the table, Nakayla was laughing at something Angela had said.

I set Nakayla's tea and scone in front of her. "I hope I'm not the reason you're laughing."

Angela looked up at me, her bright blue eyes sparkling. "I was telling Nakayla about my introduction to barbecue, North Carolina style. Yesterday, Collin suggested we meet for lunch and have barbecue. I kept asking him what we'd have to eat. He kept answering barbecue. I asked barbecued what? It was like Abbott and Costello's 'Who's On First?' I'd always known barbecue as a verb, and it usually involved a hot dog or hamburger."

I shook my finger at her. "Then you don't want to get into the difference between western North Carolina and eastern North Carolina barbecue. It's been known to break up families."

"I get it," Angela said. "Up north it's the Giants versus the Jets or the Mets versus the Yankees that can destroy the harmony of Thanksgiving dinner."

I sat beside Nakayla and squeezed her thigh under the table. She'd managed to have Angela bring up Collin McPhillips in a completely neutral context. "How's the article coming? Tough that Collin lost access to his photographs."

Angela brushed her blond hair off her forehead. "We hope to get some of them back. At least the ones of you with the tour group before…" She paused and closed her eyes. "Before that terrible moment."

"Anyone agree to publish your story?" Nakayla asked.

"Not yet. That's what created the barbecue meeting. Collin is anxious to move on it, but I think the story is about what happened up to that moment at the bridge when a well-intended event went horribly wrong."

"Sounds like Collin wants it to be an investigation story instead of a background piece," I said.

Angela's blue eyes turned icy. "It's not a background piece. The tragedy of the twins and what we hoped to accomplish on their behalf is the centerpiece. Yes, I'll follow the investigation, but if I approach it as strictly a crime story, the news reporters will have the advantage and I'll be left with warm leftovers."

Angela's rationale for her approach made sense. The human interest story was the boys and the community that rallied around them. For her, the murders were entwined amid the custody conflict. She would view the investigation into a long ago case here or in Durango as a sidebar.

"So, are you and Collin not working together?" I asked.

"Collin is a great guy with a great eye. I'm happy to work with him. It's just I'm taking the story in a different direction, but I'll still need photographic support. I'll bring him in when I finish a first draft."

"Well, he seems to know his way around Asheville," I said. "He's a good contact for someone new to town."

"I agree," Angela said. "He can get me to people I'd never see on my own. I hope he'll introduce me to Nelda and Cletus Atwood."

"How's he know them?" Nakayla asked.

She leaned over her coffee and checked the nearby tables before answering. "Know them? He's related to them. He said his father and Cletus are first cousins. Clyde was his second cousin."

Nakayla and I exchanged a quick glance. Angela had just linked the Atwoods to Collin McPhillips, the man who took the incriminating picture that D.A. Carter planned to enter into evidence against Hewitt.

"I'm surprised Collin would work on a fundraiser his family didn't support," I said.

Angela shrugged. "You'll have to ask him."

Two hours later, Nakayla and I welcomed Collin into our office. He wore faded black jeans and a black turtleneck. His camera bag dangled from his shoulder, and I realized I'd never seen him without it.

"Do you sleep with that thing?" I asked.

He blinked with confusion. The camera was so much a part of him he didn't know what thing I meant.

"Your camera."

He laughed. "No. But it stays by my door so I have to trip over it before leaving. My equivalent of a policeman's gun."

Nakayla gestured to our leather sofa. "Sit there and you can keep the camera right beside you in case a photo op breaks out."

Collin stopped and cocked his head. "That's a great idea. A day in the life of a private detective."

"I was kidding," Nakayla said nervously.

"Well, I'm not. And the fact that you're a team makes it all the more interesting."

I took his arm and steered him to the sofa. "We'll think about it."

He sat and Nakayla and I each took a chair. Collin studied the room like he considered buying it. I was afraid he was already framing shots.

I got right to the point. "As I said on the phone, we have a potential case that's going to require some photography. Nakayla and I are swamped at the moment and might need you as backup."

Collin nodded with excitement. "Sure. Whatever I can do. Will I need a P.I. license?"

I stifled a laugh. "No, because you won't be representing yourself as a detective."

"Okay." He rubbed his palms on his thighs, clearly eager to learn more. "What kind of time are you looking at?"

"Probably late afternoon till midnight. The client thinks her husband is cheating on her. She wants us to watch the house of his secretary."

The prospect of an assignment had been the bait I'd used to lure Collin to the office on such short notice. Since I'd just talked to him about the murders the day before, calling another meeting on the same topic could spook him.

"Sounds simple enough," he said. "Can I shoot from the car?"

"There's on-street parking. I don't know what you're driving, but if it's not too distinctive, you should be fine."

"A silver Honda Civic," he said. "A car so invisible pedestrians step right off the curb in front of me."

We then spent a few minutes talking about his rate and expenses for the mythical job that would never happen.

"When do you think you might know?" he asked.

"We're giving her an estimate and then she'll decide," Nakayla said. "We should know pretty quickly."

"Do you have something pending?" I asked. "We talked to Angela Douglas and she said you wouldn't be shooting for her until after the first draft of her story."

Collin slipped the strap of his camera bag over his shoulder and stood. "If then."

Nakayla and I rose, and I edged to my right to block his path to the door. "What do you mean?"

"Just that she might be one of those writers who researches a story to death without getting around to writing it. At some point, you have to put your butt in the chair and write the damn thing."

I understood why the rift between the two developed. Collin covered stories with deadlines.

"It's only been a few days since the murders," I said.

"And you think she'd be hounding the cops for information, or camped on your doorstep if you're working with Donaldson."

This was my opening to explore Collin's tie to the Atwoods. "Is she pumping you for information?" I asked.

"What information?" he asked.

"About the Atwoods. She said you were related."

Collin's face colored and his eyes cut from me to Nakayla. "I have nothing to do with that family and she knows it."

"You're not related?" Nakayla asked.

"I didn't say that," he snapped. "My father and Cletus are first cousins. My great aunt married an Atwood when she was sixteen. Cletus was born six months later."

Collin didn't have to draw us a family tree. If what he said was true, back then his family would have held no love for the Atwood who impregnated their daughter.

"So, how did Angela find out? Research?"

He shook his head. "I told her. When we first met at Clyde's trial. I thought she was cute and I was looking for some angle to keep the conversation going."

"Why was she there?" I asked.

"She was planning an article on spousal abuse." He paused as a new thought crossed his mind. "Maybe she's folding all that together—the trial for domestic assault, the custody battle, and the murders. Write some story about hillbillies out of control."

"Did she ask you to introduce her to Cletus and Nelda?" Nakayla asked.

"No. Not that I'd have any kind of in. I mean Clyde and I were civil to each other, but we had nothing in common. For him, the lumberyard was all the job he wanted. Everything else was drinking, hunting, and fishing. You know the type."

"What about your dad's cousin Junior? You have any dealings with him?"

Collin grew wary. "Junior? What's he got to do with anything?"

I shrugged. "Probably nothing. I ran into him when I was talking with Pastor Brooks. I understand he was career military."

"Yeah. Twenty and out. Junior's the one who got the brains in the family."

"Book smart?"

"People smart. I guess you learn to read people in the Army. If Junior wants something, he'll damn sure figure a way to get it."

"Were he and his nephew Clyde close?" I asked.

"Nah. Junior thought Clyde was lazy. He told me so, and, believe me, Atwoods don't speak ill of themselves to a McPhillips."

"Then he wouldn't have cared if Clyde had gone to jail?"

Collin scrunched up his face as he mulled the question. "He probably wouldn't have cared about Clyde, but he would have worried about those twins. Junior never had any kids, and those boys were like his own sons. I reckon he'd be more upset than Cletus and Nelda if he couldn't see Jimmy and Johnny."

I stepped back, clearing the way to the door. "Thanks, Collin. We'll be in touch when we hear something about that assignment."

As soon as the door closed, Nakayla whispered, "What do you think?"

"I think Collin and Junior might be closer than he let on. And if Junior's as smart as Collin said, we might be facing a formidable adversary."

Chapter Twenty

I spent about an hour that afternoon at Helen's Bridge trying to recreate what must have happened. The switchbacks up the mountain to the houses and condominiums were just on the other side of the arch of the bridge from where I'd waited in my car. If the killer had come up the opposite end of Windswept Drive, he would have driven down and stopped on the road closest to the bridge surface. I wouldn't have seen or heard him at all.

The crime scene tape had been removed and I steered my CR-V off the edge of the pavement until the vehicle was nearly off the road. The undergrowth to the top of the bridge had been trampled down. If the killer brought the body in the afternoon, he would have had a few tense moments parked on the road while he unloaded the body and wheelchair and then hid them out of sight.

The old carriage path traversing the bridge was also overgrown, but without significant trees impeding the way to move the body once in the wheelchair. Traces of plaster dust showed where the forensics team had pulled their most promising casts. One set emerged from the woods across the path from the road, lending credence to the theory that Molly's body had been hidden off the trail. Plaster also outlined a distinct depression that looked like a heel mark, but no discernible feature signified either style or brand. The damp leaves hadn't been the kind of material to hold an imprint. As I suspected, the lack of identifying characteristics explained why no mention of foot-prints existed in the early discovery documents.

I walked to the middle of the bridge and studied the dirt surface of the old carriage way. Dead leaves and spots of crabgrass covered a thin layer of soil. I turned and looked over the stone guard wall. The paved road had to be at least thirty feet below. The wall itself was about a yard high. I examined the spot where Molly's body came tumbling over. Scratches beneath one of the more prominent and extruding rocks showed where the grappling hook had been wedged in the dug-out crevice to secure the rope. I lay down beside the spot, getting a sense of what the killer must have done.

The wall provided ample protection from eyes below and enough room to crouch behind while pushing the body over. Anyone worried about being seen could have bared his forearms or worn black gloves and sweats to be practically invisible.

I rose and paced back and forth across the bridge four times, scanning the ground for anything that might have been missed. I realized it wasn't so much what was missed as what was missing.

I punched in Detective Newland's cell phone number.

"Sam. What's up?"

"Can you talk?"

Newly knew I didn't mean did he have the time but rather was he alone.

"Just pulled into the police lot. Efird's inside."

I sat on the wall. "I'm at Helen's Bridge and noticed that there's no litter. The place draws enough of the curious that I thought there would at least be a beer can or candy bar wrapper."

"We bagged everything," Newly said. "Most of it had obviously been there a while, but the killer might have touched something if he cleared a spot for himself and the body."

"Have you been through it all?"

"Checked for prints. No hits that I know of."

I thought back to Friday night—the halogen lights, the forensic team combing the area, and Newly's nephew Al not wanting to leave the scene when Newly told him to talk to Nakayla. What was it one of the techs had yelled? Check Al's shoe covering to see if a fragment had ripped free.

"Newly, did the team find whose shoe cover had been torn?"

"Shoe cover?"

"When they thought it was Al's."

"I don't know. If not, you think it was the killer's?"

"Did you get any heel marks or other identifying characteristics off the footprints?"

"No. I'll check it out."

"I hope it's not gone missing," I said.

Silence for a few seconds. "I said I'll check it out." This time the words were low and angry.

Our conversation had ended. I knew he had jumped to the same possibility I had. His partner, Tuck Efird, would have no trouble getting shoe covers or any other accessories to prevent contamination of a scene where he committed the crime.

◇◇◇

A little after five, I picked Nakayla up from in front of our office building. Rush hour isn't particularly heavy in Asheville, but both of us preferred to be fifteen minutes early rather than five minutes late. She set a file folder on her lap as she buckled her seatbelt.

"What's that?" I asked.

"My afternoon's work. I ran deeper background checks and thought I'd brief you on the way to Pastor Brooks."

"Sounds good. Fire away."

She opened the file and lifted the top sheet. "Nothing additional on Jerry Wofford. I found some more clippings on his wife. She was on the advisory board of Denver's children's hospital, but she gave that up in 2008 after her ALS diagnosis. Her name surfaced on some charity benefits for ALS research, so I guess she focused her energy there."

"Anything support Wofford's claim that the young people I saw in the photograph with her were a niece and nephew?"

Nakayla pulled out another page. "No picture for you to see, but her obituary of 2013 listed a niece and nephew, evidently the children of her younger sister."

"Any chance they were adopted?"

She turned in the seat, and from the corner of my eye, I saw the frown that told me I was bugging her.

"Yes. I guess there's a chance. But if you've got any connection to Colorado's child services, be my guest. You know Hewitt assigned that to Peterson and he ran into a stone wall searching for what happened to the Pendleton orphans."

"Calm down. I'm not criticizing you. I just thought maybe there was something there."

"Well, there isn't." She turned over a new sheet. "And I ran a check on Peterson as well. He has an honorable discharge. He earned his law degree at Northeastern in Boston thanks to Uncle Sam and then repaid his obligation as a JAG officer. That all fits with what Cory told me."

"Did she say why he came to Asheville?"

"He told Cory he'd had enough of cold in the Boston winters and enough of heat in Afghanistan. He met a guy in the service from here who couldn't wait to get home."

"Who? Do we know him?"

"Cory didn't have a name. Tom told her the guy had been killed by an IED. Tom took a trip here before his discharge and fell in love with the place. Cory said Tom's a mountain person at heart and the climate here is the perfect blend of four seasons."

"I think he has another agenda," I suggested.

"What?" Nakayla asked.

"He might be angling for a job. Hewitt's not getting any younger, and if he ever takes a partner, now might be the time."

"Peterson could be the young blood he needs," Nakayla said.

"Do you know where he grew up?"

"Some little crossroads outside Des Moines. He told Cory it was so flat that water always stayed in puddles."

We left I-40 for Highway 23, retracing the route we had taken on Sunday morning.

"What about Angela Douglas?" I asked.

Nakayla thumbed down a few pages. "There's not much. So many people her age are heavy into social media, but I couldn't find a Twitter or Facebook account. An Angela Douglas had a byline for some web articles on post-traumatic stress."

"Military publications?"

"No. They seemed to be resources for support groups—victims of child and spousal abuse."

"Consistent with her eagerness to help the Atwood twins," I said. "Collin McPhillips told us she was more interested in feature stories than hard news." I took a quick glance at the papers in her lap. "So, what about Collin?"

Nakayla separated out about five pages. "Collin has a much more detailed history. He's local. He went to T.C. Roberson High School and was a member of the National Honor Society."

"College?"

"He went to Asheville-Buncombe Technical Community College."

"I would have thought as an honor student he'd go to a four-year school."

"Could have been a money thing," Nakayla said. "Many students go to a community college the first two years and then transfer their credits to a university in the UNC system. It's a lot cheaper."

As someone who rebelled against his father and went straight into the Army out of high school, I wasn't up on playing the college game. "Did he?"

"No. Evidently he took a course in photography and got hooked. He interned at the *Asheville Citizen-Times* and then went freelance after completing his associate degree."

"Nothing that ties into Molly or Lenore?"

Nakayla closed the file and set it on the floor of the backseat. "No. But he was arrested once."

I whipped my head around. "You saved that for last?"

She laughed. "Keep your eyes on the road. Collin went to Raleigh in the summer of 2013 to cover the Moral Monday protests."

Moral Mondays were grass roots protests that descended upon the North Carolina legislature when they made slashes to progressive social programs and refused to accept federal funds to expand Medicare to the poor. Nearly a thousand people were arrested over the course of the Monday demonstrations. None were violent and the movement has since spread to other southern states.

"He was protesting?" I asked.

"He claimed he was a photo-journalist on assignment covering the Asheville contingent and got swept up in the mass arrests. He wrote about it in an op-ed page column, and if he'd been neutral before, the experience turned him into an unabashed sympathizer and supporter."

The city of Asheville was probably the most liberal in the state. The surrounding mountain counties, the most conservative. I could see how Collin's upbringing would be challenged as he started hanging out with social activists.

"Did the newspaper let him go?"

"He was never full time," Nakayla said. "They just never gave him that assignment again."

I wondered if the Raleigh arrest had radicalized him somehow. Even so, how did that tie in with Helen's Bridge?

"Does he have a girlfriend? Or a boyfriend?"

"Not that I know," Nakayla said. "I think you were right. He sleeps with his camera."

We rode in silence until the turn onto Heavenly Way.

"Are you going to take the lead?" Nakayla asked.

"Yes. I've got the military connection with Junior and I requested the meeting. But jump in if you think I'm missing anything."

We parked close to the front door. Only a few cars were in the lot.

I glanced at my watch. "We're fifteen minutes early. Should we wait till it's closer to six?"

"No. When I was investigating insurance fraud I always showed up early. Sometimes it was good to catch them off guard."

Catching Pastor Brooks and Junior off guard proved to be elusive. As we ascended the steps, the doors swung open and Wheezer greeted us with a cheery, "Howdy, folks."

"Sorry if we're a little early," Nakayla said. "Traffic wasn't as heavy as we feared."

Wheezer waved us inside with a thin bony hand. "That's no never mind. Pastor Brooks told me y'all were coming. Junior's not here yet, but I'll take you back."

"We know the way to his office," I said.

"I know you do. We ain't going to his office." Wheezer started walking. "Pastor Brooks wants to meet in his rooms."

I looked at Nakayla, shrugged, and gestured for her to fall in step behind the lively old man.

"Does Pastor Brooks have an apartment here?" Nakayla asked.

"I reckon ya could call it that. He's got a sitting room and a bedroom. He uses the church kitchen and bathrooms."

We passed by Brooks' office and continued down the hall. At the far end was a door I thought led outside, but when Wheezer opened it, I realized an annex existed on the back corner of the building.

Pastor Brooks sat in an armchair with a floor lamp positioned over his shoulder. He looked up from a book, smiled, and laid the volume on an end table. "Welcome to my abode." He stood and shook hands, first with Nakayla and then me.

"Thank you, Wheezer," he said. "When Junior gets here, tell him to come back."

Wheezer nodded and closed the door behind him.

"Why don't you take the sofa?" Brooks suggested.

In addition to the armchair, an upholstered beige sofa and matching chair completed a semicircle around a slate coffee table. A flat-screen TV hung on the wall opposite the sofa. The room was approximately twelve by twelve with what appeared to be an outside entrance at one end and a door to what must have been the bedroom at the other.

Two windows broke up the wall behind the sofa. Hanging between them was a portrait of a young woman and a toddler. The artist had added a soft abstract background that focused all attention on the smiling faces. I knew they were the wife and child killed by the hit and run that happened right in front of

Pastor Brooks. I looked away, afraid the preacher would see me staring at them.

"It's all right," Brooks said softly, as if reading my mind. "I'm sure someone told you about my wife and little boy."

"Yes," Nakayla said. "We're so sorry."

He studied the portrait a moment. "For years I couldn't bear to look at it. Just too painful. Then I realized how wrong I was to bury their goodness. I could take comfort in their love, but only after I'd discarded the hatred I held for the person who had taken them from me."

I just nodded. I couldn't think of anything to say that rose to the level of this man's suffering.

"Thank you for your efforts to help with the Atwood twins," Nakayla said.

Brooks motioned for us to sit. "I hope that proves to be the best course of action. I told Cletus and Nelda they can only control the impression they make on the boys and that speaking negatively about Helen Wilson won't do anyone any good."

"Discard the hate," I said.

Brooks gave me a wry smile. "Reconciliation can't happen any other way. You can take all of those theology books in my office and their hundreds of thousands of words, and they all come down to one—reconciliation. Person to person, person to God." He held up his hand. "Better stop me before I go preaching at you."

A knock sounded from the door and a man I assumed to be Junior Atwood stuck his head in. "You wanted to see me?" His dark eyes widened with surprise as he saw Nakayla and me. Apparently Brooks hadn't told him we were coming.

"Yes," Brooks said. "Do you know Nakayla Robertson and Sam Blackman?"

Nakayla and I stood and shook the reluctantly offered hand. Junior looked to be in his late forties and was built like a chiseled block of stone. I sensed a military bearing and some physical training regimen that he must have continued to keep in shape. He was all muscle. His gray hair was cut short in a military buzz. His handshake was firm, but not one trying to demonstrate strength.

"They asked me to introduce you because they think you might be able to help them with some audio problem." Brooks turned to me. "Did I get that right?"

"Yes. Thank you for coming, Mr. Atwood."

"You can call me Junior." He slid into the vacant chair by the sofa. "What kind of problem do you have and how can I possibly help?"

Nakayla and I sat and I pulled my cell phone from my belt. "When we were at church last Sunday, we were very impressed with the audio set up. Wheezer told us that was all your doing, and that you had been an audio tech specialist in the Army."

"That's right," Junior confirmed.

"I was a chief warrant officer and sometimes worked with audio techs when it involved a case. You guys know your stuff."

Junior straightened in his chair, obviously flattered by the compliment. "I heard you were CID. Lost a leg too."

"We all did what we had to," I said.

He nodded. "True. Some more than others. You have my respect, Mr. Blackman."

"If I'm calling you Junior, you're calling me Sam."

For the first time, a smile flashed across his lips. "Okay, Sam. So what is it?"

"We got this message on our office answering machine." I pushed the play icon on the audio app and set the phone on the slate top coffee table. I kept my eyes focused on Junior's face while Nakayla watched Pastor Brooks.

"Mr. Blackman. You have crossed Helen's Bridge into the valley of the shadow of death. You and your black harlot. Be warned that the scythe of justice is sweeping away all who are found guilty."

When the message hit "black harlot," Junior's eyes jumped to Nakayla and his face reddened. I picked up the phone as the clip ended.

Junior looked at Brooks. "What kind of scumbag would leave a message like that?"

"I guess they're hoping you can find a way to identify him," Brooks replied.

I saw Nakayla give a subtle shake of her head to cue me that Brooks' reaction hadn't been suspicious.

"The police have analyzed it," I said. "The ambient background sound appears to be from a bar and they say the clip has been filtered to disguise the voice. We were wondering if you could reverse the process."

Junior held out his hand. "Let me listen to it again, this time close to my ear."

I handed him the phone. "I also went to a bar we think might be the location and recorded ambient sound to try and match the location."

"Good. I'll listen to that as well."

For about five minutes, Junior worked my phone. He'd listen to the message and then jump down to the cuts I made at the Thirsty Monk.

He handed the phone back. "Interesting."

"Can you do anything?" I asked.

"I'd like to pull copies. I think the voice filter was used to lower the original voice. But that's not the interesting part."

"What is?" I asked.

"The voice has been filtered but the background hasn't been. That means the voice and background were recorded separately. Someone took the trouble to mix the tracks together before sending them to your answering machine."

"Why would they do that?"

Junior shook his head. "That's the question, isn't it? Either to establish a location for the time of the call that wasn't the real location, or to make sure the location was recognizable because he wanted it to be identified."

"Or both," I said.

"Or both," Junior agreed. "Whichever, you have a very clever adversary."

Chapter Twenty-one

Nakayla and I sat stunned by Junior's analysis. The background of the call could have been recorded any time earlier that evening or even days ahead.

"You're positive?" I asked. "The police didn't mention the discrepancy."

Junior waved his broad hand as if to dismiss the entire Asheville Police Department. "Once they identified the background as a bar they got too focused on the voice. I guess I was more open to the possibility because I'd seen it before."

"In the Army?"

"Yeah. A homicide investigation where you CID boys thought a sergeant was good for the murder of his wife. Neighbors said there had been rows in the past. This was off-base near Fort Bragg." Junior leaned forward, his eyes bright as he recalled the event. "But a message from the husband on the victim's phone was recorded in the middle of the window that the ME had established as the time of death. You know those Moe's restaurants?"

"The burrito place?" Nakayla asked.

"Yeah. Whenever you walk in the door the staff all yells, 'Welcome to Moe's.'"

"He used that as an alibi," I said.

"You got it. You can hear the words plain as day behind him. He tells his wife he's running late and to go ahead and eat. He'll be home later. Later was around eleven because after Moe's he stopped at a bar. He found the backdoor of his house broken into and his wife strangled in the den. The silver and her jewelry were taken."

"What put you onto the message?" I asked.

Junior rubbed the back of his neck like the reason puzzled him as well. "Something about the sound. His voice was too clear. I didn't have any technical proof. The investigators hadn't found witnesses at Moe's who remembered seeing him, but the bartender testified he'd been drinking beer till around ten thirty. I played a hunch and took my recording to Moe's on my own. I had the staff listen to it one at a time. Several people recognized themselves, and one guy, an African-American with a distinctive baritone voice, was predominant in all the 'Welcome to Moe's.'" Junior grinned. "The trouble was he'd been off the night of the supposed call. I gave the info to CID and it sealed the case. I got a nice write-up in your CID newsletter."

"Impressive," I said. "That's the kind of newsletter you send home."

He actually blushed. "Well, I guess it was a highlight."

"I know one of your relatives who must have been impressed."

His expression turned wary. "Who's that?"

"Collin McPhillips. We got to know him working on the fundraiser. He thinks a lot of you."

Junior seemed uncertain how to respond. Interjecting Collin had momentarily thrown him. He looked at Pastor Brooks. "Collin's like a second cousin. Good kid but a little too much in the liberal Asheville camp. He did send me a congratulations note, although we rarely cross paths these days."

I turned to Nakayla, signaling her to add anything she wished.

"This has been very helpful," she said. "Do you think there's any chance you could reverse engineer the filters on the voice?"

"Did the police try that?" Junior asked.

"Yes," Nakayla said. "They said the voice went through at least a two-phase alteration that they couldn't undo."

Junior nodded. "Whatever frequencies were lost can't be accurately replaced. If you find the original project on someone's computer, you might be able to undo those changes, but if the guy's got any brains he deleted all the files."

"How about the background?" I asked. "I recorded three locations—a ground level bar, the cellar bar, and the cellar restroom."

"We're talking about the Thirsty Monk, aren't we?" Junior winked at Pastor Brooks. "Not that I've ever been there."

"Yes," I admitted.

"I don't think it's the restroom because that sound is more muffled. If I had to take an educated guess, I'd say the upstairs. The sound's more hollow with the outside door."

It was the answer I was hoping for.

"Thank you both for seeing us," I said. "I'll let you know if we have any luck."

"Do you think you're in any danger?" Brooks asked.

"No, I think someone's trying to confuse things, not threaten us."

Junior cocked his head and gave me a hard stare. "This is about those ghost story killings, isn't it?"

"Yes," I said. "But please keep our conversation confidential. The man behind the voice might be the man behind the murders. We don't want to spook him."

"You have my word," Junior promised.

"You have my prayers," Pastor Brooks added.

Back in the CR-V, I asked Nakayla, "Can we cross Junior off our list?"

She scrunched her lips, weighing the question. "He seemed to have an innocent reaction, and I think he was genuinely surprised to see us."

I started the engine and backed out of our space. Evening worshipers were beginning to arrive. "Can you think why Brooks told him to come by but neglected to say we'd be there?"

"Only one reason," she said. "Brooks suspected we'd be asking something about the murdered women and he was as curious as we were to see Junior's unprepared reaction."

"And if Junior left that voicemail, why reveal the truth about the background?"

"Covering himself," Nakayla said. "Maybe he didn't know what we knew and decided to play it straight. One thing for sure, it changes the whole character of the phone message."

"A spoofed number and a falsified location time," I said. "But I don't see how it could have been planned. Even Hewitt didn't know he'd wind up at the Thirsty Monk."

"All our guy needed was a cell phone and a laptop," Nakayla argued. "People carry those like they carry wallets. He witnessed Nathan and Hewitt go into the bar, followed, and made the ambience recording unobserved while they were in the lower bar. Then, he could record his voice in his car where no one could overhear him. He doctored it, mixed in the background, and sent the message when it was late enough that the bar had thinned out. The staff would remember Hewitt and if the call came from a reasonably close proximity, the cell tower records would support the location."

Nakayla's theory made logical sense as far as a sequence of events, but one question still gnawed at me. "Why? To what purpose? It's not like the evidence ties Hewitt to the murders."

"Face it, Sam. Someone hates Hewitt and is exploiting every opportunity to make his life miserable. Maybe he thought calling me a black harlot would drive a wedge between you and Hewitt."

"Maybe." I pulled my phone from my belt and handed it to Nakayla. Dusk was falling fast and I didn't risk driving and dialing. "Call him. His number's in recent calls as Hewitt's cell."

He must have answered on the first ring.

"Hewitt. It's Nakayla. Okay if I put you on speaker?" She held the phone on the console between us and pressed the speaker icon. "Can you hear me?"

"Yes." His voice sounded tinny but the connection was good. "Where are you?"

"We just left the church," I said.

"You feeling righteous?"

Hewitt's sarcasm struck me the wrong way. "Brooks is all right. Thanks to him Junior gave us some valuable information."

"Like what?"

"The background audio on that phone message was recorded separately from the voice. The voice was filtered but the bar was meant to be heard."

Silence.

"Hewitt, did you hear what I said?"

"I heard what you said, but what does it mean?"

"Someone recorded the sound at the Thirsty Monk and then mixed in a filtered voice later. They didn't have to place the call from the bar at all. They avoided being seen after the bar thinned out."

"Hot damn," he said so loudly it distorted the speaker. "If Carter presents that message we can blow him out of the water."

I sensed wherever Hewitt was he was dancing.

"No," I said sharply. "I don't think that's the way to play it."

Again, silence. Hewitt wasn't accustomed to having his court-room strategy challenged.

"All right," he drawled at last. "Then what do you suggest?"

"I understand your inclination is to ambush Carter if he tries to play this card. But the message proves nothing. Rather than engage in a game of Gotcha, we need to find the real killer. In my mind, the doctored voicemail confirms the existence of a conspiracy. If we can fuel Newland's doubts about your guilt, then not only can you undermine his testimony if Carter puts him on the stand, but you increase the friction between him and Carter. I bet if it comes to a head, the police chief will back his detective and buck the prosecutor."

Without hesitation, Hewitt said, "I'm sold. Come by the Rhubarb Bar. We're still here."

Nakayla gave a definite shake of her head. She was done for the day and the last thing she wanted was a night drinking with Hewitt.

"Thanks, but I want to get to Newly as soon as possible. We'll see you in the morning." I clicked off before he could argue.

"Thank you," Nakayla said. "I'd like for you and me to split a bottle of wine and take-out Chinese at my house. Then we'll see what develops."

I sped up. "Now that's an offer I can't refuse."

"Do you want me to call Newland?" Nakayla asked. "Maybe he can see us first thing in the morning."

"Yes. His number should be on the recent call log."

Their conversation lasted less than a minute She spoke three sentences. "This is Nakayla... Sam's with me... We'll be there."

"Don't tell me," I said. "The wine and Chinese are on hold."

"Newly wants us at the station. He has something he thinks we'll find interesting."

"You didn't even try to tell him about the recording."

She flashed a broad smile. "Whatever he's got, I want to trump it."

"Getting a little competitive, are we?"

She handed me my phone. "I've always been competitive. I just don't consider you competition."

I knew I should shut up while I was behind.

We were buzzed through to Newland without any fanfare— no reporters, no satellite trucks, no problem. Although the bullpen was relatively deserted at mid-shift, Detective Newland led us back to the same interview room, only this time without the dramatics of turning off the lights and reversing our seating arrangements.

He sat, motioned for Nakayla to take the seat beside him, and left me to sit in the interviewee chair across from them. He laid an unzipped, leather portfolio binder on the table.

"What's new from your side of things?" he asked.

"You invited us." Nakayla eyed the legal-pad size binder in front of him.

Newly scraped the legs of his chair on the hard floor as he angled to see both of us. "Well, I know this is going to come as a shock, Nakayla, but Sam had a good idea."

Nakayla drew back in mock surprise. "There must be some mistake."

Newly flipped open the portfolio. Tucked in the left inside pocket opposite a clean legal pad was a clear evidence bag. He pulled it free and handed it to Nakayla.

"Sam remembered one of the techs at Helen's Bridge asking if Al had torn his shoe covering. I'd let that slip my mind, and at your partner's suggestion, I went back through the litter collected at the scene. This is what I found."

Nakayla gave the plastic pouch to me. At first glance, the fragment appeared to be shaped like the state of North Carolina, wider at one end and narrowing to a point at the other. The fabric was light green like some hospital scrubs I've seen, and the edge of the wider portion showed a small strip of silver, evidently a part of where the reinforced sole had ripped free.

I held the fragment close to my eye. The edges were frayed, demonstrating a tear rather than a clean cut. A symbol was embossed on the silver—a vertical line with a diagonal line attached to one end forming an acute angle. The diagonal line was interrupted by an edge of the tear. It could be a tread pattern to prevent slipping. It could be part of a letter with a sharp angle like an M or N.

I slid the sleeve across to Newly. "I take it this piece is not one of yours?"

The detective tucked it back in the leather pocket. "No. And the techs made a bad assumption that it was. Ours are blue and have the word POLICE repeated across the sole so that any imprint made at the scene can be clearly delineated from others."

"Do you know where this came from?" I asked.

"Best guess is some hospital. We're checking medical supply catalogues and all facilities within a fifty-mile radius. That sole design could be a brand name. It could be an M for Medical. The only thing we know for sure is that the shoe cover isn't ours. Unfortunately, on the wet leaves, no shoe prints left an impression."

"I assume you've analyzed it for soil traces."

"Yes. Nothing other than what was at the scene. The rip appears to have originated at the edge of the sole. Scrape marks are consistent with a rough rock surface."

In my mind, I returned to my examination of the bridge earlier that afternoon. "He probably wedged his foot against the rock wall as he heaved Molly's body over. It had to be an awkward position to make sure his face stayed hidden."

"And yet purposefully expose a portion of his Hawaiian shirt," Nakayla added.

Newly shifted his gaze between Nakayla and me. "You're going with this elaborate frame of Donaldson?"

I spread my hands wide, palm up. "You think someone else coincidentally wore a Hawaiian shirt in October? Did you get an exact match on the pattern?"

"No," Newly admitted. "The shirt was too blurred and magnification only degraded it into a smear of colors—but colors consistent with what Donaldson wore that night."

"I thought you believed Hewitt was being set up," I said.

"Unlike Carter, I believe it's a possibility. But we now have the credit card receipts for Molly's dress and the rope and hook, we have the wheelchair in his garage, we have the hate call from the Thirsty Monk, and we have a possible motive."

Nakayla shot me a look of surprise.

"Motive?" I exclaimed. "Since when?"

"Since we verified the handwriting we found in the diary tucked in the nightstand by Lenore Carpenter's bed."

Ice crystallized in the pit of my stomach. No longer was Hewitt facing hearsay that Tuck Efird might claim Molly told him. A diary would be damning testimony in the murder victim's own words.

"What did she say?" I braced myself for a phrase like, "I fear for my life."

Newly simply shrugged. "Just that she needed to cool off the relationship. How she realized the age gap was insurmountable, and she would only be in her sixties when Donaldson was in his late eighties. She was afraid he wouldn't take the breakup well."

"Take the breakup well?" I repeated. "That can mean anything from hurt feelings to breaking down in tears."

"I admit it's not a smoking gun."

"Smoking gun? Hell, it's not even a loaded gun."

Newland's expression turned deadly serious. "You can tell yourself that, but it's a motive Carter will run with all the way through closing arguments. Lenore broke up with him and refused to join him at the proposed love nest at Grove Park. He confronted her at her home Friday morning where and when we've established his presence. They argued in front of Molly, and in his rage he killed both women."

"What about the timing of the diary entry?" Nakayla asked.

"Two days before he ordered the dress and hardware. The real confrontation could have occurred then. That's what Carter will argue and if he can sell that point, everything afterwards looks like the execution of a plan."

"Any subsequent entries describing Hewitt's reaction?"

"No. But Lenore didn't make entries every day, or sometimes she went back and filled in the missing ones."

It was time to halt Newland's defection into the prosecution camp. I pulled my cell phone from my belt. "Listen to this." I played the clip I'd recorded in the upstairs bar of the Thirsty Monk. After about thirty seconds, I clicked it off. "Recognize it?"

"I guess it's close to those background sounds on your voicemail. What's your point?"

"That is the point. Basically, it's the same sounds, unadulterated and unfiltered. So, the question is how did the caller manage to filter his voice while leaving the background unfiltered?"

Newly stared at my phone and the wheels in his head must have been spinning at double speed.

"He didn't," he said. "The two had to be recorded separately."

"Exactly. Now why in God's name would Hewitt do that? And don't give me he's creating confusion for the jury. We're way beyond confusion."

"I don't know. It supports the theory he's being framed. But now Carter won't submit the voicemail into evidence."

"But we will," I argued. "And you can bet Hewitt will subpoena you to talk about your forensics analysis and how that analysis works against the state's case."

Newly tapped my phone with his forefinger. "You discovered this on your own?"

"No way. If your guys missed it, I would never have found it in a million years." I summarized the conversation with Junior Atwood and how he'd done some forensic audio work in the Army.

Newly started writing notes on the legal pad in his portfolio. "So, Junior has the technical skill to have created the message he later identified as being a composite."

"Yes," I said. "Unlike Hewitt who has to have Shirley help him change his password."

"There's one other thing," Nakayla added. "When I asked Junior if he could reverse engineer the voice to approximate the original, he asked whether the police had done that."

"Interesting," Newly remarked. "He could have been fishing whether his voice had been revealed and you were leading him into a trap."

"Yes," I said. "But his reactions held not even the slightest tinge of duplicity."

"I agree," Nakayla said.

"We've all faced consummate liars," Newly said. "I think what he told you about the recording keeps him in play. Neither he nor his brother Cletus have an alibi for last Friday night."

"And there's one other thing." I told Newland about the kinship to Collin McPhillips and the fact that Collin was the only person who framed his shot to catch the top of the bridge.

Newly drummed his fingers on the table and thought a few moments. "You didn't hear this from me," he whispered, "but Carter's trying to reverse engineer the voice message to match Donaldson. We have his statement on audio for reference. I'm going to submit the oral statement we received from McPhillips as well. Your information about the separate tracks gives me reason to bring in Junior Atwood to put his assessment on record, and get his voice in the process." Newly tapped the shoe cover fragment. "The real success will be linking this clue directly from the killer to either one of them."

Newly was right. The scrap was a critical piece of evidence. Suddenly, the back of my neck prickled and I stared past Nakayla and Newly to the two-way mirror on the wall. I couldn't see through it, but images played across it, projected by my memory onto the reflective surface.

Jerry Wofford opening the door to the brewing room to check on the cleaning. Two figures moving behind him, each in protective clothing, each wearing shoe covers.

"What?" Nakayla and Newly asked in unison. They'd read my startled expression.

"Wofford uses those throw-away coveralls and booties in his brewing room. I saw them yesterday afternoon."

"The same color as our bridge scrap?" Newly asked.

"I'm not sure. Definitely different from your team's."

Newly stood, too fidgety to stay seated. He paced back and forth in front of the mirror. Then he stopped and spoke to our reflections. "So, you think McPhillips and Wofford might be linked together somehow? Maybe a conspiracy where the Atwoods and Wofford have a common interest?"

"At this point, I don't know what I think. You need to check out Wofford's operation. If you've got any contacts in the Denver Police Department, ask them about a scandal in the foster care services about fourteen years ago."

"Why?"

"The detective in Durango alluded to it. The Pendleton children went into foster care and Wofford's wife worked with children's charities. It's a long shot, especially when we don't know what we're shooting at."

"I can do that," Nakayla volunteered. "The story should have generated a lot of press."

Newly wheeled around to face us. "Okay. I'll work the police angle and we'll follow up with Junior Atwood, McPhillips, and Wofford. Efird and I'll bring them in for a round of questions and we'll add their voices to Carter's efforts to match your phone message."

"Efird's still on the case?" I asked, knowing full well he was.

"Yes. When I pulled Donaldson's phone records, I also pulled Efird's. When the calls went out about Molly's body last Friday night, cell tower records put him in Candler where he lives. No way he could have gotten from Helen's Bridge to that area of the county in time."

"That's good," I said. I meant it. The world didn't need another dirty cop.

Chapter Twenty-two

I was back atop Helen's Bridge, this time looking at the murder scene well after dark. Mist swirled around me, forming dancing patterns of light and dark as I stepped carefully through the moon shadows. No sounds, no smells. I was alone. Yet, as I approached the bridge, the mist seemed to coalesce and hover over the place where the grappling hook had anchored Molly's body.

It was like I had traveled back to last Friday when I'd called out for Helen and Molly had dropped from this very spot. Had she joined Helen in the midnight wanderings of a lost soul? "Molly, come forth!" I shouted the words into the darkness of the other side of the bridge. "Molly, come forth! Molly, come forth!"

The pillar of mist shimmered and a shrouded figure stepped toward me. Suddenly, my feet were anchored to the ground.

A moonbeam hit Heather Atwood's tear-streaked face, the face she had turned to me in the courtroom. "Thank you for what you said and did." The last words she had spoken before Clyde Atwood shot her in cold blood. Her voice was the breeze of a whisper, felt as much as heard.

"I'm sorry," I said. "I did nothing."

Her eyes widened. "Like Clyde, they are coming." She raised an arm clothed in the dress Molly had worn. The whisper turned into a shriek. "Coming for you!"

I twisted around, breaking my left stump free of my prosthesis. A black-cloaked shape rushed toward me as I fought to keep my balance. "Stay back," I cried, not afraid for myself but for Heather. I plunged my fist into a void as the attacker passed right through me.

Heather screamed—

"Sam!"

Nakayla shouted my name a second time.

I bolted up in bed, heart racing, mind trying to reconnect with reality.

Nakayla flipped on her bedside lamp. Helen's Bridge was gone. We were in her bedroom.

"I'm Okay. Nightmare."

She studied me, her forehead creased with concern. "Iraq?"

"Yes," I lied. The one word was answer enough.

"It's two-thirty and we're meeting Hewitt early. Do you think you can go back to sleep, or do you want to talk about it?"

"I'm fine now. You can turn out the light."

But I wasn't fine. Every time I closed my eyes, Heather's frightened face loomed in front of me. So, I lay staring at nothing and wondering what she had tried to tell me.

◇◇◇

Nakayla and I met with Hewitt in his office at seven. I'd already had two cups of black coffee in an effort to combat the lack of sleep.

We didn't want to spring Lenore's diary on him in front of the others, but we couldn't sit on it either. We needed to learn how damaging the entries would be.

I expected Hewitt to take the news hard, but I wasn't prepared for the magnitude of his despair. Blood drained from his face. He rolled his chair back from his desk as if trying to put distance between us. He made a futile effort to speak, but gave up and wiped tears from his eyes with the palm of his hand.

I felt compelled to fill the silence. "Detective Newland said Lenore's words were fairly innocuous. Mainly about your age difference and a sense of not wanting to hurt your feelings."

"A sense of not wanting to hurt my feelings?" he asked bitterly. "What the hell's that supposed to mean?"

Nakayla crossed the room and knelt beside him. She took his hand. "It shows she cared for you. Carter will try and blow it out of proportion, but from what Newland said, there's no fearful or disparaging remarks. Just the regrettable fact that you two are almost a generation apart."

He took a deep breath and swallowed. "She never said anything to me."

"I know," Nakayla said. "There's no entry that says she did. How could you have gotten angry if you didn't know?"

Hewitt gnawed on his lower lip a few seconds, then nodded. "You're right. Let's get to work. I'll break the news about the diary to the others."

When we entered the conference room, Shirley, Cory, and Tom Peterson looked up expectantly, knowing we'd been sequestered in Hewitt's office.

"We've had some developments," Hewitt stated.

He paused out of habit for Shirley to interject some wisecrack, but his razor-witted colleague held her tongue.

"Some good, some not so good." Hewitt laid out the changing legal landscape—the diary, the relationship between Junior Atwood and Collin McPhillips, the shoe cover clue and potential link to Jerry Wofford, and the exculpatory phone evidence that Tuck Efird couldn't have been at Helen's Bridge.

He finished, folded his hands on the table, and studied his team. "Any thoughts?"

Without hesitation, Peterson said, "Cory and I need to get a look at that diary."

"Agreed," Hewitt said. "But make a general request for any correspondence, journals, or diaries the prosecution might have uncovered. Include not just Lenore, but also Molly. That way we protect our backdoor source and put Carter in a position of lying if he tries to spring it as a late piece of evidence."

"Good," Cory said. "We'll head to the courthouse first thing."

"I'd like to make another run at the Durango case," Peterson said. "If Wofford's involved, there has to be some link. The foster care files of the Pendleton children are sealed, but there could be a way in through any evidence that might have been presented at a trial. Surely someone was prosecuted."

"I planned to work that angle," Nakayla said.

"Leave that for Tom," Hewitt ordered. "He'll navigate the court system better. I'd rather you and Sam pursue every lead you can on Junior and Collin."

I could tell Nakayla didn't like being sidelined when her instincts told her otherwise. The investigation into Junior and Collin was now dependent upon what Newland uncovered. We were reacting, not acting. And our local inquiries into Molly and Lenore had netted no enemies, no work issues, and no conflicts other than Molly's breakup with Detective Efird and Lenore's planned breakup with Hewitt. Both women were well liked and admired. The entire Asheville community had been shocked by their deaths.

"And let me say this," Hewitt continued. "Tom, I want to apologize for my initial reluctance to bringing you onboard. You were right that I need outside counsel. I can't imagine arguing about Lenore's diary in front of a jury. Talk about self-serving. The jurors need to see me through your eyes and your questions. So, I'm grateful for your contribution. I look forward to putting this behind us and perhaps working for a real client together."

Coming from Hewitt, the words were unprecedented praise. Peterson mumbled his thanks. Cory reached out and clutched his hand, unable to conceal her delight. I realized what a strain her romantic involvement with the young attorney must have put on her working relationship with her boss.

Hewitt turned to me. "What's your agenda?"

"I'm staying close to Newland. I expect he'll have both Collin and Junior into the station as soon as he can. But I'm not sitting on my hands. I'm going to work some CID contacts to see if anyone knows Junior from the Army."

"I can do that," Peterson offered.

"No," Hewitt said. "Sam's closer to the investigators. Let him pursue it."

Hewitt's perspective wasn't entirely accurate. I'd worked with many JAGs who actively participated in the field, visiting crime scenes and sitting in on witness interviews.

"Anything else before we break?" Hewitt asked.

"What about Lenore's car?" Peterson asked. "Did it ever turn up?"

Hewitt looked at me for an answer.

"No. Newland's theory is that the killer moved it from her house so that if any friends dropped by Friday, they'd think she was out."

"And Molly's car?" Peterson asked.

"In her apartment lot. Whether she was abducted from there or was at Lenore's and the killer returned her car is unknown. Logistically, shuffling vehicles is a problem for one person. I know that's bugging Newland."

"The car could be important," Peterson said. "I'm surprised it hasn't turned up in some place obvious."

"Obvious how?" I asked.

"Obvious in a connection to Hewitt. The killer's tagged everything else to him."

I shot a glance at Nakayla. The young attorney made a good point. We'd left that legwork to the police, but maybe it was time to take the lead.

"Lenore drove a silver Honda Civic," I said. "So does Collin McPhillips. Those cars are so common they're practically invisible. If Tom's correct, Hewitt, the Honda's somewhere you frequent or will have something personal of yours in it. Did you ever drive her car?"

"No. But you can bet some of my errant hair strands have been planted in it. I'm sure the police have scoured my neighborhood looking for it."

"Have they done Biltmore Village?" Peterson asked.

"How the hell should I know?" Hewitt exclaimed. "Why there?"

"It's the area you covered the night of the fundraiser. Let's say the bodies were crammed in the trunk of the Civic. You want the car in close proximity to your van's position so you can switch vehicles without driving all over Asheville. A Honda Civic would also be very forgettable if it were parked for a while in the housing lot above Helen's Bridge."

Hewitt nodded. "Goddamn, you are a prosecutor."

Peterson smiled. "It's the case I'd try to build. The location of the car could be the missing piece of the puzzle, the puzzle where the killer makes sure you are the only solution."

"I'll ask Newland where they've searched," I said. "And do some checking on my own."

Hewitt slid his chair away from the table. "All right. Let's get cracking. Cory, you call me if anyone in Carter's office stonewalls that diary. I'll go to the judge if I have to. I can always say I knew Lenore kept one."

Cory grabbed Peterson's hand again. "We can handle it."

When Nakayla and I returned to our office, she immediately logged onto her computer. I knew without asking what she was up to. Her curiosity about Denver's foster care scandal wasn't extinguished just because Hewitt gave Peterson the assignment.

I got on the phone to Newly. The detective was already at the station and had calls into Junior, Collin, and Wofford.

"Are you bringing them in as a group?" I asked.

"Not to be interviewed together. But I'll make sure they see each other in the halls. If there's a connection between two or even all three of them, I hope to create enough fear to turn one of them. I'd put my money on Collin McPhillips as the weakest link."

"What about Wofford and his shoe booties?"

"A uniformed officer is going to stop by the brewery once Wofford's with me. Then we'll know immediately if there's a match to the fragment on the bridge and I can leverage that against Wofford while he's here at the station."

His approach made sense.

"Good luck. Any developments with Lenore Carpenter's Honda?"

"No. That whole car thing is a mystery. Our best guess is the killer used the Honda to move the bodies. It's probably abandoned on some mountain dirt road or been pushed over a ravine."

"You're talking two or more people."

"I know," Newly said. "But the logistics of the double murders point to that conclusion."

I pulled a note pad from my desk drawer. "Give me the tag for the Honda. I'll keep an eye out."

I jotted down the number, ripped the sheet free, and stuffed it in my pants' pocket. "Call if anything breaks."

"Sam, you're on my speed dial. When I know something, you'll know something."

I hung up and for a moment, I sat thinking how Newly had climbed out on a limb by feeding me all this inside information. I doubted he'd shared our arrangement with his partner Efird, and D.A. Carter's head would explode if he learned the lead detective was speed dialing his chief suspect's investigator.

I also had to admit I enjoyed working with Newly. After thirteen years as an MP and then a chief warrant officer, I felt at home pursuing suspects. Justice meant convicting the guilty, not playing the system for any way possible to get a client off. I realized Hewitt and I would never see eye to eye on that point. I understood where Tom Peterson was coming from when he said he preferred working the prosecutorial side.

Nakayla was immersed in some archived, online newspaper story and only grunted when I said I was going out to look for Lenore's car. The truth was I had at least a couple hours before I'd hear from Newly and I needed to run by my apartment to drop off a bag of dirty clothes that had collected at Nakayla's. And there was the temptation of a morning catnap. Then I'd swing through a couple shopping centers around Biltmore Village where cars could sit unnoticed for a few days.

I drove up the back way to the Kenilworth Inn Apartments, planning to lug my laundry through a door avoiding the lobby. The rear lot was nearly empty as most residents had left for work. I spotted several spaces close to the door.

"Sam, you idiot," I muttered. "It was right under your nose."

I pulled beside a silver Honda Civic. Although it was parked facing out, I had no doubt the plate would match the number in my pocket.

Chapter Twenty-three

"Maybe you would have found the car earlier if it had been tied up with a big red bow." Detective Tuck Efird knelt and peered under the Honda's front bumper.

"It wasn't my job to find it," I said. His sarcasm didn't bother me. Lenore Carpenter's car was literally in my backyard.

"Damn Japanese cars. None of them ever leak any oil."

Efird was checking what I'd looked for before phoning Newland, signs for how long the vehicle had been parked.

He stood and brushed the dirt from his knees. "So, don't tell me. This is another attempt to frame Donaldson. The killer left Lenore's car in the vicinity where Donaldson was assigned last Friday night."

"Hewitt Donaldson isn't stupid."

Efird stepped closer to me. "No, he's not. He's cunning. He knows he's going to be a suspect so he frames himself. He's a guy who can convince a jury black is white and Adolf Hitler was misunderstood."

I let him rant. Newland and I would have a more productive conversation later. He'd stayed at the station for his interviews and let Efird take charge of the forensics team at the car.

"Speak of the devil." Efird looked past me to the other side of the parking lot.

Hewitt's Jaguar swung wide of the patrol cars and stopped in a space at the far edge. The morning sun glinted off his

NOT-GIL-T license plate. It had been a statement about his clients. Now it was his own plea.

Efird licked his finger and stuck it in the air. "Go keep your pal downwind. I don't want him claiming any hair or fibers we might find blew off him while he was standing by the car."

I stared at him a few seconds. "Really? Then I expect a full disclosure on everything you find as soon as your team's finished. Red bow or no red bow, I found the car less than an hour after Newly gave me the tag number. You had six days." I spun around and headed for Hewitt's Jaguar without waiting for a reply.

I'd phoned Hewitt immediately after notifying Newland. I knew he'd come to see for himself, but I was surprised when Tom Peterson emerged from the passenger's seat. Hewitt led his new protégé by a few steps, his eyes intent on the Honda.

"Hold up," I said. "Efird doesn't want us any closer."

"I don't see any crime tape," Peterson argued.

"No, but I was given a direct order. There's nothing to be gained by antagonizing them."

"Okay," Hewitt said. "What can you tell us?"

"Not much. I kept my distance and I kept my prints off the car. But I don't believe it's been here the whole time."

"How can you be sure?" Peterson asked.

"Because that's where I parked last Friday night. The weather was bad and I was surprised to get a spot so close to the door. Nakayla was with me." I turned to Hewitt. "You called us from the Thirsty Monk at eleven. We'd already been here half an hour. The earliest Lenore's car could have been parked was six-fifteen the next morning after I drove to the office."

"Was Nakayla with you then?" Hewitt asked.

"No. Her car was here and she came in later."

Hewitt stared across the lot to the Civic. "Did you tell Efird that?"

"No. But I'll have to tell Newland."

Hewitt nodded. "Somebody's being a little too cute. He probably didn't want to move the car in the middle of the night on the off chance someone would come in and remember it.

But early morning wouldn't be that unusual and the search for Lenore's car really hadn't gotten underway."

My phone vibrated. I checked the number. It was familiar but I couldn't place the caller. "I'd better take this." I stepped a few yards away. "Sam Blackman."

"It's Collin." The photographer's voice was tense. "We need to talk right away."

"What about?"

"I've been summoned by the police again. I told you something that wasn't true, and I want to talk to you before I see them."

"Didn't tell the truth about what?"

"Angela Douglas. That's all I'm going to say till we meet."

"Where?"

"Are you at your office?"

"No, but I can be there in twenty minutes."

"Good." He hung up.

Hewitt and Peterson had been watching me and I'd made no effort to hide my surprise.

"That was Collin McPhillips. I'm going to meet him."

"Has he already talked to the police again?" Peterson asked.

"No. He wants to clear something up with me first."

"What?" Hewitt asked.

"He said he told me a lie about Angela Douglas."

"What lie?" Peterson exclaimed.

"That's all he said and that's all I know." I started for my car. "I'll brief you later."

Although I made it to the office in only fifteen minutes, Collin was already there. He must have phoned from the front of our building. Nakayla had served him a cup of coffee and they were making small talk while waiting.

"There's a fresh pot," Nakayla told me.

"Thanks. I'm still coffeed out."

Collin stood up from the sofa and we shook hands.

"So, what's up?" I gestured for him to sit and I took the chair beside Nakayla.

"There's a message on my phone from Detective Newland. He called at seven-thirty this morning when I was in the shower. He's got more questions about that photograph I took."

"I'm not surprised. Yours was the only one showing a piece of the killer's clothing. They'll introduce it at the trial."

Collin patted his camera bag beside him like it was a beloved lap dog. "I know. And I won't take credit for something I didn't do."

His statement confused me. I leaned forward, anxious for an explanation. "What didn't you do?"

"Choose the framing. Angela told me to include the top of the bridge. Everyone jumped to the conclusion I'd composed the photograph. The truth is I'd have shot horizontally because I knew Molly was supposed to walk out from behind a bridge support, but I didn't know from which side of the road."

The prickle in the back of my neck alerted me that the investigation had taken an unexpected and dramatic turn. "Did she say why?"

"Yeah, that she wanted the shot to line up better with a vertical newspaper column. I was going to humor her and then get more photos with the framing I knew was best. But when the body fell…"

"Everything went crazy," I said. "The framing would be the last thing you'd remember."

He nodded. "Not until you asked about it, and since it seemed like a good thing, I took the credit."

"But you don't want to say that under oath," Nakayla said.

"No. But that's not my main concern. Suddenly, I get the feeling I'm a suspect. I think the police believe I knew in advance Molly's body was going to drop from the top."

Because you are a suspect, I thought. At least you were. "Has Angela said anything about that photograph?"

"No. And we haven't spoken since Tuesday." He wiped his palms on his knees. "And that's why I'm here. I don't mean to get her in trouble, but if the police are suspicious of me, then they should also be suspicious of her."

"Did she say anything else to arouse suspicion?" Nakayla asked.

Collin gritted his teeth as if the question pained him. I remembered the young man had been attracted to Angela and I wondered if this whole conversation was a reaction to spurned affection.

"No, she didn't say anything." He emphasized the word say. "It's what she wrote."

"I thought she hadn't finished her article," I said.

"She hasn't. And she hasn't written anything else I can find. When we disagreed over the style and direction of the story, I searched for other things she'd done. Maybe I was wrong and her instincts were correct. But nada, man. No newspaper bylines, magazine credits, scripts like she touted at our organizational meeting, none of it exists."

Nakayla started to rise from her chair. "I can show you some short pieces she posted on abuse."

Collin waved her to sit. "I saw those. They're blogs at best, like ten million other amateurs write. Unless she wrote under another name, the woman is a fraud. Claiming to be a writer is the easiest job to fake. I mean who the hell reads anymore?"

"Did you confront her?" I asked.

"No. I just lost interest in the project. Until all the fuss about the photograph. What do you think I should do?"

I looked to Nakayla. She nodded for me to take the lead.

"Go straight to Detective Newland. Tell him you talked to us and we advised you to share your thoughts—not accusations. He'll make of it what he will. If this turns out to be a misunderstanding, you never accused Angela Douglas of anything."

Collin visibly relaxed. "Okay. He was the one who contacted me. I'm just anticipating what he's going to ask."

"Exactly. Nakayla and I will explore this through our sources. Do you know where Angela lives?"

"She's got an apartment at River Ridge. I don't know the number."

"The ones near the city golf course?" Nakayla asked.

"Yes."

Nakayla stood. She was anxious to get to work. "I should be able to find the address without any trouble."

"Anything else?" I asked.

Collin grabbed his camera and got to his feet. "No. I'd better get going."

I walked him to the elevator. "I advise you to avoid any contact with Angela until this is sorted out."

"No problem." He stepped into the elevator and turned to face me. As the doors closed, he said, "I can smell a big story, Sam. Keep me informed."

I let the doors close without answering him.

When I returned to the office, Nakayla handed me a slip of paper.

"What's this?"

"Angela Douglas' address. I have a friend who works in the rental office. Angela signed a short term lease."

"Then I'm going to see her now. What's your priority?"

She turned back to her computer. "Playing a hunch. Collin said Angela might have written under a different name. I want to determine if that's the case. I also want to look for a link between Angela and Jerry Wofford. One thing that's always bothered me is the match of the Hawaiian shirt to the one Hewitt was wearing."

"Everyone knows Hewitt has a penchant for Hawaiian shirts, even in cool weather."

"Yes, but the same colors? Someone had to have seen him earlier in the day and planned accordingly. Wofford stopped by when Hewitt was picking up his two-way radio from Nathan, something that Junior Atwood didn't do. We've got to take a look at Angela and Wofford, not Collin and Wofford or Collin and Junior."

"Then go for it. Call me if you learn something I can leverage against either one of them."

Although I'd never been to the River Ridge apartments, I'd seen the entrance in pursuit of other interests, namely the Highland Brewing Company and its neighbor, Troy and Sons Distillery. One of Asheville's first craft breweries, Highland had a tasting room and a venue for live music. Troy and Sons special-ized in moonshine. Not the rot-gut made in backwoods stills or radiators, but a quality whiskey that I'd serve at the White House if I were president. They couldn't sell their wares on the premises, but a tour of their operation included sampling the fruits of their labor.

I glanced wistfully at their sign as I turned right instead of left and entered the landscaped grounds of River Ridge. True to its name, the apartments had been constructed in clusters on the side of the ridge. I imagined rents got higher the farther up the mountain and the more spectacular the view.

Angela Douglas' cluster was about halfway up. I located her ground floor unit on the end of a two-story building. Her cement walkway looped around the side where her entrance was protected from the view from the parking lot. Plenty of spaces were available, and I had no idea if her vehicle was one of the few left.

I pulled beside a pickup with oversized tires that raised the cab so high the driver must have needed an oxygen mask. As I approached Angela's front door, I noticed the blinds were open, but I saw no movement behind them. I knocked on the front door. It swung open a few inches. The latch hadn't been fully engaged.

"Angela? It's Sam Blackman."

No one answered.

"Angela," I shouted. "Your door is open."

I tensed. She was a single woman living alone who shouldn't leave her front door unlocked at any time. I nudged it wider until I could peer inside.

The apartment appeared nearly vacant. To the right, a worn brown sofa sat against the far wall with a scarred coffee table in front of it. No pictures hung on the walls. To the left was a card table and four folding chairs. A cup and saucer were near the edge closest to the kitchen.

"Angela, I'm coming in."

A hallway lay directly across the room from the front door. I stepped to the left, moving closer to the kitchen where I would be out of the line of fire should someone spring from what I assumed must have been a bathroom and at least one bedroom. My Kimber pistol was in my desk drawer back at the office.

Stopping at the card table, I dipped my finger into the coffee that half filled the cup. Still warm. I strained to hear the slightest sound. A dog yapped outside and someone yelled, "Quiet, Grady." A small plane droned overhead. Nothing came from the back of the apartment. My apprehension grew in the silence. Two women connected to the ghost tour fundraiser had already been murdered.

"All right. I'm leaving." I walked to the door and closed it from the inside. I stood motionless for a full five minutes. Then I moved quickly to the hall, saw an empty bathroom on my left and a single bedroom on the right. Bed sheets were rumpled into a pile beside a mattress on the floor. There was no frame or box springs. The dresser with three open drawers looked like it had come from the same salvage store as the rest of the furniture. A closet held only empty hangers.

I returned to the bathroom. The mirrored medicine chest was open, but it too was bare. A small white waste bin under the sink contained only a squeezed tube of Crest toothpaste.

Back in the kitchen, I checked the refrigerator and found a lone can of Diet Coke and a quart of milk sitting on the top shelf. There was nothing else. On the counter, a small coffee maker and bag of ground coffee explained the lukewarm contents of the cup. If Angela lived here, she certainly didn't own much. Not even a television.

"Grady, don't step in your own poop." The words of wisdom sounded outside the front door.

I opened it. A lanky, gray-haired man bent over the adjacent grass with his right hand encased in a plastic bag and his left holding the leash attached to a black miniature schnauzer who had his own idea where he wanted to go. The man picked up the dog's droppings, reversed the bag, and turned at the sound of the door's creak. The schnauzer started barking.

"Quiet, Grady!" The man pulled the dog closer to his side. "Sorry, you startled us."

"It's okay, sir. Maybe you can help me. I came by to visit my friend and found the door open. There's no sign of her."

"The blond woman?"

"Yes. Angela. Do you know her?"

"Not really. We've said hello a few times when I was walking Grady."

The dog wagged his tail and tugged at the leash. I knelt down. "It's okay. I'm a dog person."

The man gave the dog some slack and Grady licked my outstretched hand.

"I hope she wasn't your girlfriend," the man said.

"Why's that?"

"Grady and I saw her when we started our walk about fifteen minutes ago. She was carrying suitcases and a bunch of hanging clothes to her car. She must be going on a trip. Did she know you were coming by?"

I stood. "I thought she did, but maybe I got the time wrong. I guess it's a good thing I did come by. At least I can lock the door."

The man chuckled. "Can't be too careful these days. That's why I have a killer schnauzer."

I went back inside what I now suspected was Angela's abandoned apartment. I phoned Nakayla.

"I think she flew the coop."

"When?" Nakayla asked.

"About twenty minutes ago. Her apartment's stripped, and there wasn't much to begin with."

"Do you think someone tipped her off?"

"I wonder if Newly talked to Wofford or Junior and spooked either one. We don't know what kind of alliances have been formed."

"Maybe," Nakayla said. "I found what might be a possible connection. Jerry Wofford's wife Margaret signed an open letter along with twenty-five other people to the Colorado Department of Social Services protesting the foster care situation in Denver.

It was published on the Op-Ed page of the Denver paper. And we know the Pendleton children were in foster care about that time. I'm going to make my own inquiries using some of the other names that appeared."

"Good plan. I'll call Newly and then I want to follow up with Wofford. Keep me posted."

I got Newly's voicemail. He was probably still conducting his interviews if he was seeing Collin, Wofford, and Junior back to back. I left a message that Angela Douglas might have skipped town and to call me immediately. Then I headed for the office to cool my jets until something broke.

I didn't make it. A few blocks short of Pack Square, Nakayla phoned.

"Sam. I talked to one of the women who signed that letter. She'd been a counselor to some of the girls who had been sexually assaulted by the man who was the chief perpetrator of the abuse. Some of them were so traumatized they went to great lengths to eradicate any connection to that sordid experience."

"Great lengths how?"

"Leaving Colorado. Changing their names when they came of age. I followed up with a search of petitions for name changes in the Denver area during that time period. Because applicants are no longer minors, I could access the requests. On her eighteenth birthday, Sandra Pendleton's daughter Eileen legally applied to change her name. She was successful. Eileen Pendleton and Angela Douglas are one and the same."

Chapter Twenty-four

"What about her brother Timothy?" I asked. "Did he apply for a name change?"

"Not that I could find," Nakayla said. "He was three years older and I expanded the search parameters, but he seems to have disappeared."

"And that woman you spoke with had no information on him?"

"She only worked with the girls."

The revelation of Angela's true identity would be a major upheaval. Even D.A. Carter couldn't explain it away as a coincidence.

"Great job," I said. "I've got to get this information to Newly."

"You headed for the office?"

"Yes. I want to talk to Wofford but not until Newly finishes with him."

"Then I'll press on," Nakayla said. "I'm going to try another approach with Denver foster care."

After we hung up, I scrolled through my contacts for Newly's number again. "What the hell," I muttered to myself, and clipped the phone back on my belt.

I pulled into a spot reserved for police vehicles only. Time was too critical to circle the block looking for a parking space.

The duty officer buzzed me through without hesitation. The first person I ran into was Efird.

"Get Newland. The three of us need to talk now."

Efird crossed his arms. "He's in with Junior Atwood, and if this is about the car forensics, you'll get them when I say."

"Forget the damn car. Nakayla found the link connecting Lenore and Hewitt."

"That Kyle Duncan trial? We've been through that."

"Do you want Molly's killer or do you want to piss around with some vendetta against Hewitt?"

Efird's face turned pink. He uncrossed his arms and rocked forward on the balls of his feet. He was probably deciding whether to help me or hit me. "All right. We'll get a room, but you'd better not be jerking us around."

He led me to the observation booth on the other side of the two-way mirror looking into where Newly was interrogating Junior.

"Stay here," he ordered.

The audio feed was cut off so I couldn't hear the conversation, but body language told me Junior was annoyed with Newland. He kept shaking his head, either denying something or expressing frustration with the whole situation.

Both men looked up as Efird entered. Now Newly was annoyed. He stood and gestured for Junior to stay.

Newly stormed in with Efird trailing behind.

"What's so damn important?" he growled.

"We found Sandra Pendleton's daughter."

"Yeah? Where?"

"Until about an hour ago, she was at her apartment in River Ridge. That's here in Asheville. And her name's Angela Douglas."

Even in the darkened room, I could see the eyes of both men widen. Newly's lips formed a small O as he sucked in a breath.

"Are you sure?" Efird asked.

"At the age of eighteen, a woman named Eileen Pendleton changed her name to Angela Douglas. What's the odds that's a coincidence?"

"Less than me winning the next Powerball." Newly looked through the glass. "Any connection to Junior?"

"Possibly. It would be an alliance against Hewitt for different reasons. But there's an intersection with Jerry Wofford." I went through the background Nakayla uncovered—the letter Margaret Wofford signed and the sexual abuse the girls suffered.

"I wish I'd known this before I spoke with Wofford," Newly said.

Efird started pacing. "But what's his motive? I get it about the wife and the girl, but murder?"

"The dying wife," I corrected. "Who knows what she made him promise. She and the girl could have seen all the trouble starting with one event—the hung jury of Kyle Duncan that was caused by Hewitt and Lenore. Setting a guilty man free in Asheville meant a murder in Durango."

Efird shook his head. "You're saying Wofford made a promise to his wife to exact revenge."

"Revenge, justice, whatever. It must have become an obsession."

"Come on," Efird objected. "How could they know Clyde would kill Heather in the courtroom?"

"It's called being in position for an opportunity," Newly said. "If it hadn't been that, it would have been something else. They probably couldn't believe their luck that both their targets wound up working on the fundraiser."

"Not so unexpected," I said. "The two have a history, Asheville's still a small city, and Shirley is Hewitt's office manager and was close to both Molly and Lenore."

"So, why Molly?" Efird asked. "She had nothing to do with the Duncan trial."

"Best explanation is she showed up at Lenore's while Wofford and Angela were preparing to move Lenore's body," Newly said.

"Or they murdered her to divert any link to the Duncan trial," I said. "Make it all about the ghost tour and create confusion by throwing suspicion on the Atwoods."

Efird's face set into a hard grimace. He moved toward the door. "Then why the hell are we standing here? If Wofford tipped off Angela, then he's probably skipping town with her."

I stared through the glass at Junior. He'd gotten out of his chair and was walking back and forth like a lion in a cage.

"What?" Newly asked me.

"Did you get those booties from the brewery?"

"No. Wofford came in first thing this morning. My man went by but it was too early. No one was at work yet."

"I wonder how tech savvy Wofford is? Somebody with some expertise doctored that voicemail message."

Efird yanked open the door. "Well, why don't we just ask him?"

"I'll cut Junior loose for now," Newly said. "Sam, you're coming with us." He shot Efird a look that said don't argue. "You discovered Angela's identity, you can spring it on him."

We rode in Newly's unmarked car, I in the backseat like their prisoner. I wondered if I'd have to share it with Wofford on the return trip to the station.

When we arrived, Newly and Efird stood to the side of the door out of range of Wofford's security camera. I pushed the buzzer.

"Sam?" Wofford's voice vibrated through the small speaker. He didn't sound alarmed, just curious.

"I need to speak to you a few minutes. It's urgent."

"Of course." He released the electronic bolt.

I opened the door and stepped aside to let Newly and Efird lead. If Wofford bolted, their good legs would have a better chance of running him down.

Wofford stepped out of his office. At the sight of the detectives, his mouth opened with surprise, but there was no panic, no involuntary flinch at a perceived threat.

"Detective Newland? Did we leave something uncovered?"

"There's some new information we need to go over. You remember my partner Tuck Efird."

Wofford offered his hand. "Yes. Good to see you again." He turned to his doorway. "My office is small. Would you rather talk in the tasting room? I'm happy to treat you to lunch."

Either Wofford was completely innocent or he was the smoothest murderer I'd ever met.

"We'd better stay here," Newly advised. "You and Sam can sit. Tuck and I'll stand."

We crowded in. Wofford walked behind his desk but didn't sit. I moved beside the guest chairs, Newly stood directly across the desk from Wofford, and Efird closed the door and leaned against it. Wofford wasn't going anywhere.

"So, what's this information?" Wofford asked.

"Your wife signed a letter published in a Denver newspaper protesting abuses in foster care."

Wofford blinked with confusion as if Newly had spoken in Chinese. "My wife's deceased."

"I know, sir," Newly said gently. "She and others signed an open letter around thirteen years ago."

"You mean the screening lapses that allowed a pedophile and his wife into the system?"

"Yes."

Wofford transformed from confused to bewildered. "What's that have to do with anything?"

"We believe your wife was close to one of the girls involved who is now a person of interest in our investigation."

"Margaret didn't know any of those girls. Their names were kept from the public. One of Margaret's friends on the children's hospital board asked her to sign it."

Newly turned to me, uncertainty flickering in his eyes.

"We know about your connection to Angela Douglas." I forced unfelt confidence into my voice even as my brain told me our theory was collapsing around us.

"The writer," he said. "I met her through the fundraiser. You know that, Sam."

"I do," I agreed. "But more importantly you know Eileen Pendleton."

Immediately, the blank expression returned. He threw out his hands. "Gentlemen, I'd love to help you, but I have no idea what or who you're talking about."

"You didn't call Angela Douglas after we met this morning?" Newly asked.

"Definitely not. I haven't talked with her since our last planning meeting." The fact finally dawned that we were treating him like a suspect. He pulled his cell phone from his clip. "Check the log. I spoke to my brewery supervisor to tell him I was on my way. We met here for about thirty minutes going over supply orders."

"Could we speak to him in the brewery?" I asked.

Wofford reddened. "Well, since it appears my word isn't good enough, I'll take you to him."

Efird stepped aside as Wofford brusquely moved past him. I trailed the two detectives down the hall and into the heart of the brewery.

A young man in his mid-twenties sat on a stool at a make-shift writing board that was hinged to the wall. He studied an electronic tablet and appeared to be entering data through the touch screen. He wore clean blue jeans, a lighter denim shirt, and his brown hair was pulled back in a short ponytail.

Wofford stopped just inside the door. "Tony, these men would like a word with you."

Tony looked up and frowned at the interruption.

Newly flashed his detective shield. "Just a few moments."

The young man glanced at Wofford who gave him a slight nod.

"Okay." Tony slipped off the stool and came toward us.

"Should I leave?" Wofford asked.

I decided there was nothing to be gained in embarrassing Wofford in front of his employee. "No. You can verify his answer to my question."

The two detectives eyed me suspiciously for jumping into their business, but they said nothing.

"When I was here the other day, I saw you flushing out one of the tanks. You were wearing protective clothing and shoe covers."

"Yes. Mr. Wofford says the key to excellent beer is pristine equipment. We're like an operating room in here."

"Do you use only one kind of shoe booties?"

"They're nothing special, if that's what you mean."

"Can we see them?"

Again, he looked at his boss for approval.

"Bring the box from the supply closet," Wofford said.

Tony walked to a door in the far corner, stepped out of view for a minute, and returned with a box in both hands. The label read "Super Track Boot Cover—Non-skid & Water Resistant." I pulled one from the box. It was darker in color than the scrap from the bridge. The bottom had no lettering, only rough ridges to prevent slipping on wet surfaces. I passed it to Efird and pulled another for Newly.

"And you don't have any other brands in stock?" Efird asked.

"No," Wofford said. "I order these by the case. It's what we used in Colorado."

Newly took the bootie from Efird and handed the pair back to Tony. "Thank you. Sorry to have bothered you. Mr. Wofford said you were inventorying supplies."

"Getting ready to place the order for the holiday run of our seasonal ale," Tony explained. "That's why I was flushing out the number one kettle."

"Count on me coming back to buy some," Newly said. "Thank you for your time." He nodded to Wofford that we were finished.

As soon as we stepped out onto the sidewalk, Efird turned on me. "Well, so much for your theory."

"Angela Douglas is still Eileen Pendleton," Newly reminded his partner. "There's got to be a connection somewhere."

"If it's to Wofford, he's a hell of an actor," Efird argued. "He didn't bat an eye when Sam threw out Eileen Pendleton's name."

I waited by the curb while Newly unlocked the unmarked car. We were overlooking something. "Still no luck tracing that partial pattern on the sole of the shoe cover?"

"No," Newly said. "It's either M or N. Too sharp an angle to be the P in POLICE. If that were the case, I'd say someone on the forensics team had an off brand that got torn and they never noticed it."

I slid in the backseat and thought about the letters.

"M could be Medical," Efird suggested, "but that's in operating rooms where there's no need to distinguish ground impressions."

M and P aligned in my mind. "MP. Military police."

Newly and Efird spun around and stared at me.

"Goddamn," Efird said. "I think you're on to something. Junior worked with MPs. He was involved in that whole doctored audio case. And people are always pilfering things from military supplies. He could have gotten a couple boxes of those shoe covers."

"We need to pick him up again," Newly said. "And I'd like to get a warrant to search his house."

My mind headed in another direction. "Let me out and I'll walk to the office so as not to hold you up."

I stood on the sidewalk until the car turned at the next block. Then I headed for the Thirsty Monk.

The crowd had thinned. I had a clear view of the bar and was disappointed not to see Hank serving drinks.

One of the waitresses approached. "Just one, sir?"

"Actually, I'm looking for Hank."

"He's downstairs."

"With the Belgians," I said.

She flashed a smile. "So, you've been here before. Well, if Hank served you once, he'll pour your favorite as soon as he sees you coming down the stairs. He's amazing."

"That's what I'm counting on."

Chapter Twenty-five

"Nakayla, I think I've broken the case." I nearly shouted the words as I opened the office door.

No one was there. I leaned against the wall and caught my breath. I'd hoofed it so fast from the Thirsty Monk that my left leg stump was aching from pounding on the concrete sidewalk. I'd held off phoning because I wanted to see Nakayla's face when I explained my theory. Then she could unleash her computer skills to search the Internet for corroborating evidence.

Her purse was still by her chair so she couldn't have gone far. I hurried down the hall to Hewitt's office.

Nakayla and Cory stood at Shirley's desk. Shirley was seated and held the receiver of her desk phone in her hand.

"Sam. I was just about to call you. Have you seen Hewitt?"

"Yes. Earlier this morning. He and Tom came to Molly's car."

"We haven't seen them since," Cory said. "Tom was supposed to meet me at the D.A.'s office at noon to pick up the photocopies of Lenore's diary."

Shirley dropped the receiver in the cradle and stood. "Hewitt had a luncheon with Nathan Armitage, but he never showed. I know he's distracted but he's not one to miss an appointment."

Both women were clearly upset. A knot tightened in my stomach. I tried to keep calm and be reassuring.

"They probably just got tied up with the car and lost track of time."

"But it's well after two," Cory said. "Neither one is answering his cell."

Nakayla gave an almost imperceptible nod toward the door. For some reason, she wanted me outside.

"Tell you what," I said. "I'll call Efird. He was the last person with them." I stepped out in the hall. "I'll let you know what I find." I walked away, listening for Nakayla's footsteps to follow.

She came in the door behind me. "Sam, I'm worried about Hewitt. There's something funny about Tom Peterson."

My mouth dropped open. "How did you know?"

"You too?"

"Yes. Wofford has nothing to do with this. He's just a beer guy from Colorado. The shoe cover at the bridge is probably from the military. Newly and Efird are going after Junior, but Peterson was in the JAG Corps and told us how much he liked working with the MPs. I just came from Hank at the Thirsty Monk. He remembers seeing Peterson with his Bells Amber Ale in the upper bar last Friday night, the night Hewitt and Nathan were downstairs. Junior said that audio background trick made the CID newsletter. JAGs read it too. Peterson saw his opportunity and made the recording. The guy's brilliant. He's exploited everything he could."

"What do we do now?"

"What put you on to him?" I asked.

"I spoke to the foster care agency in Denver. I was hoping they'd share any records they might have after Eileen or Timothy turned eighteen and were no longer minors. I said I knew they'd already had inquiries, but we had information we only wanted to confirm."

"And they knew nothing about any inquiries," I said.

"Exactly. Peterson never asked."

"Of course not. Hewitt handed him a gift when he assigned Peterson the responsibilities for finding the Pendleton kids—the area where he was most vulnerable for being discovered. He's got to be Timothy Pendleton and we have to prove it."

Nakayla's eyes widened. "Oh, my God. I connected something earlier to Angela but completely missed the relevance to Peterson."

"What?"

She pointed to a stack of printouts on her desk. "I reviewed all the stories about the Pendleton murder and the sex scandal. The papers identified Sandy Pendleton's late husband as P.D. Pendleton. I did a further check. His full name was Peter Douglas Pendleton. Angela Douglas."

"And Tom Peterson. Peter's son. And he went into the military like his father."

"He went as Tom Peterson so the name change had to happen in college."

"Or before," I suggested. "I wonder why it didn't show up?"

Nakayla hurried to her computer. "Because Colorado only allows you to change your name in the county in which you're a resident. Angela still lived in Denver, but if Tom had moved, it would be in the records of a different county."

"Hit the counties of the state universities. I'm calling Newly."

"Sam, he's got Hewitt."

"I know. We don't have much time."

As I speed-dialed Newly, I heard Nakayla's fingers typing furiously on her keyboard. The phone rang until I went to voicemail. "Call me now," I said. I immediately redialed. Again, voicemail. I dialed a third time.

"What?" Newly shouted. "We're executing a search warrant at Junior's."

"You won't find a thing. It's Tom Peterson and he's taken Hewitt."

"What?" This time the word wasn't angry but astonished.

I quickly detailed what I'd learned from Hank and what Nakayla discovered in Denver. "He had to be the one who tipped Angela. He was there this morning when I got the call from Collin about her. Neither he nor Hewitt have been seen since."

"How the hell did he manage to be at the Grove Park and the bridge at the same time?"

"Newly, we can't worry about that now. Whatever they were planning is going to be accelerated."

If it hasn't been already, I thought.

"All right," Newly said. "I'll issue a BOLO, send officers to his home and office, and put a watch on the airport and bus station. I already have men looking for Angela."

"Found it!" Nakayla ran to my door. "El Paso County. He changed his name from Timothy Pendleton to Tom Peterson in the county of the University of Colorado at Colorado Springs three years before Angela."

I repeated the information for Newly.

"I'm headed back to the station," he said. "Ask Nakayla to look for any background she can. Does he own a cabin, have a favorite vacation spot, bank accounts in other states? I'll put our people on it, but she's already up to speed."

"Okay," I agreed. "But first I think she should tap another source."

I looked up at Nakayla. She frowned because she knew where I was going.

"What?" Newly asked.

"His girlfriend. Cory DeMille."

I hung up with the promise to call Newly immediately if we learned anything.

Nakayla wiped tears off her cheeks. "You're right. We have to find out what Cory knows. But she's going to be devastated."

"I think you should be one-on-one with her. She can cry or scream or whatever."

Nakayla smiled in spite of her tears. "You're just chicken."

I stood. "I am. But I'm not totally taking myself off the hook. While you talk here to Cory, I'll break the news to Shirley."

Nakayla stepped close and embraced me so hard I couldn't breathe. But we stayed that way for a moment, infusing each other with courage.

I broke away first. "Your brave soldier's going to hide around the corner of the hall until you get Cory to come see you. Then I'll stay with Shirley until either Cory returns or you call me."

"Okay. Once I get her through the initial shock I'll try to glean any information I can as to where they might have taken Hewitt."

I stayed out of sight on the far side of the elevator, but not so distant that I couldn't hear Cory's heels clicking on the hardwood floor. As soon as our door closed, I trod as softly as I could to Hewitt's office.

Shirley sat at her desk, staring blankly at the wall. It took a second for her to register that I'd entered.

"Did you speak to Efird?" she asked cautiously.

"No. But I do have some information." I tapped my left knee. "I'd be more comfortable in the conference room if that's okay."

Shirley wet her lips. "Nakayla called for Cory. Something happened to Hewitt and Tom, didn't it?"

"Let's just go to the conference room."

Her black eyeliner started running into the white makeup like ink spilling across parchment. I led the way and then stepped aside when we reached the round table, pointing for her to take the nearest chair. I sat next to her.

"Nakayla and I have found the children of Sandra Pendleton."

"The woman murdered in Durango?"

"Yes. They are Angela Douglas and Tom Peterson."

Shirley gasped, and then threw her hand to her mouth to stifle a sob.

There was no sense holding back. The faster it all came out, the better. "We believe they've abducted Hewitt."

Her shoulders shook like electricity ran through them. "Oh, God. They'll kill him. You've got to find him, Sam."

I laid my hand on top of hers. "We're doing everything we can. Detective Newland is all over it. Nakayla's talking to Cory for any hint of helpful information she might have, whether she's aware it's valuable or not."

She took a deep breath. "He murdered Molly and Lenore and then sat in this room and pretended he was helping us, helping to find their killers, helping Hewitt. And all the while he was framing him." Her dark eyes fixed on mine. "What kind of person does that?"

The answer came to my mind, not in my voice, but the voice of Horace Brooks talking about his destroyed family.

I could take comfort in their love, but only after I'd discarded the hatred I held for the person who had taken them from me.

"A person who never let go of their hatred, Shirley. A person to whom life dealt only tragedy, and so they fed on it, and on each other, until Hewitt and Lenore became the embodiment of everything evil that happened. Not imagined things. Real things."

"But Hewitt was just doing his job. Lenore was serving her civic duty, and Molly was what? Just Lenore's friend."

"Better to let ten guilty persons go free than one innocent suffer? And when those ten go on to kill again, who are the innocent that suffer? A boy and a girl whose lives are upended and then dumped into a system that betrays them. They're not right and they don't have the right to do what they're doing. But I understand. It's their sense of justice, the specter of justice that's haunted them all their lives."

"And they'll execute him," Shirley whispered.

"No. Because we're going to stop them."

While Nakayla and Shirley dug into Peterson's college and law school days, Cory followed up on anything she could from what he'd shared as personal history. She'd been distraught when confronted with Peterson's duplicity, but her concern for Hewitt rapidly transmuted that despair into anger. However, she soon discovered everything he told her about himself was a complete fabrication, and she was left with little to do except keep coffee going and be the liaison with Detective Newland and the police.

I'd been on the phone crisscrossing the country, backtracking Tom Peterson's military career. To find any information of value meant we had to look where he didn't want us to look. He'd tried to be the interface between our team and the search into Junior Atwood's military career. I took that as a sign he didn't want his name popping up in a general inquiry.

I first went to a former colleague and chief warrant officer stationed at Fort Bragg. He didn't know Peterson, but he passed me along to a JAG officer who worked in assignments. That led to several former commanders who all said the same thing: Tom

Peterson had been a tenacious prosecutor and a half-hearted defender.

My last conversation was with a Captain Michelson at Fort Hood, Peterson's last assignment before discharge. Michelson said Peterson was like a pit bull who took criminal behavior as a personal affront. "It was like he was judge and jury," Michelson said. "As a former chief warrant officer, you understand the Uniform Code of Military Justice is different from civilian proceedings, but Captain Peterson pulled every lever he could for a conviction. The man wasn't a prosecutor, he was a crusader. And he had a backup plan for every case."

"Did he ever prosecute a murder?" I asked.

Michelson laughed. "He lived for them. He told me his favorite part was the sentencing and if the Army had the guts to carry out executions, he'd volunteer to be a member of a firing squad, to slip the noose around a neck, or push the plunger for lethal injection. It didn't matter which, as long as the public saw justice being done."

Shadows were lengthening across Pack Square when I finally hung up the phone. Michelson's words, "As long as the public saw justice being done," rang in my ear.

Nakayla came to the door. She shook her head slowly.

"I know," I said. "I haven't had any luck either."

"Cory, Shirley, and I talked about grabbing something to eat downstairs. We figure it's going to be a long night. You want to come?"

"Thanks. I'm not hungry. You go on. I just want to think a little."

She bent down and kissed my lips. "You did everything you could."

When the door had closed and I sat alone in the shadows, I thought, you did everything you could, Sam, but it wasn't enough. Tom Peterson bested you. He beat all of us. His and his sister's crusade won. They got their public display of justice.

If that were true, then Hewitt wouldn't be killed on some backwoods mountain road or buried in some shallow grave. Hewitt had been targeted for more than execution. He'd been set up for public humiliation. Murder charges to destroy his life before his death. But how could Peterson be sure of a conviction? What was the backup plan he always carried into action?

I picked up a pen and the printout sheets Nakayla had given me summarizing the evidence against Hewitt. I reviewed all of it. I didn't find a backup plan, but I did see an incomplete plan and a possible ending. The one ending that terminated Hewitt while tarnishing his reputation forever. Suicide. A man driven by guilt to despair. And Tom Peterson and Angela Douglas would have walked away clean.

If I were correct, the end game would be the final link connecting Hewitt to Molly and Lenore.

I walked to the window and looked over Pack Square to Beaucatcher Mountain. Lights were sprinkled across the dark ridge as dusk approached night. There was no time to rally backup, not when stealth was my only option.

I went to my desk, retrieved the Kimber forty-five, slammed one of two magazines home, and loaded a cartridge in the chamber.

On the way out, I dropped a note with three words on Nakayla's keyboard.

I love you.

Chapter Twenty-six

I kept my low beams on as I drove up the back of Windswept Drive to the condominiums atop the ridge. I wanted to keep the headlights from sweeping through the trees, but descending fog also made the low beams more practical.

During my scout of the area the previous afternoon, I'd walked through the woods from the upper parking lot to Helen's Bridge. Now I would have to traverse it without light and in total silence.

I parked the CR-V at the far end, hood facing outward, and took the shortest route to the cover of the forest. It had just swallowed me when headlights from a vehicle ascending from College Street swept the parking lot. I stepped behind a tree trunk and tucked the Kimber into my waistband to keep both hands free to gently push brush and branches away from my body.

Although the descending fog compounded problems of visibility, the dampness helped muffle my footsteps on the newly fallen leaves. I walked like I was back in Iraq, each step potentially triggering an IED.

After fifteen minutes, I estimated I would soon intersect the old carriage path headed for the bridge. Trees thinned and visibility improved as the low hanging clouds reflected the lights of Asheville burning at the foot of the mountain.

I heard a grunt. Then the sound of something being dragged across the ground. My hand clutched the grip of my semi-automatic. Then, not a grunt, but a groan.

I went into a crouch. There might be only seconds. I emerged from the forest into the clearing that spanned the final few yards to the top of Helen's Bridge. One dark shape lay in the middle. A second figure bent over it, holding a length of rope in one hand.

"Don't move. It's over, Pendleton." I waved the pistol so he would clearly see what he was facing.

The figure froze. "Sam." Timothy Pendleton barked my name with guttural fury. "Why couldn't you keep your goddamned nose out of this?"

I stepped onto the bridge. "Because what you're doing is wrong, no matter how much you and your sister suffered. Lenore was only in her early twenties, not much older than a kid."

"Yeah. And what about this son of a bitch? He used every trick he could to set scumbags like Kyle Duncan free."

"Just like you used every trick in the book to convict anyone you prosecuted. What if you sent an innocent man to jail for life or worse? Should someone come gunning for you?"

He dropped the rope and rose slowly, holding both palms open at his side. "They were guilty. Every last one of them. Just like Clyde Atwood. You think I didn't anticipate Hewitt Donaldson's little stunts? I knew he was aiding the D.A. I knew you have one leg. I knew Heather's cell phone was on and you'd heard everything Clyde was saying. I didn't walk, I ran into those traps to make sure he was convicted."

"And two little boys were orphaned. How'd that work out for you?"

He took a step forward, not in aggression, but as if anxious to be heard. "I'm sorry about that. I really am. But it set things in motion that I couldn't have dreamed would happen. Every event an opportunity. Like God meant justice to be taken. Those boys will know nothing like we went through. To have your sister raped at eleven, taken back to a bedroom in what was supposed to be a loving, caring family. To hear her crying, and to later learn if she said anything, she was told I'd be killed. And that I was beaten and told to keep silent if I didn't want my sister hurt.

We lost our mother, we lost our family, we lost our childhood." He looked down at Hewitt. "All because of this piece of shit."

A groan came from Hewitt.

"This was supposed to be a suicide," I said. "That's why he's still alive. A disgraced lawyer taking his own life. Now you can tell your story in court. It will be as much a judgment about him as about you."

Pendleton gave a hollow laugh. "Right. My story in the hands of this spin master."

"Spin master? And how are you spinning Molly's death? What did she ever do to you and your sister?"

"Like you said. She showed up at the wrong time and the wrong place."

"Bullshit! Then why the double order? The receipts you tagged for Hewitt's credit card were for two grappling hooks and twice the length of rope we found with Molly. You're a coward. You planned to kill Molly to throw suspicion elsewhere. To save your own skin. You've become what you abhor. A cold-blooded killer. A monster."

"I'm not going in." He knelt behind Hewitt's body, still keeping his hands in sight. "We'll have our justice now."

Mist blew across the ground, swirling around the two men. For a split second, I flashed to the dream and Heather's cry, "Coming for you." Or maybe it was something in Timothy Pendleton's voice.

I wheeled around as a figure in a dark hood rushed at me, arms outstretched to shove me over the bridge. With that split-second warning, I stepped aside and grabbed a wrist as forward momentum carried the attacker by me and over the wall.

"Eileen!" Timothy Pendleton screamed.

Eileen dangled in the air, thirty feet above the hard blacktop. If I dropped the gun to clutch her with both hands, I'd be at the mercy of her brother. He could have had a weapon. I knew he had the grappling hook tied to the end of the noose around Hewitt's neck.

"Do it, Timmy," Eileen screamed. "Throw him over."

Headlights raked over the bridge and froze. A car stopped on the ascending slope, its beams like spotlights illuminating a stage.

Timothy Pendleton scooped up Hewitt Donaldson, a man who had him by at least twenty-five pounds.

"I'll drop her, Pendleton. I swear I will."

Pendleton turned, using Hewitt's body as a shield against the headlights.

"Do it, Timmy," his sister urged even louder. "You promised!"

"Is this the justice you want?" I cried. "Your sister dead because you value revenge more than her life?"

Pendleton's hard expression faltered as he calculated whether I too could be capable of murder.

Fingernails dug into my wrist. With feral tenacity, Eileen took matters under her own control as she fought to loosen my grip.

"No." I struggled to pull her up.

She clawed at my wrist, digging her talons deeper until they pinched nerves and tendons. I felt my fingers opening.

"Tell her to stop," I shouted at Pendleton.

"Do it," she screeched. She violently jerked her body back and forth.

My fingers yielded. She fell through the mist and landed with a sickening smack on the pavement.

I turned, leveling the Kimber at Pendleton. He stared at me, his face pale as a ghost's. Then from somewhere deep inside, a sob of unspeakable sorrow welled up. He twisted as he lunged toward the wall with Hewitt's body.

I fired at his upper chest, the only clean shot I had. The bullet caught him in the left shoulder and his arm went limp. Hewitt toppled onto the wall. I fired again, this time at his center mass. The impact of the forty-five caliber slug knocked him back. Hewitt rolled toward the edge.

I leaped forward, grabbing for Hewitt's belt. Somehow, sheer will kept Pendleton on his feet. He looked over the wall at the sprawled body of his sister.

Then he jumped.

Chapter Twenty-seven

Less than a week ago, Helen's Bridge had been bathed in blue and red flashing lights as Molly's body dangled from the end of rope. Now the bridge was once again aglow as police vehicles and ambulances surrounded two bodies that lay side by side in the middle of the road.

I stayed on top of the bridge, clutching Hewitt's belt until Nakayla pried my fingers loose.

"It's all right, Sam," she whispered. "We've got him."

"He's drugged. They were going to hang him."

"Let the EMTs take care of him. Come with me." She grabbed my arm, and then looked more closely. "We'll have them clean those scratches."

Newly took my other arm and together they helped me to my feet.

"My gun's here somewhere. You'll need it for the investigation."

"We'll take care of it," Newly said. "One thing at a time. Let's get you checked out and then we can talk."

"How did you know to come?" I asked him.

"Nakayla called."

"I found your note," she said.

"I love you?"

"Yes. Written on the back of the copy of the credit card receipt for the rope and two grappling hooks. You'd underlined the number two, and I put two and two together. Where would they use another hook?"

I stopped and kissed her.

Newly cleared his throat. "You want me to wait in the car?"

"No," Nakayla said. "Get his statement so I can take him home."

When we reached the road, Tuck Efird ran up to me.

"You okay?"

"Yeah." I gestured up Windswept Drive. "I think you'll find their car at the top of the hill in one of the condominium lots. Probably a rental. I'm pretty sure Angela drove it up after dropping off Peterson and Hewitt. He dragged Hewitt from the closest switchback to the bridge."

"Donaldson's scratched up all right," Efird said. "They put him in a Hawaiian shirt like in McPhillips' picture. And Peterson's wearing military shoe covers matching our scrap."

"Peterson got inside our inner circle where he could get whatever he needed," I said. "I'm sure he copied the credit card information from his access to the office or Cory's purse. He could have collected strands of Hewitt's hair, seen him wear all manner of Hawaiian shirts he could buy and have on standby, and then he knew Cory's schedule for when it was safe to have the dress and hardware delivered to her address."

"He faked us out at the Grove Park," Efird said. "He parked where the surveillance camera could see the back of the van, but he could exit from the passenger's side. We'll never know but I bet Lenore's car was parked up there. He could take the walkie-talkie and her car to bring Molly's body to the bridge. He still communicated with everyone, saying he was at the Grove Park, and because no cell towers were involved, his exact location couldn't be tracked. The bartender at the Sunset Terrace only remembered Peterson was there at some point in the evening."

Efird's theory sounded spot on.

"And the untraceable walkie-talkies destroyed Hewitt's alibi," I said. "We couldn't confirm his location because, unlike Peterson, there was no surveillance camera on his van at the time Molly was thrown from the bridge."

Efird turned to Newly. "If everything's under control here, I'll take Al and Ted up to check on those cars."

"Go ahead," Newly said.

"You should find a key on Angela's body," I said.

Efird stepped a few yards toward the cluster of police cars. Then he abruptly returned and stood toe-to-toe with me. "We've had our differences, Sam. And you know why. I still can't stand Donaldson. But you did a hell of a job."

He offered his hand. Blue lights flickered across his exhausted face and I could read the toll the case had taken. He'd loved Molly and been denied confronting her killers.

I shook his hand. "We worked together, Tuck. We both wanted the truth."

I sat in back of Newly's car with Nakayla beside me and recounted everything that happened since I arrived on the mountain. Newly ran an audio recorder and let me talk uninterrupted.

When I'd finished, he flipped off the device. "I'll get this typed and you can sign it tomorrow or sometime over the next few days. Anything unaccounted for?"

"I'll have to think about it," I said. "Once Peterson and Cory became a couple, he had the opportunity to collect the evidence planted on Hewitt's property, obtain the credit card information, and exploit the fundraiser plans to murder Molly and Lenore. Molly's death was meant to throw us off, to focus the investigation on the Atwoods. He claimed Molly showed up at Lenore's at the wrong time Friday morning. Maybe. But the extra rope, hook, and dress undercut that argument. And Molly's assignment at the remote bridge location made her the easiest target."

"Do you know of anything slipping between the cracks?"

I thought for a moment more about the confrontation on the bridge. "I also think Peterson was lying about his deliberate sabotage of Clyde Atwood's case. He went scarlet when I testified about my cell phone call with Heather. I've never known anyone who could command blood to rush to his face. He could have learned from Cory later that Hewitt had schooled D.A. Carter and then claimed to have known it before the trial."

"Why lie?" Newly asked.

"I think he wanted my respect. Even at the end." I put my arm around Nakayla. "Something Nakayla noticed before I did. I'd been a chief warrant officer, a tool of the prosecution. He saw everything through that lens. Better for ten innocent people to be convicted than one guilty be freed to wreak havoc in the world. It was important to him that I understood his story. I understand that he and his sister were doomed the moment Kyle Duncan walked into their mother's house."

"No," Newly said. "The moment Kyle Duncan walked out of an Asheville courtroom."

I said nothing.

Efird rapped on Newly's window and the detective lowered it.

"We found the car," Efird said. "A Chevy Malibu rented in Hendersonville with Tennessee plates. We also found a syringe and ketamine in the glove compartment. That's how they sedated Donaldson."

Ketamine. I knew it was primarily used by veterinarians as an anesthetic. It was also infamous as a date-rape drug. Because ketamine breaks down so quickly into other chemicals, a positive trace is difficult unless the blood test specifically targets it.

"I notified the hospital so they can treat Donaldson accordingly," Efird continued. "We found a suicide note in Peterson's pocket signed by Donaldson. Peterson must have planned to leave it at the scene."

"I doubt if Hewitt will remember much," I said. "But the drug does make you compliant."

"He needs to know he came within inches of rolling off that bridge wall to his death," Efird said. "Maybe he'll think twice about who he takes as a client."

"Are we done?" Nakayla asked.

"Yes," Newly said. "Take him home."

I wondered which one, Nakayla's house or my apartment? Then I realized it didn't matter as long as she was with me.

◇◇◇

The hospital kept Hewitt Donaldson overnight and into late the next afternoon for observation. Shirley and Cory never left his bedside. I slept for twelve hours, physically and mentally exhausted from the ordeal. Saturday afternoon I went by the police station to sign my statement. I learned that Hewitt had been abducted shortly after leaving the Kenilworth, the scene of Lenore's abandoned car. Peterson had forced him into the trunk of his vehicle at gunpoint, and then injected him with the first dose of ketamine. After that, Hewitt had only foggy memories of being in the dark until transferred from one trunk to another. He had no recollection of being dragged to the bridge or how perilously close he'd come to hanging.

On Monday morning, Nakayla and I drove to his house. He came to the front door, still in his pajamas and with his hair tangled like the beaters of an electric mixer had been run through it.

He held a screwdriver in his hand. "I was just putting this away. Come in. Would you like some coffee?"

Nakayla and I both took a cup and then we sat at his kitchen table. He looked at my bandaged wrist.

"Detective Newland showed me your statement, Sam. You saved my life. Such as it is."

"We got to the truth. I just wish it had been sooner for your sake."

"Yeah, for my sake," he repeated without conviction. His eyes filled with tears and he looked away. Nakayla and I sipped our coffee in silence.

"I'm going to take a little time off," Hewitt said, still not looking at us.

"I think that's good," Nakayla said. "You've been through a lot."

He snapped his head around. "Maybe I haven't been through enough!" He sighed. "I'm sorry. I didn't mean to bark at you. I need to do a little thinking. Shirley and Cory can keep the office running, and I can work on some appeals that are pending. Keep enough cash coming through to cover their salaries. But it's time I stepped back and looked at the big picture."

I gazed beyond him to the screwdriver lying on the kitchen counter.

"I think that's wise," I said. I nudged Nakayla's knee under the table. "When you're ready to talk, we're here to listen."

We left him sitting at the table.

"Is he all right?" Nakayla asked as we let ourselves out the front door.

"He will be. He'll be different. For a while at least." I took her hand. "I want to check something."

I led her to Hewitt's garage. The Jaguar was backed in close to the door, but not so close that we couldn't see that there was no license plate. We walked to the roll-out trashcan positioned up against the side of the garage. I lifted the lid.

Lying atop the trash was Hewitt's vanity plate. He'd bent it in half. Facing up were the letters GIL-T.

Acknowledgments

Although Sam, Nakayla, and their friends and adversaries are fictitious, they are accompanied in this tale by the spectral presence of characters who might have once walked the streets and hills of Asheville but are now enshrined by decades of folklore. Each of the stories presented during the fundraising ghost tour are part of the canon of Asheville's rich encounters with spirits from the other side. I've never met any of these dearly departed, but I apologize to them for any misquotes or misrepresentations I might have made in describing their lives, their deaths, or their current ethereal whereabouts. Please do not contact me for corrections.

As for the living, thanks to my editor, Barbara Peters, who helps trim away the dead parts of my stories; to JAG officer Jonathan DeMille for insights into the realm of military judicial process; and to Linda, Melissa, Pete, and Lindsay for reading the early manuscript.

I'm grateful to Rob Rosenwald and the Poisoned Pen Press staff for their guidance, support, and talent that make working with them such a pleasure.

Finally, I must acknowledge the City of Asheville and its diversity of people for providing such a great setting. Come see them. Bring your dog, have a brew, and maybe you'll see a ghost or two!

Mark de Castrique
March, 2015

To receive a free catalog of Poisoned Pen Press titles, please provide your name and address in one of the following ways:

Phone: 1-800-421-3976
Facsimile: 1-480-949-1707
Email: info@poisonedpenpress.com
Website: www.poisonedpenpress.com

Poisoned Pen Press
6962 E. First Ave. Ste 103
Scottsdale, AZ 85251